Kudos for *Kill the Devil*

"T. K. Marion is an eloquent storyteller who peppers his imaginary Civil War saga with empathetic characters and believable circumstances. You will be turning the pages of this historical novel faster than a soldier can load his musket."

- Cynthia Brian, *New York Times* best-selling author

"Kill the Devil is a whirlwind. [The] premise, combined with admirable research, superb writing and amiable characters…makes this novel a one-of-a-kind thriller worth reading."

- Jeremy Robinson, author of *The Didymus Contingency*

"Was a pleasure reading [this] book. As one who is very interested in the Civil War…I find the times and some of the language right on. The book takes you on a journey as if you were looking down from heaven watching the story unfold. It would make an exciting movie."

- Elliott Barnett, Corpsman, U. S. Navy (Ret.)

East Wind, Rain

T. K. MARION

A Cold War Novel of Murder and Espionage

ISBN 978-0-615-29421-6
Thirteen Stars Press
Printed in the United States of America

Cover design by Deb Deysher, Double D Media, LLC
Photograph by Bill Cascaden, III

You are invited to visit the author's web sites:
www.tkmarion.com
www.authorforacause.com

For those who have served in the United States military.

THE VICTIM

CHAPTER 1

"I love you!"

Marlene's jaw dropped; the silence that followed was almost deafening. It was as if time had slammed on the brakes and come to complete standstill. She hesitated, as if unsure what to say in return, but then snuggled closer, enjoying the sensation of her firm breasts pressed against his warm body. Even her pink cheeks seemed aglow, curiously visible in the gray shadows of the moonlit room. His "I love you" was the perfect conclusion to a fabulous night of lovemaking. Like sweet dessert after a sumptuous full-course meal.

"Why did you say that, Bill?"

"Because it's true," he said proudly.

She liked the sound of that too. Smiling, she pillowed her head on his chest, enjoying the steady rhythm of his heartbeat. Although it was the first time they had made love, she knew it would not be the last. There was something different about this man. He was tender with her, his feelings for her sincere and not fabricated, not like the others she had known before him. And there was nothing rushed or primitive about his lovemaking style. Her body tingled by just the slightest caress of his fingertips. Mostly, it was the way he kissed her over and over. He had such warm, sweet-tasting kisses.

For him, their night of sexual adventure had seemed surreal. They had started awkwardly, like newlyweds, almost as if afraid of each other. Yet that was to be expected, and it didn't take long for her to relax in his arms, and him in hers. The passionate lovemaking that followed seemed so natural, so perfect.

He was smiling at the ceiling, as if lost in some kind of private world, and she wriggled to get his attention. He turned to face her, and they gazed into each other's sparkling eyes. She noticed a smudge of red lipstick at the corner of his mouth, wetted her thumb and wiped it off.

"What are you thinking about, darling?"

"But I just told you."

"I don't remember," she said, suppressing her laughter. "Tell me again."

"Okay." His grin widened. "I love you, Marlene."

"Are you sure it's love and not lust? Besides, we've only known each other for a few weeks."

"And because of that, you don't believe I could be in love with you?"

She blushed, appearing strangely vulnerable.

"Well, what I mean is…"

He didn't let her finish. Instead, he dragged his lips across her forehead and kissed the tip of her nose, barely making contact. She giggled.

"You're spectacular, Marlene. We're perfect together, don't you agree?"

"Yes," she said, suddenly feeling helpless to say anything else. "I've never felt so relaxed and comfortable with a man. You're so warm and pleasant to hold. I feel safe in your arms. I can easily see myself falling in love with you too."

"Didn't mean to startle you by saying that, but I just had to get it out of my system. In fact, I wanted to say it the first moment we met."

"You're not serious?"

"Of course I'm serious. I've just been afraid to tell you." He unleashed a thoughtful sigh. "Man, I'll never forget *that* day."

"You remember the date?"

"Absolutely! It was a Sunday afternoon. June twenty-ninth, nineteen sixty-nine." Another sigh before he added, "Virginia Beach hasn't been the same for me since."

"I still can't believe you feel this way about me. Really, that only happens in the movies."

"Why can't it happen in real life?" he countered. "No, don't kid yourself, baby. I'm crazy about you. And I know you have strong feelings for me too."

"I do, darling, I do!" She kissed his cheek. "You're very special to me."

She lodged her head between his neck and shoulder as he ran a soft hand over her silky blond hair, then finger-tipped his way down her spine, ending up at the small of her back. She giggled when he reached down and gently pinched her buttocks.

"You're naughty," she told him.

"Actually it's all your fault why I feel this way."

"How do you mean?"

"Well, when I first saw you at the beach in that red bikini, I almost went out of my mind. You were the most spectacular creature on the oceanfront that day. I knew right then and there I wanted to meet you."

"Well, you certainly succeeded."

Grinning, he tickled her stomach, making slow circles around her navel, enjoying watching her squirm.

"When I first met you, Bill, I was hoping you'd ask me out."

"I wanted to, but my friend beat me to it, remember?"

"Yes, I remember. What was his name again?"

"Roger Morrison."

"Oh, yes, Roger—I liked him too. But when I saw you with him, I wanted to be with you, not him."

"Roger said I stole you away from him. He was very bitter about it."

"You're kidding?"

"No, I'm not. In fact, he didn't speak to me for about a week afterward. Crazy, isn't it?"

"Childish, you mean. Does he speak to you now?"

"Yeah, he and I are still good friends. Roger was the only person I knew when I was transferred to Oceana last year. We used to spend most of our free time together. We'd go to the beach on weekends, then to the bars at night to pick up girls."

"I'm jealous," she said, though the tone in her voice proved otherwise.

"Actually Roger had more success than I did. He's a slick operator, loves flirting with the opposite sex."

"But he was too pushy for me. I liked you because you weren't."

"Roger told me he'd get you on the rebound." He planted another kiss on her cheek. "But that's never going to happen. I'm never going to let you go."

"You don't know that, Bill. You could change your mind someday."

"No, I'll never change my mind. I've never met anyone like you, Marlene. You…you're so spectacular."

"Is that your favorite word to use to sweet-talk a girl into wanting you?"

"As a matter of fact, it is."

They laughed together and she squeezed him with affection. She sighed, her warm breath floating across his chest like a lazy summer breeze.

"Tell me, Bill, how's your friend Roger doing now?"

"Don't know, haven't seen him in a while."

"You think he's still sore at you?"

"No, that's all over with."

"So why haven't you seen him?"

"Because he's out of the service."

"Oh, where did he go?"

"He's living over in Hampton. You see, after he resigned his commission, he found a steady job at the Norfolk Airport. The way he told it, he's now earning double the pay he was making in the navy."

"What does he do for a living?"

"He's an air traffic controller," was his answer. "You know, those guys who work up in the control tower and direct all the incoming and outgoing planes from smacking into each other. Roger's a pretty smart guy, was in the top five percent of his class at Purdue."

"Impressive. Why did he join the navy?"

"Because he didn't want to be drafted and sent to Vietnam."

"That's understandable."

He continued, "Roger went to officers' training after college and qualified for flight school, like me. We were together at Pensacola for a while, but then he was transferred to Korea. For some reason he couldn't make it as a flyer, so the navy sent him to air traffic control school."

"And the rest is history."

"Yeah, it worked out well for him. He served on a carrier for two years, but never in Vietnam."

"And then fate brought the two of you back together."

"Yeah. In fact, if it hadn't been for Roger, I wouldn't have met you at the beach that day."

"Oh, why?"

"Because it was his idea to go to the beach in the first place. I had been sick the night before, but he managed to talk me into going along with him."

"You seemed fine to me that day."

"That's because I took one look at you in that bikini and got well in a helluva hurry." He punctuated his words with a wide teeth-filled grin. She snuggled closer.

"Oh, darling, I want to say I love you too, but I'll need more time. I just don't want to rush into something that we might regret later. Besides—"

"I know, I know—you're still married." His comment was spiked with obvious disdain, was unpleasant to her ears. He turned over on his back, facing the ceiling. "Please stop reminding me," he added in the same tone.

"Sorry."

She rolled away, her back to him. For a moment he just lay there sliding his fingers up and down her spine, but then reached closer and ran his lips across her neckline, feeling himself becoming aroused.

"Sorry I brought up the topic, baby, but it's something we need to talk about. You know it and I know it."

"I just wish the divorce was over and done with," she said, leaning back to face him. "Why is it taking so damned long?"

"Don't know. Guess it's just lawyers being lawyers."

"Strange, isn't it? It takes practically no time to get married, but when you want a divorce it takes forever. It's almost as if God is punishing me for revoking my marriage vows."

"I wouldn't worry about it. You're not the first person to go through a divorce."

She didn't respond. Instead, she reached up and caressed his chin with her fingers, provoking a smile from him.

"What about your folks?" he asked. "Didn't you tell me before that they disapproved of the divorce?"

"Yes."

"Do they still feel that way?"

"Yes. They're strict Catholics, you know. They believe divorce is a sin. They said I didn't try hard enough to make the marriage work. They believe it was my fault, not Charles'."

"You think you got married too young?"

"That's what they said. They said I should've waited until after I'd graduated from college. I only had a year to go. But they got married young. My mom was only seventeen at the time."

"But that was common of their generation. Things were different then."

"That's what they said too. It's what they always say. They're always right and I'm always wrong."

He ran his fingers through her hair like a soft comb, something she enjoyed.

He said, "Hope you don't mind me asking, but why did you and your husband split up in the first place? I can't imagine any man in his right mind ever wanting to let go of a gorgeous woman like you."

"Bill, let's not talk about it, okay?"

"Marlene, we have to talk about it eventually."

He left it at that, waiting for her to carry the conversation instead, feeling content by just being near her. He glanced over her shoulder at the alarm clock on the night table—it was five minutes past midnight—and dreaded that he would be leaving soon, much sooner than he wanted.

She said, "The reason Charles and I split up was because we couldn't get along anymore. We had very little in common. The marriage was a mistake from the beginning. We were both stupid and naïve."

"Naïve maybe, but you're not stupid. And neither is he. He was first in his class at the Naval Academy, isn't that what you told me?"

"Yes."

"And now he's a lieutenant-commander stationed aboard the *Roosevelt*."

"Yes, he was promoted the week before we broke up."

"And you married him right after he graduated from Annapolis. Man, I'll bet that was some wedding."

"Yes, the wedding was fabulous but the marriage…" She stopped for some reason, but then continued in a trembling tone, "Charles always smothered me, never gave me any freedom. He was the jealous type too. He never trusted me when we were apart."

"I'll bet he was a wreck when he was at sea."

"The longest he was away was five months. But it was awful for me too. I wasn't the type to just sit around the apartment and wait for him to come home, not like the other navy wives."

"Did you ever get the urge to fool around when he was away?"

"Well, I did have some tempting offers."

"I'll bet you did," he said with a smirk.

She went on, "There was this one sailor who was always flirting with me. His name was Larry Phillips. He was a good friend of Charles but they were on different boats. Larry was stationed on one of those submarine ships."

"So when your husband was away, this Phillips guy came on to you?"

"Yes, he tried several times but I didn't accommodate him. He wasn't my type." She giggled.

"So you played out your role as the faithful navy wife."

"Yes. Instead of fooling around, I got a cashier's job at the Little Creek commissary. It helped me pass the time. Besides, I liked it."

"But your husband didn't like it when he came home from sea duty."

"No, he didn't like it one bit. He blew his cork and accused me of cheating on him while he was away. He said I took the job so I could flirt with the sailors."

"He thought you were cheating just because you got a job at the commissary?"

"Yes. He told me to quit. *He* was going to support us, he said. But I refused to quit. Then, when I was promoted to assistant manager last year, he lost his temper. Then he…"

"What?" he urged.

She seemed hesitant, as if unwilling to explain the rest, but then swallowed the lump in her throat and said, "He hit me in the face."

"You mean with his fist?"

"No, it was more like a slap. But it hurt, left a dark bruise on my cheek."

"Then what happened?"

"Well, after that we argued almost every time we saw each other. Sometimes the arguments got ugly and he slapped me from time to time. Then, when we stopped sleeping together, he started to drink heavily. Then the arguments got worse."

"Why didn't you file for divorce then?"

"Actually I did see a lawyer. He told me I had a very good case because of his abusive behavior. But I didn't need to file for divorce because Charles beat me to it. But that was fine by me because I saved a lot of money. Lawyers can be very expensive, you know."

"Was your husband always a heavy drinker?"

"Well, sort of," was her cryptic reply. "After he was transferred to Norfolk, we used to go out to this nightclub in Portsmouth called The Gunslinger. They played country music there, which we both liked. We usually went out double dating with his friend George and his wife. Larry used to tag along sometimes too. Charles would get stoned a lot and..." She started to cry, unable to go on, the tears tumbling across his shoulder.

"Sorry, baby, didn't mean to bring up bad memories."

"No, it's not that. I was thinking of something Charles told me on the day we broke up. He said if he ever found me with another man..."

"What?" he urged.

No answer, and he grew impatient.

"Tell me, Marlene."

"He...said he was going to kill me."

He didn't like the sound of that and proved it when he said, "You didn't believe him, did you?"

"Yes, I did."

"But he's filed for divorce. Why would he make a stupid threat like that?"

"Don't know. Maybe he just wanted to scare me or intimidate me for some reason."

"But it doesn't make sense. You told me he's already shacked up with another woman."

"That's right."

"But why would he threaten to kill you?"

"Don't know, I tell you. At first I ignored him. He always made strange remarks when he was angry, or when he was drunk or stoned from smoking too much pot."

"He smokes marijuana?"

"Sure, who doesn't these days?" She stopped to swipe the tears from her face, but then continued in a quivering tone, "I remember one night when we were at The Gunslinger. Charles got so jealous when George or Larry asked me to dance, I thought he was going to murder them both. It was the way he looked at them."

"Did you dance with them?"

"Of course, I was just being polite. Besides, it was fun. I love to dance."

"I'll bet you're something to look at in a pair of cowboy boots. Do you have a cowboy hat too?"

She nudged him playfully in the ribs, her way of telling him to behave.

"Will you be serious, Bill Gallagher?"

"Sorry."

"Anyway, when we got home that night, Charles ripped off my clothes like a wild man and screwed the hell out of me."

"Did you resist?"

"Of course! Charles is a big man. He's six feet tall and weighs over two hundred pounds." She wiped away more tears, adding glumly, "I just closed my eyes and endured it."

"In other words, he raped you."

"No, they don't call it rape when you're married. He hurt me that night, almost broke my arm. He was so stinking drunk. Afterward he passed out and I found him the next morning asleep on the couch, stark naked."

He pulled her closer and she clung to him like glue, as if afraid something bad would happen to her if she let go.

He said, "Where did you go after you left him?"

"I moved in with my friend, Lisa," was her answer. "She works with me at the commissary. You met her at the beach, remember?"

"Oh, yeah, the cute skinny redhead."

"That's right. I didn't live with her long, though. I wanted my own place, so I asked my parents for some money so I could rent this apartment. My mom sent me just enough for a deposit."

"How are you getting along with the bills?"

"Not bad. A month ago I started a savings account at the bank. There's not much in there, but it's better than nothing at all."

"You think you'll get alimony?"

"Maybe, maybe not. But I really don't want his money. I don't want anything from Charles anymore. I just want to forget the past and move on with my life."

"And how do I fit into your plans?"

There was no hesitation this time as she slipped her hand behind his neck, pulled herself closer and kissed him fiercely on the mouth, forcing it open. A half minute later she leaned away, smiling at him.

"Right now I'm just happy I found you, Bill. But like I said, I'll need more time. I just want to forget that horrible marriage before I take another step in my life."

"You're a wonderful person, Marlene. I'll certainly respect your privacy. If you want to be left alone for a while, I'll understand.

Just say the word."

"No, no, don't get the wrong idea, lover. I enjoy every moment we spend together. I just can't make a full-time commitment right now. At least not until the divorce is settled."

He smiled again. Though he didn't want to leave her, duty called and he was due back at the base. He let go of her reluctantly and slipped out of the bed.

He heard her say, "Have to go now, I suppose?" Her voice was gloomy.

He didn't respond, was too busy dressing himself.

"Wish you didn't have to leave, Bill. Next time we do this, make sure you don't have the duty in the morning, okay?"

"I will—I promise." He surveyed the floor, frowning. "What happened to my other sock?"

She reached across the bed and switched on the night lamp. She stared at him, enjoying the sight of his good looks and lean body, the strong arms which had held her close all night. It was then she noticed the slight bulge at the front of his white skivvies. She giggled.

"What's so funny?"

"Are you sure you want to leave?" She pointed at his groin. "Seems to me we could put *that* to good use before you go."

He wagged a scolding finger at her.

"You naughty girl, didn't you have enough?"

"Nope."

"Well, I did. You wore me out."

"Don't believe you."

"Well, whether you do or don't, I still have to go. If I don't leave, I'll never make it back to Oceana in time." He stared at the floor again, shaking his head. "Where is my sock?"

"You mean *this* one?"

She produced the black sock she had been hiding under the sheets and held it up, taunting him. When he reached for it, she flung her arms around his neck, yanked him down on the bed and kissed him on the mouth.

"Mrs. Pike, we don't have time for this." He broke free and snatched the sock from her.

"I don't like it when you call me that," she said, her voice close to anger.

"Sorry."

She slipped out of the bed, wearing only her perfume and a silver ankle bracelet. They embraced.

"Bill, come back tomorrow night. I'll make dinner for you and we could—"

"That's very tempting, baby, but...well, I'll call you later. Gotta go."

"You sailors are all alike—love 'em and leave 'em."

"Correction, I'm a marine, not a sailor."

"Oh, yes, how could I forget? Lieutenant William Francis Gallagher, United States Marine Corps." She stepped back and gave him a sexy salute.

Smiling, he kissed her as she'd kissed him just moments earlier. When they finally let go of each other, he grabbed her nightgown from the bed and wrapped it around her.

"I better leave now before my mad passion gets the better of me again. Good night, baby."

She didn't say another word, just watched as he headed for the door. She followed him, he waved goodbye when he was outside, and she blew him a kiss in return. She closed the door and returned to the bedroom. She removed the nightgown, slipped back into bed and pulled the sheets up to her chin, smiling hugely.

* * *

Gallagher spotted his red '65 Mustang convertible waiting for him in the parking lot and started toward it. The night air was pleasantly warm as he yanked out his car keys from his pants pocket and unlocked the door.

As he climbed in and switched on the motor, the man slouched at the wheel of the navy-blue '63 Chevrolet Impala parked four spaces behind him sat up and watched with interest. He waited as Gallagher accelerated and headed toward the alley that would funnel him onto East Bayview Boulevard. When the Mustang turned the corner and disappeared, he made a wide smirk as he reached for the new pack of Camel cigarettes on the dash.

He opened the pack, pushed one between his lips and saw the bedroom light vanish in Marlene's ground floor apartment, his face wrinkled in the shape of a snarling lion. He waited a while longer before turning the ignition key, smiling with pride when the eight cylinders burst into life. He let in the clutch and drove out of the parking lot, but didn't light the cigarette or turn on the headlights until he reached the highway.

CHAPTER 2

Bill Gallagher's love affair with flying had begun while he was still wearing three-corner pants.

First to capture his imagination was the squadron of toy planes he found waiting for him under his first Christmas tree. This unique breed of aircraft was manufactured out of balsa wood and propelled across the floor by the raw power of a rubber band engine.

He remembered attending the military air shows in Pensacola each summer with his parents and kid brother. The Navy's flying circus better known as the Blue Angels was his favorite. From toddler to teen, his bedroom décor evolved from toys and teddy bears to a museum of posters, magazine clippings and model airplanes of the World War II era, including the American P-51 Mustang, British Spitfire, Japanese Zero and the German ME-262 jet.

During those impressionable years he spent much of his free time at the library devouring books on the history of flying. His favorite action-adventure movie was the Korean War thriller, "The Bridges at Toko-Ri." He had pictured himself so many times catapulting off the deck of a carrier in a Saber jet and strafing enemy targets like William Holden, and then coming home to a loving Grace Kelly look-alike who would greet him at the door with passionate hugs and kisses.

His first flying lesson happened as a gift on his sixteenth birthday. Unfortunately the family budget permitted only three others to follow. In spite of that, Bill had fallen in love with aviation, knew it was his calling in life. He was going to be the top fighter ace of the next war. That he promised himself.

At the time of his high school graduation, his passion for flying still boiled inside him. By then, though, college had become his number one priority. He took a year off after high school and found employment with the sole intent of stockpiling enough cash for his first year's tuition. His daylight hours were dedicated to a sweaty construction job, while at night he waited tables at a local eatery not far from the shrimp boat piers. At Florida State University he majored in mechanical engineering and graduated in the top ten percent of his class.

Following college, pursuing a postgraduate degree seemed the obvious next step, only he had other plans in mind. He was weary of the school routine and yearned for his independence. He wanted to fly, see what the world had to offer him, which meant he needed money and a way to go about it. Of course the military was the logical, the only choice possible.

His father, a veteran of the Second World War who had experienced the horrors of the *kamikaze* attacks at the Battle of Okinawa in 1945, suggested that he follow in his footsteps and join the Navy. "They need flyers as much as the Air Force," he told his son. The idea of catapulting from a "flattop" in a swift Navy fighter and sparring with Russian MiGs seemingly more feasible than ever, Bill scheduled an appointment with the local recruiting office. He discussed his military future with two veterans. One was a chief petty officer boatswain's mate with a long line of hash marks wearing on his sleeve; the other a marine officer who happened to be a former flyer. The Marine Corps, the captain said, needed pilot candidates too.

Not surprisingly, his interview with the marine went more smoothly, better than expected. "We'll send you to officer training, then flight school if you qualify," he was told. Although the CPO had a similar strategy in mind, Bill decided that the marine uniform would fit better and completed the requisite paperwork. A year and a half later he was living out his boyhood dreams in the skies over Vietnam as a fighter jock, bagging five enemy kills in his first six months of combat. Following his tour in Southeast Asia, the hot-shot ace was transferred to mainland Japan where he stayed for a year before returning to the States, this time to work as a classroom instructor at Oceana Naval Air Station in Virginia Beach.

After leaving Marlene's apartment, Gallagher returned to his permanent dwelling at the Bachelor Officers' Quarters. He showered, shaved and reported for his duty watch at three bells (1:30). Following the tedious four-hour affair, he went back to the BOQ and slept for five hours. He and his roommate, a navy cargo navigator from Boston who, according to his dog tags, was called Chester Greaves (pronounced Graves), enjoyed Sunday brunch together as they always did before ending up at the officers' lounge to play a round of pocket billiards.

They were midway through their second game of nine ball

when Greaves, a tree stump of a man with midnight black hair and sky-blue eyes, said, "So, Bill, what do you got planned for today?"

"Don't know, Chet, haven't really thought about it."

"What do you say we go to the beach?"

"No, I'm not in the mood."

"The moon landing's today," Greaves reminded him. "Are you going to watch it?"

"Of course."

"What do you say we watch it here tonight with the rest of the guys?"

"Can't do it, buddy. Marlene invited me to her place."

Greaves made a smirk as he studied the confusion of colored balls on the green felt table. Finally he leaned over, took aim with his cue stick and buried the six ball in the side pocket. He grinned hugely, showing cream-colored teeth.

"So you're planning to see her again tonight?"

"She invited me for dinner."

"Dinner, huh? Sounds like you're getting pretty serious with this chick." Greaves missed his next shot and swore. "Your turn, boss."

Gallagher pondered the motif of colored balls as he applied chalk to his cue stick. He positioned himself behind the cue ball, leaned down, squinted and followed through. The seven ball, his target, dropped like a rock in the corner pocket. It was promptly followed by the cue ball.

"Damn!"

"Not enough backspin, man," taunted Greaves. Then quickly added, "But that's understandable. Don't think your mind's on the game."

"I'm telling you, Chet, I'm crazy about her. She's just so…so different. Know what I mean?"

"No, I don't. But she's beautiful, that I do know. You showed me her picture, remember?"

"That photo doesn't do her justice, buddy. You should see her in the flesh."

"I'd like to!" Greaves chuckled before he pocketed the eight ball with his next shot.

"I've never felt this way about another babe," Gallagher said to his cue stick.

"But she's married, Bill. Sounds to me like you're playing with fire. What if her old man finds out about you?"

"So what? Why would he care about me? Besides, Marlene said he's already shacked up with his new girlfriend, has been for several months."

"Yeah, but that doesn't mean he won't cause trouble. Did you ever think that he might be the jealous type and take his anger out on her? Hell, you read stories all the time about jealous men harassing their ex-wives."

"Are you trying to scare me?"

"As a matter of fact, I am."

"Whatever this guy is, he's not stupid, Chet."

"Yeah, I know, you told me all about him. Some sort of super genius or something."

Gallagher watched helplessly as Greaves deposited the nine ball into the side pocket, ending the game.

"Well, that's two beers you owe me," gloated the grinning sailor. "Shall we try another game? Double or nothing, what do you say?"

"No, I surrender. Let's get some beer."

At the bar, Gallagher paid the bartender when he had delivered the first round, waited for him to leave, then startled Greaves when he said, "I'm going to marry her, Chet."

Chester Greaves was a smaller man than Gallagher. Even while perched on the bar stool, he had to look up at his friend when he spoke.

"Are you serious, man?"

"Of course I'm serious. I love her! I'm crazy about her!"

Greaves watched him for a long moment, frowning, as if not liking the picture he saw. He leaned over and sipped the head off his cold Schlitz.

"Bill, do you know what you're saying? You've only known this chick for, what, three or four weeks?"

"So?"

"Let me put it another way. Have you ever been in love before? I mean *really* in love?"

"I've had other babes before."

"That's not what I meant."

"I know what you meant, Chet. I'm telling you, this is the real McCoy. This girl is perfect for me."

"Why, because she's good-looking and has a terrific body? Or is it because she lets you sleep with her?"

"No, there's more to it than that."

"I'm sure there is. But think of this. Maybe she goes to bed with you because she's horny from being lonely. Hell, it happens all the time with married people who break up with their spouses."

"So you think she's just using me temporarily, on the rebound, so to speak?"

"It's possible."

"No, you're wrong, Chet. Marlene could have any guy she wants. She gets propositioned all the time."

"Yeah, well, I can understand that. She's a looker."

Bill finished his beer and ordered another. As the bartender turned away, he said, "Believe me, I know what I'm doing, buddy.

I just have a feeling about her that won't go away. She's not what you think she is."

"Has she told you she loves you?"

"Well, not exactly. She wants to take things slow before she makes a commitment."

"So in the meantime, there's no harm in screwing around?"

Gallagher stared at his friend at length, but not in a way that suggested affinity.

"You make it sound as if I'm breaking the law. Hell, Chet, she's legally separated. The divorce papers have already been signed. They're just waiting for the court date. Anyway, I told you, her hubby already has a new girlfriend. And from what Marlene told me, they're pretty serious about each other too."

"How would she know?"

"She has her sources. You know how women are."

Greaves reached up and scratched the top of his head, but not because he had an itch.

"Married life in the military," he said thoughtfully, as if speaking to himself. "Have you considered that maybe *that* was the reason they broke up?"

"Yeah, I thought about it."

"And that doesn't scare you?"

"No, why would it? Hell, Chet, there are thousands of married couples in the service who have normal lives. They got homes, families. Your old man was a lifer, right?" He shook his head with emphasis, adding, "No, I'm not scared, not one bit."

"But what happens when you get married and all of a sudden she decides the military life is not what she wants anymore? Would you be willing to give up your career to accommodate her?"

"Don't know, but maybe that's something we'll need to talk about before I ask her to marry me."

"And when do you plan to do that?"

"Soon—but not too soon. I'll have to be patient and wait for the right moment."

"Gee, I don't know, Bill. I just can't picture you in a civilian job."

"There're many opportunities out there for a pilot, Chet. Like flying for one of those big commercial outfits, like TWA or Pan Am. Those pilots make a pretty good living. We wouldn't starve, that's for sure."

"No, that's not your style. You're a marine. You fly because you love it and money's got nothing to do with it. You're motivated by old-fashioned glory and honor and moving up in rank. You're a thirty-year man, Bill, just like my old man was. The service is where you belong."

"Yeah, well, whatever the future holds, I want Marlene to be a part of it."

"Well, for what it's worth, good luck, man. I hope you do the right thing." Greaves finished his beer and nudged his glass forward, provoking movement from the bartender. "Now, Lieutenant, about that other beer you owe me?"

Gallagher telephoned Marlene when he returned to the BOQ.

"I'm making spaghetti tonight," she told him.

He left the base at four o'clock with the convertible top down, enjoying the pleasant afternoon air and the many jealous looks from the passing drivers. Eighteen minutes later he heard "the Eagle has landed" from the radio, meaning that the Apollo 11 lunar module had landed safely on the surface of the moon.

He arrived at Marlene's Norfolk apartment forty-five minutes later. She greeted him at the door wearing a huge smile, pink blouse, denim shorts that seemed to strangle her thighs, and bare feet. They bear-hugged, kissed, and when they finally let go, he told her the news of the historic lunar landing.

"That's nice," was her flippant response.

By half past seven they had finished dinner. He helped her with the dishwashing afterward, and they followed it up with a stroll around the neighborhood holding hands, enjoying the warm evening air.

Back at the apartment, they parked themselves on the couch in front of the television and watched the latest news report on what was happening a quarter million miles away. At precisely 10:56 p.m. eastern daylight time on that twentieth day of July 1969, they held their breaths as the gray silhouette of Commander Neil Alden Armstrong hopped off the ladder of the spacecraft and onto the barren lunar surface, proclaiming, "That's one small step for man, one giant leap for mankind." The greatest feat in the history of the human race had happened as planned. They celebrated by making love.

"That was beautiful," she told him afterward. "Better than last night even."

He smiled but said nothing in return. To her, he seemed pensive, lost in some kind of private world, eyes riveted on the ceiling.

"What is it, Bill?"

"Nothing important," he told her. "Was just thinking about something."

"You're not going to tell me?"

"Like I said, it's not important."

"My husband called today," she said, snatching his attention.

"Oh?"

"Yes." She didn't elaborate and he became impatient.

"Aren't you going to tell me why he called?"

"No, because you won't tell me what you were thinking about."

"I was thinking about us."

"And that's not important enough for me to know?"

He ignored the question, seemed impatient again, almost angry.

"First tell me why your husband called, and then I'll tell you what I was thinking about, okay?"

"Actually we talked about a lot of things. The divorce, alimony, who would get what. Things like that."

"But there was something else, wasn't there?"

"Yes." She hesitated.

"Well?" he urged.

"He knows about you, Bill."

"You mean you told him?"

"No, he found out from someone."

"Who?"

"He didn't say. He just said he knew about you. He described your hazel eyes and brown hair, and that cute dimple you have on your chin. Said you were tall and lean. He even knows you're in the marines."

Gallagher thought about it, feeling strangely uneasy.

"What else did he say about me? Does he know I'm stationed at Oceana?"

"He didn't say," was her answer.

He leaned away, head resting on his arm, and thought some more. After a while he looked back, his face a picture of concern, eyes nervous.

"What else did your husband say about me? Is he going to make trouble for you?"

"Oh, he made his usual threats and I just laughed back. But he wouldn't dare touch me now since we're so close to the divorce settlement. Besides, like I told you, he's already shacked up with his new girlfriend. What trouble could he possibly make for me now?"

"He threatened to kill you. Have you forgotten that?"

"No, but he's not crazy enough to do something stupid like that." An impatient sigh. "Now tell me, what were you thinking about?"

"Wait a minute!" He sat up, frowning at her. "How can you take this guy lightly? He's threatened you more than once, then calls today and—"

"Bill, darling, don't worry yourself for nothing. I can handle him." She pulled him down and stared into his handsome eyes. "Now, if you don't tell me what you were thinking about, I'm going to get mad."

"All right—you win." He took a deep breath and said when he exhaled, "Marlene, I need to know how you feel about me."

"But you already know that."

"Yes and no. I need to know if you love me as much as I love you. Sorry, but I've got to get this off my chest. I want to marry you as soon as you're divorced. I love you so much, baby!"

"Darling, I love everything about you. The way you hold my hand when we walk along the beach, the way you kiss me, the way you make love to me."

"But there's something holding you back from marrying me, isn't there?"

"Bill, you have to picture yourself in my shoes. I'm divorcing a man who treated me horribly for five years. My life with Charles Pike was absolute hell. You and I need more time to get to know each other, to make sure marriage is the right thing for us."

"You're afraid of getting involved with another serviceman, aren't you?" She didn't answer, and he carried on glumly, "Well, I can understand how you feel. Let's face it, the military is not very popular these days. Almost everybody hates the war. All you see on the news anymore are students burning their draft cards, campus protests, street rioting. And ever since *Life* magazine came out with those pictures of Vietnamese civilians massacred by American soldiers last year…" He stopped suddenly, unable to finish.

She snuggled closer, clinging to him like a magnet.

He heard her say, "Charles once told me that the war was a sideshow meant to keep the defense contractors in business. He said the real war is the Cold War with the Russians. Said Vietnam drags on 'cause a lot of people are getting rich from it, including people in the government."

"Ironic, isn't it? Good men are dying in Vietnam every day, and yet we're landing men on the moon."

"Yes, wasn't that exciting?"

He ignored the comment, said instead, "Did your husband ever serve in Vietnam?"

"No."

"So what's your opinion?"

"About what—the war or the moon men?"

"Forget the astronauts for a moment. What's your opinion of the war? How do you feel about it?"

"I hate it," she said, the tone in her voice backing up her statement. "It seems so ridiculous. Young boys barely out of high school fighting and dying for no real reason. I believe in our generation, Bill. We should love each other, not kill each other. Love is the way, not hate."

"You sound like a Joan Baez song. I just wish it were simpler than that." He let loose a disgusted sigh, but then returned to the main topic. "So tell me the truth. Are you afraid to get involved with me because I'm in the marines?"

"No, that has nothing to do with it. But I promise you, after the divorce is over, we'll talk about the future. Okay?"

"Oh, Marlene, I want you so bad, it hurts. But you're right—I need to be patient. If we're meant to be together, it will happen, one way or the other."

"Now *that's* what I like to hear." She reached down and gently massaged the soft skin around his navel, then climbed on top and kissed him on the lips. "Better?"

"You like this position, don't you?"

"Oh, yes, very much so. Would you like me to prove it again?"

He reached up, combed his fingers through her hair and watched with a grateful smile as she closed her eyes, lifted her head and purred like a spoiled kitten.

He said, "Wouldn't you rather watch the astronauts some more?"

"What astronauts?" She kissed the tip of his nose. "By the way, you have to stay tonight."

"Oh, is that an order?"

"Yes," she said, dragging her lips across his face. "As a matter of fact, it is!"

A half hour later the man sitting in the driver's seat of the Chevy Impala watched as the light in her bedroom window disappeared.

"So," he heard himself say, "you've decided to spend the night."

He reached for the pack of Camels on the dash, shook one out, jammed the cigarette between his lips, started the motor and drove out of the parking lot.

CHAPTER 3

On Wednesday the 23rd, Bill Gallagher had just finished his morning lecture on evasive fighter tactics in surface-to-air combat when the telephone rang in his office. The caller was his commanding officer.

"Hello, Bill, it's me."

"Good morning, sir. What can I do for you?"

"Need to talk with you, Lieutenant. You free for dinner?"

"Sure am."

"Good. I'll meet you at lounge in ten minutes."

When Gallagher walked into the officers' lounge twelve minutes later, he found the place abuzz with excited chitchat over yesterday's historic moon landing. His boss, Navy Commander Stephen Jack Watson, was sitting at a corner table by himself, an enamel mug of steaming black coffee in front of him.

Watson was a young forty-three-year-old fair-haired, straight shooter of a man whose belt size was an inch longer than it had been the year previous, something he was not proud of. Like his protégé, Watson was a fighter ace of a different era, the Korean War, the conflict which had formally introduced the jet plane to the world as the new warlord of the heavens. Watson's present job was training coordinator of all attack fighter groups in the Second Fleet district. He offered a broad smile as Gallagher took the seat opposite.

"Have you ordered yet?" Bill asked him.

"No, wanted to wait for you," replied the sailor.

Gallagher studied the lunch menu. The special was grilled swordfish with sautéed sea scallops.

"Special looks tempting," he said.

"Did you watch the moon landing last night?"

"Yes, I did."

"Quite a show, huh? Makes one proud to be an American again."

Nodding, Gallagher changed the subject when he said, "So what's up, Steve?"

"Bill, how would you like to go to San Diego?"

"San Diego?" He chuckled. "You're joking, right?"

"No, I'm not. Had a meeting in Norfolk yesterday with my boss, Gene Waverly. You remember him, don't you?"

"Yeah, I met him once or twice."

"Anyway, the Navy's made some modifications to the F-16. Gene wants me to send a jock over there for hands-on training, preferably a veteran pilot with a better-than-average track record. Training is scheduled for next week."

"What kind of modifications?"

"Don't know all the details, but it has something to do with the computer navigation system."

The mess steward arrived to hear their lunch order. Gallagher ordered the special, Watson a turkey club sandwich with a side order of coleslaw. Bill asked for coffee, the steward withdrew and returned two minutes later with a cup of fresh-brewed joe. The Filipino left and Gallagher picked up where he had left off.

"Why me, Steve? Why not send Rob Jenkins or Chubby Washburn? Both have seniority over me."

"I've two reasons, actually. First of all, Rob's on leave. And I can't spare Washburn at the moment. His wife's expecting their second child any day now. I just don't have the heart to ask him to go."

Gallagher blew on his coffee and sipped.

"And the other reason?" he asked.

"Because I know you're bored here."

"Oh, who told you that?"

"Chet Greaves. He told me you wanted to get back in the air again. Even said you're thinking of going back to 'Nam."

"Well, since it's no secret any longer, you're absolutely right—I *am* bored. Don't think I'm cut out for this teaching routine anymore. You should have professional teachers doing what I do."

"You're right. But you and I both know that teachers don't join the service. They join the antiwar demonstrators."

"Yeah, they're just educated hippies too smart to fight for their country."

Watson observed his friend closely, not liking what he had heard, could sense the animosity stewing inside him. It was most evident in his voice when he spoke.

"I have to be honest with you, Steve. I'm not crazy about this San Diego trip. I'm a trained pilot. I was born to be a flyer, not a bookworm."

"And you're certainly one of the best we have. But that's

precisely why you're doing these classroom lectures. We're losing sky jocks to the civilian airlines every other day." Watson laughed without mirth, but continued, "Ironic, isn't it? We train these men for air combat, they do a tour in 'Nam, and then they desert to Pan Am or TWA 'cause that's where the *real* money is."

"Yeah, it's a revolving door in the service anymore."

"And getting tougher all the time to find replacements. Let's face it, the war's out of fashion."

"You can say that again. Two of my high school buddies were killed last year in that bloody Tet offensive." He shook his head in disgust. "Vietnam's not just a war, it's a…a…"

"Go on, say it, you're among friends here."

"It's a sewer!" snarled the marine. "Nixon's promised to end the war, right? But when? GIs are still dying over there in that godforsaken jungle of a country. And look what's happening in our country. I'm almost afraid to leave the base with my uniform on. If I wear civvies, my haircut gives me away. The rest of the country is walking around with their hair down to their knees, laughing at us."

"Yeah, it's getting tougher all the time to distinguish the boys from the girls."

Gallagher added nothing to that, and Watson carried on, "Bill, I'm a career sailor. I've been in the navy nineteen years now and love what I do. Yes, the war's wrong. I know it, you know it, the whole country knows it. Actually I don't blame those pilots for putting in their time and then leaving for a cushy civilian job."

Gallagher had no time to respond when the mess steward arrived with their dinner platters. He waited until the man had left the table before he resumed the conversation.

"Steve, I've been in the service four years now. I had planned to make it a career. But lately the war's got me depressed. It just doesn't make sense anymore."

Watson took a bite out of his sandwich, chewed, swallowed and said, "Exactly what are you trying to say, Lieutenant?"

"Well, to be honest, sir, I'm not sure anymore if I want to stay in the marines for the duration. Like you said, a flyer can make a helluva lot of cash on the outside." He gobbled down a slice of swordfish and chased it with a sip of water. "Fish is a little dry."

"Don't change the subject. Greaves said you're getting pretty friendly with some local girl. Said you were even thinking about marriage."

"Chet has a big mouth."

"Oh, it's not his fault. You know how persuasive I can be."

"Yes, I know," said Gallagher, inciting a reluctant grin from his boss. He continued, "But Chet was right—I *am* thinking about marriage. I'm also thinking about an alternate lifestyle for me and my girl."

"Well, I can understand what you're going through. The military has wrecked a lot of marriages. I once had a friend who had sea duty for five months. About three years ago, I think it was. Anyway, when he came home, he found his devoted wife shacked up with another sailor."

"So much for 'till death do us part.'"

"Yeah, it takes a strong marriage these days for a couple to remain faithful to each other, especially with all that hippie free-love propaganda out there." Watson shook his head lazily, as if disgusted with himself, but then returned to the main topic. "So, do you want to go to San Diego or not? I need to know before tomorrow."

"Sir, if you want me to go, I'll go."

"Good, that takes a load off my mind."

"Actually it might be kind of fun," added the marine, reaching for his coffee. "I've never been there before."

"Consider it a working vacation."

"All right, Steve, but do me a favor while I'm gone."

"Anything."

"Arrange me a transfer. I want to get back up in the clouds where I belong. Maybe I can do this teaching stuff down the road when I'm older, but not now. I just want to get everything I can out of flying while I'm still young and able."

Watson threw back his head and laughed with gusto, attracting a few curious stares from the surrounding patrons.

"All right, Lieutenant, you win. Besides, it's the least I can do for you."

"Thanks, sir." Gallagher harpooned a scallop with his fork. "So when do I leave?"

Bill telephoned Marlene after work and told her about his forthcoming trip to the west coast. Her reaction surprised him.

"That's wonderful, darling."

"But I'll be gone for a week. Doesn't that bother you?"

"No, why would it? I've had a lot of experience not having a mate around, remember?"

"So I'm your mate now, huh? Sounds like you want to make that a permanent thing."

"I do."

Later that night as they lay in bed, she told him she had been thinking of him all day and that she was ready to take the matrimonial plunge again as soon as her divorce was final.

"How come the change of heart?" he asked, skepticism accenting his words.

"Well, I spent most of the day with my friend, Lisa. We talked about you and I told her how good you were to me. She said she had never seen me so happy."

"Are you?"

She kissed him on the mouth, smiled and answered, "What do you think, darling?"

He frowned at her, still seemed skeptical.

"So let me get this story straight. You've decided to marry me because of what your friend told you today?"

"No, of course not, silly. I made the decision just before you called me about your trip to California. You see, about an hour before you called, I had a long chat with my husband."

"Oh, what happened?"

"The usual—we had another fight. Only this one was the worst of 'em all."

"What did you fight about this time?"

"He said he'll cancel the divorce if we get back together. In fact, he begged me. Can you believe it? Anyway, when I told him no, he lost his cool and started ranting and raving. Then he started making his usual threats, one after the other."

"Did he threaten to kill you again?"

"Yes." The tears began to trickle from her eyes, and he pulled her closer. Her body trembled, like her voice when she said, "I got scared, Bill, *really* scared. There was something in his voice that sounded different from the other times he'd threatened me."

"You should have called the cops."

"Why, what could they have done? It would have been his word against mine."

"Still, to report it and have it on file could work to your advantage, especially during the divorce hearing. You could claim harassment...or mental cruelty."

"You're right. Maybe I should've called the police." She squeezed him with affection, as if not wanting to let go.

He said, "So that's why you decided to marry me?"

"Yes. We love each other, Bill. You're a good man and I know you'll always be there for me. I don't want to wait any longer than I have to. I don't want to lose you."

"Don't worry, baby, you won't lose me. I love you so much, I'll never let you go. Never!"

His words seemed to relax her, and they lay there for a while without conversation. Before long they switched gears and talked about their future together: what kind of wedding they would have, whom they would invite, and where they would spend their honeymoon.

"I've always wanted to see Jamaica," she told him. "Do you think we can afford it?"

"Don't know, honey. I'll look in my pockets later and see if I have any loose change in them."

She giggled.

"Actually I really don't care where we go, Bill, as long as we're together."

She squeezed him again, and he kissed her on the cheek. He then surprised her when he brought up another important topic.

"Marlene, what would you say if I told you I'm thinking of leaving the service?"

"You're not serious?"

"Believe me, it's not what I want to do, but I was thinking about us. Let's face it, the military's hardly a normal life. There's so much travel involved. So far I've been stationed in five different places since I joined the marines."

"But what would you do? You said you loved flying."

"Yes, but I could get a job almost anywhere, maybe even latch on with one of the major airlines. My buddy Roger is making a pretty good living as an air traffic controller. I'm sure I could do the same as a flyer. There are many opportunities out there with independent companies that hire ex-military pilots. We could live almost anywhere we want. We could even stay here in Tidewater if you want."

"But would you be happy?"

"As long as I'm with you, I'll be happy."

She leaned closer, staring into his sparkling eyes.

"I just can't believe you're thinking of leaving the marines. You told me before you wanted to make it a career. You said there's security in the service and that you can retire before fifty if you want. A civilian job sounds scary to me."

"Yes, it *is* a little scary. But I'll do anything to make you happy. That's the most important thing to me. I'd be willing to take a chance."

"I think we should talk about this when you get back from San Diego, okay?"

"Okay, you win."

A fleeting smile before she asked, "So when do you leave?"

"Friday."

"You mean I won't see you this weekend?"

"'Fraid not, baby."

"What time Friday?"

"Seven o'clock."

"Morning or night?"

"Night."

"From Oceana?"

"No, Norfolk airport. I'm taking a commercial flight."

"Well, at least we'll have two more days together before you go. Can I see you off at the airport on Friday?"

"Don't see why not. In fact, I'll let you take care of my car while I'm gone. Would you like that?"

"You mean you'll let me drive your precious Mustang until you get back?"

"Sure, why not? I trust you."

"Groovy!" She purred as she snuggled closer. "You really must love me a lot."

"Baby, I love you so much, I'm now going to prove it."

As the light disappeared from her bedroom window, the man in the Chevrolet Impala turned the ignition key and drove out of the parking lot. After a pleasant drive along Bayview Boulevard, he stopped at the Crab Cake Diner, which was located at the corner of Independence and Shore Drive, just across the street from the Little Creek Naval Amphibious Base. He got out of the car and headed for the door.

He was a strapping, good-looking man, six feet tall and two hundred pounds, his wavy blond hair cropped short at the ears. The waitress who greeted him, a skinny, fairly attractive dark-haired young woman, was sure that he was a serviceman stationed at one of the many bases that honeycombed the greater Tidewater region. She even considered flirting with him—there was only one other customer in the diner—but when he sat down at the counter and lit a Camel cigarette, she abandoned the idea. She was not particularly fond of men who smoked; they made lousy kissers. Still…

The sailor with the gorgeous blue eyes ordered a cup of coffee and powdered doughnut. They chatted for a while about nothing in particular between sips and bites before he paid the bill and left the restaurant. The tip he left behind was double the price of the meal.

Back in the car, he started the motor and watched with a grin as the waitress served her lone customer a bowl of clam chowder.

When she was finished, she stared out the window, smiling at him. He waved to her, put the car in gear and drove away, deciding that he would return tomorrow night for another coffee and some friendlier conversation.

It rained Friday afternoon, and it was still spitting drizzle as Bill Gallagher braked his Mustang to a stop in front of the main terminal entrance of the Norfolk Airport. He left the motor running in neutral, turned toward her and kissed her on the mouth. When he leaned away, there were tears in her eyes.

"Why the long face, baby? I'll only be gone for a week."

"I'll miss you terribly," she said, sniffling.

"When I get to San Diego, I'll mail you a postcard," he said. "By the way, would you like me to bring back a souvenir or something?"

"No, just bring yourself back." They kissed.

"You're so beautiful, Marlene, even when you're crying."

"You better go now or you'll miss your plane."

He wanted to say more, she could tell, but refrained from doing so. He slipped out of the car, grabbed his suitcase from the back seat, waved goodbye and headed for the terminal. He waited at the door as she waved to him, then watched sadly as she put the car in gear and drove off. He turned reluctantly and marched into the terminal.

On the way home, she stopped at the local delicatessen to do some food shopping. It was five minutes past eight when she returned to the apartment. She found an empty parking space and slipped out of the car, hefting two grocery bags.

The man in the Chevy Impala was surprised to see her alone. Where was her lover? He watched as she stepped into the apartment, saw the kitchen light go on, then moments later the one in her bedroom window. It had stopped raining a half hour earlier, so he cranked the window down to enjoy a cigarette. It was 11:15 and two more cigarettes later when the light in her bedroom vanished.

He waited another five minutes—he was a patient man—and opened the door and climbed out of the car.

There were dogs barking somewhere in the night as he made his way across the street. When he reached the front door of her apartment, he glanced over his shoulder, hoping no one had seen him. As far as he could tell, no one had. He put on his black leather driving gloves, took a deep breath and inserted the skeleton key into the door lock. It opened with a soft click.

Eight minutes later he exited the apartment, panting. He glanced around—still no one about—and hurried across the street. He slipped into the car, removed the trembling gloves, reached for the pack of Camels, lit one after several attempts, started the car and drove away.

CHAPTER 4

Detective Inspector Matthew "Fuzzy" Hostetler had witnessed the sight of dead bodies many times. He still recalled the first stiff he had seen in the line of duty. It had happened on a balmy starlit evening in August of '53.

He was walking his beat in Norfolk's Ghent section when he noticed the cocker spaniel sniffing at something behind the wall of ash cans in the alley. He remembered staring at the disheveled male corpse, and then turning away and vomiting until his stomach was dry. It took him another five minutes to compose himself and call the station for assistance.

The incident had left an ugly scar in his memory, and he wondered if he would ever get used to the sight of another dead human being. Time had solved that problem, yet nothing in his two decades of loyal service on the force had prepared him for what he was staring at then.

The beautiful young woman lying naked in the rumpled pink sheets had lush silky-blond hair. Her unblemished face was the kind commonly worn by models in mail order catalogs and cosmetic magazines, her figure that of a *Playboy* centerfold. But the days of vomiting at the sight of another murder victim had long since passed for Fuzzy Hostetler. What he saw in front of him was just a routine part of the job, another case that needed answers to many questions.

He stepped away from the bed and sighed. There were two other cops in the apartment, Ralston and Jablonski, both rummaging for clues. So far nothing had turned up. Hostetler glanced at the vanity in the corner and caught another glimpse of the corpse in the mirror. He shook his head sadly and exited the bedroom.

In the living room, he plopped down in the chair opposite the young red-haired woman sitting on the vinyl sofa with head down and knees together. She was crying. He looked away and scanned the room, his sharp eye for detail missing nothing.

Standing against the wall on his left was a not-too-new-looking General Electric television, a copy of last week's *TV Guide* perched on top. In the corner beside it was a record player sitting atop a metal stand, a stack of rock 'n' roll albums next to it. The furniture in the place was similar to the kind found at department store fire sales or neighborhood flea markets. He opened his note pad, facing the redhead.

"Miss, I need to ask you some questions now. You feel you're up to it?"

Lisa D'Angelo looked up from the floor and nodded with some difficulty at the middle-aged policeman with the salt-and-pepper hair as she sponged her wet face with a handkerchief.

There were two parallel lines of mascara that started at the eyes and ended at the bottom slope of her cheekbones. For some reason, they reminded him of railway tracks.

He said, "How long did you know the deceased?"

"About two years," she answered with a trembling voice. "We...were good friends."

"And what was your reason for coming here today?"

"Well, like I told the other policeman, I came by to pick her up for work this morning, like I always do."

"Did you knock on the door to see if she was home?"

"No, I just honked my horn a few times. When she didn't come out, I assumed she was sick, so I left for work. I didn't want to be late."

"Then, after work, you dropped by again?"

"That's right. I called her during my lunch break but there was no answer and I started to worry." She pushed back the clump of hair dangling over her forehead and continued, "After work I decided to stop by to see if she was all right. When I saw her boyfriend's car in the parking lot, I figured she was home, so I knocked on the door. When there was no answer, I went to the landlord." He jotted it down.

"Then what?"

"I told him I was worried about her, so he let me in and that's when we found her..." She stopped her voice and shook her head sadly, seeming as if ready to burst into tears again. "How could anyone do a thing like that?" she said to the floor.

Hostetler ignored her, waited as she dried her face. He cleared the gravel from his throat.

"Miss D'Angelo, we're trying to locate the owner of that red Mustang in the parking lot. You said it was her boyfriend's car?"

"That's right."

"But she was married, was she not?"

"Yes and no."

"What does that mean?"

"She was separated from her husband," was her reply. "They were in the middle of getting a divorce." He wrote it down.

"Tell me," he continued, "did you notice the Mustang in the lot when you stopped by this morning?"

"No."

Hostetler started to respond but stopped when they heard the knock at the front door. Corporal Jablonski, who happened to be standing nearby, opened the door with his gloved hand and two men in green smocks stepped into the apartment wheeling a hospital gurney. Fuzzy indicated the bedroom, the newcomers went inside and minutes later returned with the corpse, a white sheet on top. Lisa D'Angelo did not watch as they left the apartment.

Hostetler took a deep breath and said, "Miss D'Angelo, about Mrs. Pike's boyfriend. Do you know his name?"

"Bill Gallagher."

"What do you know about him?"

"Only what Marlene told me."

"Can you be more specific?"

"She said he was a pilot in the marines. A lieutenant, I think she said."

"You know where he's stationed?"

"Oceana." He jotted it down.

"Tell me, miss, were you a friend of his too?"

"Not really. I only met him once. It was at the beach, about a month ago. That's when Marlene started dating him."

"They were lovers, I take it?"

She hesitated for some reason, aware she had stopped crying, but then nodded in answer.

"What about her husband?" was his next question. "Do you know him?"

"Yes. He's in the military too, you know."

"The marines?"

"No, navy."

"Do you know where he's stationed?"

"Yes, Norfolk Navy Base. He's stationed aboard the *Roosevelt*. You know, that big ship with all those airplane jets."

"Yep, the nuclear aircraft carrier."

She leaned forward, hands on her lap, looking anxious in a desperate sort of way.

"Inspector, what's going to happen now?"

"Well, there will be an autopsy and then I'll begin the investigation. However, from what I've seen so far, there don't seem to be any clues other than the body. The man who did this was clever. He got in somehow, did his dirty work, and then left without leaving a trail. From what I can tell, she didn't put up much of a struggle either. The ring around her neck proves he was a strong man."

"You don't suppose her boyfriend had anything to do with it?"

"Don't know, miss. However, it would seem unlikely. What I mean is, why would he strangle her and then leave his car in the parking lot?"

"What about her husband?"

"Hard to say," he told her. "In fact, I wouldn't even wager a guess at this point."

"But he's still a suspect, right?"

"Miss D'Angelo, I've been on the police force seventeen years. I've worked in homicide the last ten. As far as I'm concerned, *everybody* is a suspect."

*   *   *

News of the murder of Mrs. Charles Pike appeared on the second page of Sunday morning's *Virginian-Pilot*. Front-page headlines were dedicated to anti-war protests in the District of Columbia, which had resulted in seventy-one arrests.

Fuzzy Hostetler and his assistant, Detective Sergeant Jake Wharton, returned to the scene of the crime on Monday noon as lab technicians were conducting fingerprint tests. Wharton, a native of Portsmouth, a short, compact man with a receding hairline who had worked in homicide for the past five years, couldn't get over how tidy the place was. Like his boss, he had a feeling the investigation was not going to be easy.

At the police station later, Hostetler received a telephone call from the city coroner. "I've completed the postmortem," he told the detective. Hostetler listened as the man explained what he already knew: death by strangulation. "She died Friday night sometime between late afternoon and midnight," concluded the pathologist. Hostetler thanked him for the report and relayed the news to Wharton.

"You know, Matt, this case reminds me of the one we had in February."

"The Hingston murder in Ocean View?"

"Yeah. If you recall, her neck was broken in two places. And she was good-looking too, like Marlene Pike."

"You think there's a pattern here?"

"Maybe."

"What I don't like about this already is that the Navy's going to be involved. And you know what that means."

"Yeah, red tape."

Hostetler continued, "Take Gallagher, for instance. He's not even in Virginia. His CO told me that he's in San Diego for some sort of training."

"It gives him a great alibi, you must admit."

"That's for sure," added Hostetler dolefully.

"So he's not a suspect?"

"No, I didn't say that exactly."

"My money's on the husband," opinioned Wharton.

"Why?"

"Because *he* had a motive. According to Lisa D'Angelo, he was extremely jealous of her. She also said they used to fight like cats and dogs all the time."

"That's not much of a reason, Jake, but it'll be interesting to hear what he has to say when he comes in today."

Wharton lit a cigarette and propped his feet over the edge of the desk as if it were a normal thing to do.

"What about the marine?" he asked his partner.

"Well, according to his CO, he's flying back to Virginia tomorrow. So far the Navy's cooperating, which is good news for us. Other than Gallagher and Pike, we don't have a single lead to go on, unless the lab boys can find something."

Wharton said nothing in return. Hostetler glanced at his notes.

"You know, Jake, there's something that bothers me about this whole affair."

"Yeah, what's that?"

"Well, Lisa D'Angelo said that Marlene Pike's husband filed for divorce about six months ago. She also said that Gallagher was her first boyfriend after they split up."

"So?"

"Come on, Jake, you saw the body. She wasn't just another pretty face, she was beautiful."

"That's putting it mildly. That photo album we found in her closet was something to behold. Those snapshots of her in that wedding dress, for instance, not to mention those pictures of her in that red bikini." He frowned. "So what are you getting at, boss?"

"Just this. A girl who looks like that doesn't walk around town for long without a boyfriend on her arm, not in this day and age of free love. She must have had other guys knocking on her door after she and the hubby separated."

"You think Miss D'Angelo was lying?"

"Maybe."

"That's tough to swallow, Matt. She was a good friend, or so she claims. Why would she hide information from us?"

"To protect somebody maybe. I just got a feeling there's someone else involved here that we don't know about yet. Maybe we need to talk to the deceased's parents. They might know something."

"They live in Baltimore. They're driving down later today."

"Did you ask them to stop by the station?"

"Yes."

"Good. We'll also need to talk to all the victim's co-workers."

"I'm way ahead of you, Matt. I'm driving out to Little Creek base in the morning to interview the people she worked with at the commissary, including her boss."

The intercom buzzed, startling them. Hostetler leaned over and pressed a button.

"Yes?"

"Sorry to disturb you, Inspector, but Commander Pike is here. Shall I bring him in?"

"Yep, right away, Joyce."

Hostetler released the button and glanced at his partner. "Here we go, Jake."

"I'm ready," Wharton told him.

There was a knock at the door and the homicide cops got to

their feet.

"Come in."

The door was opened by a comely brunette, who promptly stepped aside to make room for the khaki-clad naval officer standing behind her. The tall good-looking man of sandy blond hair and blue eyes stepped past her and nodded respectfully at the two detectives. To Wharton, Pike looked like the prototype for next month's recruiting poster. Hostetler noticed how the big man filled out his uniform, especially at the shoulders and chest. But it was the size of the man's hands, the type that easily could have done the killing last week, which had caught his particular attention.

"Lieutenant-Commander Charles Pike," announced Joyce, who then withdrew, closing the door behind her.

"Thanks for coming in, sir." Hostetler shuffled around the desk and shook hands with the sailor. He turned. "My colleague, Sergeant Wharton."

Nodding, Pike shook hands with Wharton, who said, "Please be seated, Commander." He indicated the empty chair at the front of the desk.

Pike thanked him and plopped down on the seat. He hoisted his right leg over the other's knee, dropped his peaked cap on top and waited as Hostetler returned to his chair before he spoke.

"So, gentlemen, how can I help you?" He produced a pack of Camels from his breast pocket. "By the way, do you mind if I smoke?"

Bill Gallagher arrived at Oceana Naval Air Station late Tuesday evening.

His brief time in San Diego had been nothing short of a nightmare. Upon his arrival, he came down with diarrhea. He spent most of the weekend in bed taking stomach medicine and reading the newspaper. On Monday he felt marginally better and managed to get through the first day of orientation. The cablegram that arrived in the afternoon instructing him to return to Norfolk appeared out of nowhere like a thunderbolt of lightning.

When he arrived at the Norfolk airport, he telephoned Marlene and was surprised when there was no answer. He left the terminal, hailed a taxi, but when they stopped by her apartment, he noticed his car was missing from the lot. Thinking she was out grocery shopping or visiting friends, he told the cab driver to take him to Oceana. From ten o'clock until midnight, he called her number three times but again had no luck in making contact. It was very perplexing.

On Wednesday morning he reported to his commanding officer, who greeted him at the door wearing a long face. Gallagher helped himself to a cup of coffee and followed him into the office. Watson closed the door for privacy.

"Sit down, Bill." Watson looked him over, not liking the picture he saw. "You look beat."

"I *am* beat." He sat in the chair by the window which overlooked the airfield. "I've been sick the past few days," he added.

"No doubt you're wondering why I called you back."

"Yeah, well, I figured I'm in deep trouble for something, or that you were able to arrange my transfer."

"Well, I assure you, it's neither of those."

"All right, then, surprise me."

Watson lit a filter cigarette and inhaled hungrily.

"Bill, I want you to get a grip on yourself. I mean a *really* good grip."

"Okay."

Watson took another breath of cigarette, exhaling the smoke through his nostrils. When he spoke, his voice quivered.

"Your girlfriend, Bill, she...was murdered."

Gallagher's jaw dropped. He stared at Watson for a moment, but then looked away and peered out the window. A fuel truck lumbering across the airfield from east to west caught his attention. Watson noticed that his face had turned ash white. He struggled to swallow the knot in his throat.

"Bill, you okay?"

Gallagher turned away from the window and muttered, "Tell me it isn't true, sir?"

"I'm sorry, Bill."

"How...I mean, when did this happen?"

"According to the police, last Friday night."

Gallagher dropped his head as he leaned forward in his seat. He took a moment to massage his aching brow before he looked back, eyes tearing, sparkling like stars.

He heard Watson say, "You all right, Lieutenant?"

"Steve, this must be someone's idea of a sick joke."

"I'm sorry, Bill, but it's true. When the police called—"

"She was murdered, you say?"

"Yes, strangled to death."

"Strangled?"

"That's what the police said."

"But how can that be? I was with her Friday night. She went to the airport with me."

"And drove your car home."

"Yeah, that's right." Bill squinted at his friend. "How did you know that?"

"The police," was Watson's answer. "They found your car in the parking lot outside her apartment. They've already impounded it. On Monday they requested a copy of your fingerprints on file. You and I are going to Norfolk this morning to see the detective in charge of the investigation."

Gallagher was beside himself. His hands trembled noticeably, like his voice when he spoke.

"No, I...I can't believe this," he said to the floor. "Why would anyone want to kill..." He stopped his words, as if making a mistake, and remembered what Marlene had told him about her husband.

"What is it, Bill? What are you thinking about?"

"I'm thinking about her husband."

"You mean she was married?"

Gallagher told him the story of how he and Marlene had met at the beach the previous month, of their love affair, and of the death threats she had received from her navy husband.

When he had finished, Watson said, "I'm sure the police will be interested to know that."

Bill drank some coffee and grimaced; it was already cold. He stood and peered through the window again, watching a cargo plane lifting off the airfield. It looked like a giant pregnant bird.

"What happens now, Steve?" he said to the window.

"Well, like I said, we got an appointment with the police this morning. As of this moment you're on indefinite leave—captain's orders. The Navy wants you to cooperate with the police until the investigation is over."

Gallagher said nothing in return, just nodded as Watson stood and joined him by the window.

"Bill, you *sure* you're all right? I can postpone the meeting till later."

"No, let's get it over with."

CHAPTER 5

"Marlene Pike was murdered on the evening of Friday the twenty-fifth," Hostetler told Gallagher and Watson later that morning.

Standing next to the file cabinet, Wharton added, "That's according to the coroner's autopsy report."

Gallagher, sitting on Watson's right at the front of the desk, asked of Hostetler, "Where did it happen?"

"In her apartment bedroom," was the answer. "She didn't have a stitch of clothing on her. Except for the dark bruise around her neck, we didn't find another mark on the body."

"I see." Gallagher thought. "Am I a suspect?"

Hostetler seemed not to have heard him. Instead, he opened the top drawer, reached inside and produced a key ring with two keys attached.

"These are your car keys, are they not, Lieutenant?"

"Yes."

Hostetler continued, "We found them on the vanity table in her bedroom. Your car was parked in the lot outside the apartment building."

"Where is it now?"

"In the shop."

"When can I have it back?"

"We'll need it for another day or two," was the detective's answer. "Our forensic experts are still searching for fingerprints and other possible clues. It's standard procedure."

"So far we've found only five sets of prints in her apartment," joined in Wharton. He stared at his notepad. "Mrs. Pike's, the landlord's, Lisa D'Angelo's, and another friend of hers—Olga Sandberg. Both women worked with her at the Little Creek base commissary."

Hostetler added, "Of course, your fingerprints were found too, Lieutenant."

"Naturally." Bill hesitated, but then said with a sharp edge to his voice, "So am I a suspect or not?"

Hostetler stared at the marine, showing his best poker face.

"Mr. Gallagher, let me make one thing perfectly clear. This is a routine interview. No charges have been filed against you or anyone else."

"Including her husband?"

"We've already interviewed Commander Pike. According to his testimony, him and his wife had been separated and living apart for several months. I'm sure you know that. We also understand that you had been dating her since the latter part of June."

"That's right. We started dating the same day we met." A brief grin appeared on the marine's lips as he recalled that glorious June afternoon at the beach. "We hit it off right from the start. We had planned to get married."

"Really?" Hostetler glanced at Wharton, who was busy writing down the new information on his note pad. "So you and the girl were serious about each other?"

"Yes. I loved her and she loved me. If anyone had a motive to kill her—" Hostetler cut him off.

"So tell me about Friday night, Lieutenant. Why did you go to San Diego?"

"Excuse me, Inspector." It was Watson interrupting. "I'd like to answer that, if you don't mind?"

"Please do, sir."

"Thank you." Watson took a deep breath, as if for added strength, and said when he exhaled, "Lieutenant Gallagher went to San Diego for retraining. The Navy had made some modifications to the F-16. Bill's a decorated fighter ace and one of my top instructors. He needed to be briefed on the modifications."

"A fighter pilot, huh?" Hostetler smiled at the marine. "I spent some time in the army, by the way. Served in Korea as a mess cook for a year and a half." He stopped to clear his throat, annoyed with himself for straying from the main topic. "Anyway, you last saw the girl when?"

"Friday night, when she dropped me off at the airport."

"In your car?"

"That's right. I had asked her to take care of it while I was away in California."

Hostetler's next question was, "Before she dropped you off at the airport, did she mention what she planned to do that evening?"

Gallagher did not answer, was busy massaging his aching forehead. Watson leaned closer, frowning at him.

"Bill, you all right?"

"Yeah, I'm all right, but my life is ruined." He dropped his head and started to cry. "I loved her—I loved that girl!" He produced a handkerchief from his breast pocket and swiped the tears from his face. To Hostetler he said, "Sorry, Inspector."

"Perhaps you'd like to take a break, Lieutenant?"

Bill nodded.

The interview resumed nine minutes later. Hostetler had the floor.

"Let me summarize what we know so far," he said, addressing Gallagher. "Mrs. Pike dropped you off at the airport on Friday night around six forty-five. You then took a commercial flight to San Diego. When you arrived there, you bought a postcard and mailed it to her."

"Correct," nodded the marine.

Hostetler continued, "Presumably, she then drove your car back to her apartment. Sometime after that she was murdered. On Saturday afternoon Lisa D'Angelo and the landlord found her body in the bedroom at approximately five-thirty. The landlord then notified the police." A brief pause. "Now, Lieutenant, please tell me exactly what you did after you arrived in Norfolk last night."

"Well, the first thing I did, I phoned her. When there was no answer, I hailed a taxi and told the driver to take me to her apartment. When we got there, I noticed my car was missing from the parking lot, so I told the driver to take me to Oceana."

Wharton said, "Did you try calling her later?"

"Yes, several times. I didn't find out about the murder until Commander Watson told me this morning."

Hostetler said, "Lieutenant, tell me what you know about her husband."

"What about him?"

"Do you know him?"

"No."

"Did you ever meet him?"

"No."

"Did you know that he's a naval officer?"

"Yes. Marlene told me he was stationed aboard the *Roosevelt*."

"What else do you know about him?"

"They were married in Baltimore after he had graduated from the Naval Academy in '64."

Wharton said, "Do you know why Commander Pike filed for divorce?"

"Yes. Marlene said they couldn't live together. They were always fighting, couldn't agree on anything."

"In other words, they were incompatible?"

Bill nodded.

Hostetler said, "According to Pike's testimony, his wife cheated on him. That's why he filed for divorce."

Gallagher went pale, was stunned by Hostetler's statement. He glared at him at length, but then glanced away and stared at Wharton with the same intensity. Hostetler's partner stared back, pen poised in his writing hand. The mask on his face was a blank picture, no emotion showing.

Hostetler continued, "Pike also claimed he hadn't seen his wife since the day they separated. According to him, he didn't know you were seeing her."

"That's a lie!" Bill's voice was close to anger. "Marlene said he knew about me."

"How did she know?"

"Because he told her. She also said he was always calling her and making threats."

"What kind of threats?" urged Wharton.

"He threatened to kill her if she didn't stop seeing me."

"Were you ever present when he called and threatened her?" queried Hostetler.

"No, I wasn't, but—"

"So you're just telling us what she told you?"

"That's right."

"When did these alleged death threats occur?"

"At various times. Marlene said he threatened to kill her if he ever found out she was sleeping with another man. Believe me, Inspector, he knew about me. I think he killed her because he was jealous of me. It was his motive."

"A motive according to the deceased, that is?"

Gallagher's eyes flared.

"Yes, that's one way of putting it," he replied testily. "She was scared of him."

"Excuse me." It was Watson intruding. "I don't want to seem out of line, Inspector, but did her husband's fingerprints show up in her apartment?"

"No. Whoever killed her was obviously wearing gloves."

Gallagher rubbed the part of his forehead where the pain had started moments earlier. Hostetler took it as a sign to end the interview.

"I think we've had enough for one day, gentlemen." To Gallagher he said, "I would appreciate that you make yourself available if we find the need to question you again. As far as the funeral arrangements are concerned, her parents plan to take her body back to Maryland and have her buried in their church cemetery."

"Can I see her body?" Gallagher asked him.

"Don't see why not," was Hostetler's reply. "Just tell the desk clerk outside. She'll arrange it."

*   *   *

After leaving the morgue, Gallagher and Watson started back to Oceana. Watson decided to bypass the freeway traffic and use the less stressful route of scenic Shore Drive. Neither had said a word since leaving the city.

They were waiting for the traffic light to change at the intersection of Great Neck Road and Virginia Beach Boulevard when Watson ended the silence.

"Bill, you okay?"

"I...I'm not sure, Steve. Maybe you should ask me that tomorrow." He turned away from the window, the scene at the morgue of Marlene's pale, lifeless face still frozen in his mind. "So what now, sir?"

"Well, like I said, you're on indefinite leave. The Navy wants to keep a low profile on this. Just cooperate with the police until the investigation is over."

"But what am I supposed to do in the meantime?"

"Just take it easy for a while. Spend some time at the beach, take in a movie or two, but stay close. I'll need to know where you are at all times."

"Steve, I'd like to go to the funeral. You think it'd be okay?"

"Don't see why not. I'm sure Hostetler won't object. From the impression I got, I think he believes your story. He can't possibly believe you committed the crime."

"I don't think he believes Pike murdered her either—but I do. I got a bad feeling about him."

"Why, because Marlene said he threatened to kill her?"

"That's right."

The light changed, and Watson leaned on the gas pedal.

"So you think Pike lied to the police when he told them he hadn't seen his wife since the time they split up?"

"Yes, I do."

"I'm not sure I agree with you, Bill. Let's face it, Pike's an officer. Maybe he did abuse her during the marriage, but I don't think he'd be stupid enough to kill his own wife in cold blood."

"Yeah, well, he may be an officer and some kind of super genius, but he's still a human being. And humans kill for all kinds of reasons." He shook his head, then added between clenched teeth, "I'm telling you, Steve, I got an eerie feeling about him."

"Seems to me you've already made up your mind about him. Don't you think you're jumping the gun? Hell, anyone could have killed her. For instance, like a burglar who broke into her apartment and then killed her so she wouldn't be able to identify him to the police."

"You could be right, sir, but I still believe Pike killed her."

"Well, try not to worry about it. Let the police do their job. It's what they're paid for."

Later that night Fuzzy Hostetler was lying awake in bed, staring at the ceiling. Lying beside him, his wife put down July's *Reader's Digest,* frowning at him.

"What's on your mind, dear?"

"Work—what else?"

She slipped her hand under the sheet and rubbed his stomach in a slow circular motion, just above the navel.

"Want to talk about it?"

"No."

"Please? I won't be able to sleep unless you do."

"It's about the new murder case."

"You mean the young woman who was strangled to death?"

"Yep, that's the one."

"And?" she urged, moving her fingers lower. He turned.

"Look, sweetheart, if you keep that up, I won't tell you

anything more."

"Sorry." She reluctantly removed her hand. "Now, go on, tell me."

"Well, we've already hit a brick wall. We have no clues. Even Jake's baffled."

"No suspects?"

"Only two so far—the husband and her boyfriend. Jake thinks the hubby killed her."

"And what do you think?"

"Not sure," he replied, speaking to the ceiling. "We've already questioned them. Both had credible alibis on the night of the murder. The boyfriend thinks her husband killed her too."

"Well, whoever killed her, I'm sure you and Jake will find out eventually."

"Yeah, sure, like we did with the Hingston case." He briefly massaged his forehead, sighed and went on, "Maybe I'm losing my touch, Betty, or maybe the killers are getting smarter." An insincere chuckle before he added, "Maybe I should look for another line of work."

She ignored the comment.

"So what are you going to do, Matt?"

"Don't know. According to the boyfriend, her husband had threatened to kill her several times. Even her best friend said they used to fight a lot when they lived together. They're the only leads we have so far."

"Gee, this would make a good TV program. Maybe you ought to get Perry Mason to help you out." She giggled as she slipped her hand under the sheet again, where he liked it. "Now, let's try to get some sleep, okay?"

"Later," he told her. He wriggled closer and smirked, adding, "I got something else in mind."

CHAPTER 6

Bill Gallagher got drunk Wednesday night. On Thursday, 1 August, after a slow start due to the constant riveting in his head, he spent the afternoon enjoying the sunshine and surf of Virginia Beach. Supper that night included a superb clam chowder, marinated red snapper and chocolate mousse cake. Upon returning to Oceana later that evening, he went for a walk and ended up at the officers' lounge, where he stayed until closing.

Just after ten o'clock on Friday morning, he received a phone call from Jake Wharton. The homicide cop told him that his Mustang was ready for him and would he please drop by to pick it up. Bill's roommate, Chester Greaves, who was without hangover and had nothing else to do, provided him a lift into town.

At the police station, Gallagher bumped into Fuzzy Hostetler, who informed him that Marlene's body had been released to the family. "The funeral will be in Baltimore next Tuesday," the detective told him. Later in the afternoon he received telephone permission to attend the funeral from Steve Watson.

That evening he got plastered again, a feat he repeated the following night. After Sunday brunch, he packed his gray suit and other essentials needed for the trip to Maryland. His plan was to arrive in Baltimore Monday afternoon, attend the viewing that evening, and then return to Virginia Beach following the funeral the next day.

It rained Monday morning. Gallagher arrived in Baltimore just after noon and booked a room at the downtown Holiday Inn. He lunched at the inner harbor, purchased a copy of the *Sun* and returned to the hotel to relax before preparing himself for the viewing. For dinner he enjoyed fried calamari and shrimp at a bar not far from the hotel, for dessert a tall Budweiser. Three hours later he was still perched on the same bar stool, a wall of empty beer bottles standing in front of him.

He woke up the next morning with a jackhammer of a headache and barely made it to the church in time for the funeral. Unlike the previous morning, the sun was out and shining over The Old Line State.

At the cemetery, he counted twenty-two people in attendance. He was recognized by Lisa D'Angelo, who introduced him to the bereaved family as a "close friend of Marlene's." Bill waited at the grave site until the coffin was lowered into its eternal crypt before deciding to leave. It was not much later when he spotted the man standing next to his Mustang.

The stranger was handsome, tall and broad-shouldered, sported a navy-blue pinstriped suit jacket and matching bell-bottom pants; had curly, military-length blond hair and piercing eyes of the bluest variety. There was a kind of stoic demeanor about him that suggested he was a man of uncompromising principles: a man of confidence and steel who demanded constant perfection of himself, and nothing less.

As he stepped closer, they eyed each other over like boxers about to do battle. The blond had large, powerful-looking hands. Without a doubt, Bill knew the big man could easily beat the stuffing out of him without taking too much time in the process. It was at that moment when he realized who the man was and why he was there. Surprisingly, it was the blond who spoke first, breaking the stalemate between them.

"So you were the boyfriend." He had spoken as if reading from a book, calmly, matter-of-factly, without trace of emotion.

"The name is Gallagher," Bill told him. Then quickly added, "And you were the husband."

No response from the blond. Instead, he reached inside his jacket pocket, yanked out a pack of Camel cigarettes, tapped one out and offered it to the marine.

"Cigarette?"

A non-smoker, Gallagher shook his head.

"I believe it's time I introduced myself," said the blond. "My name is Charles Pike."

"Yes, I know who and what you are," came back Gallagher, the tone of his voice a mixture of sarcasm and contempt. "However, if you're expecting a salute from me, you're badly mistaken."

"Indeed!" Pike calmly struck a match to the cigarette. "So you've already formed an opinion of me?"

"That's right."

"And you believe I killed my wife, of course?"

"If I said so, would it change anything?"

"No, I suppose not. You despise me. It's as plain as the nose on your face. My wife—may she rest in peace—had a way of manipulating others to side with her point of view. She was very gifted in that department."

"Tell me, Commander, is there anything I should like about you?"

"Mr. Gallagher—or do you prefer Lieutenant?"

"Bill will do just fine."

"Very well, I'll be frank. I honestly don't care what you think of me. It's a free country. You're entitled to your opinion. However, it's time you learned a few facts about my wife and me."

"Sorry, but I hardly think this is the time or place to discuss this."

"Look, Bill, we're both intelligent human beings. My wife and I had a stormy marriage. I don't deny it. In fact, I'm sure Marlene gave you a blow-by-blow description of her version of the marriage. But there are two sides to every coin, and my story is quite different than hers. Trust me, my wife was no saint."

"Exactly what are you trying to say?"

"That you're not the only man she slept with after she and I separated."

"Why tell me all this? Why don't you tell your sob story to the police?"

"The police already know everything about my wife and me, just as they know about you and her, I'm sure."

"All right, so she wasn't a saint. And neither are you, or so I've been told."

"No, I'm not. I have my vices, particularly when it comes to beautiful women. But I was faithful to my wife before we broke up. I loved her dearly. But being the faithful navy wife wasn't her cup of tea. And that's why I filed for divorce."

Gallagher said nothing in return, just waited, expecting to hear more. Pike inhaled through his cigarette as though he had all the time in the world. He exhaled the smoke through his nostrils before he spoke his next words.

"Tell me, Bill, did my wife ever confide in you that she was once pregnant?"

"No, so what?"

"Well, she was, but not by me."

"Look, you've already said she was unfaithful. Now she's barely in her grave and you're telling me she was a tramp?"

"Yes, that's exactly what she was. She was impregnated by another sailor who was once a friend of mine. He spilled the beans to me the day I got back from sea duty. Guess he felt guilty about it. Anyway, he arranged for her to get an abortion out of state. Not an easy thing to do, especially for a Catholic girl."

"So that's when you decided to leave her?"

"That's right."

"Well, her version, if you don't mind me saying so, is quite another matter. She said she left you because she got tired of you beating the crap out of her. She also got tired of your drinking and—"

"That I threatened to kill her?"

"Yeah, that's right. So you freely admit it?"

"Yes, I admit it. But death threats don't convict a man of murder, Bill. Yes, I threatened her many times, but it was because I loved her and didn't want to lose her."

Gallagher had heard enough. He took a brave step toward the sailor, aware of his trembling body, his heart drumming furiously against his rib cage. Yet when he spoke, his voice was firm, not at all anxious.

"You're despicable, Commander! You're a lout—that's what you are! If you truly loved her, you wouldn't have beaten her up all the time or made all those threats. Did you ever think that maybe she cheated on you because you weren't giving her the attention she needed?"

"You're blind, Gallagher. You're blinded by hate and your admiration for a girl you barely knew."

"Since we're both being open and frank, and since we're both officers and gentlemen, why don't you tell me the truth, Pike? Everyone's gone now, the police aren't here, no one's taking notes. So tell me, did you do it? Did you kill her?"

"No, but that won't change your opinion of me."

"Yes, you're absolutely right about that. I *know* you murdered her. And I'm going to prove it, one way or another."

"What's that supposed to mean? Are you starting your own investigation?"

"Maybe I will."

Pike smirked, seemed unfazed by Gallagher's rejoinder. He inhaled through the cigarette for the last time and flicked the butt away.

"I was wrong about you, Bill. You're not just a fool, you're a pig-headed one. If I were you, I'd go back to base, forget the past and get on with my life. You've absolutely no proof that I killed her. Even the police are convinced I'm not guilty. If they thought otherwise, we wouldn't be chatting right now. If you persist in slandering me with false accusations, I could make it very difficult for you."

"So now you threaten me, like you threatened her?"

"No, it's not a threat, just a simple suggestion."

Pike turned to leave, but then stopped suddenly and looked back, as if forgetting something.

"By the way, Lieutenant, if we ever meet again, it'll probably be in uniform. If and when that day happens, I will expect that salute." Another wide smirk. "Good day to you."

* * *

At the same time Gallagher and Pike parted company, Fuzzy Hostetler was leaving the office of the chief of police after an unrewarding hour-long meeting. Back in his office, he reorganized the mountain of paperwork on his desktop while nursing a cup of black coffee. Finished, he stepped over to the window overlooking the Elizabeth River and watched a commercial tug plowing its way north toward the Roads.

"That's what I need, a simpler life," he heard himself say.

Jake Wharton appeared at the door. Hostetler's right-hand man was in white shirtsleeves, black tie and gray slacks, a cigarette in one hand, a folder stuffed with notes in the other. He walked into the room without fanfare, grabbed an empty chair from the corner, positioned it closer to the desk and sat down. Hostetler stared at him beneath a wrinkled brow, a mask of resignation attached to his long face. Wharton deduced that his meeting with the chief had not gone well.

"Was it that bad, Matt?"

"It was absolutely awful," was Hostetler's answer. "To put it mildly, he's not happy with the way we're handling the case."

"Oh, anything in particular?"

"Yeah. He couldn't understand why we hadn't made any progress."

"By that, you mean, an arrest?"

"Yep."

"So what did you tell him?"

"What *could* I tell him? We've got no leads, no clues. Our prime suspects have rock solid alibis." He shook his head, adding, "We're chasing a ghost, Jake."

"It's starting to look like the Hingston case all over again, isn't it?"

"That's what the chief said. And that's what bothers him. The press are breathing down his neck. They want results. So does the mayor."

"Don't tell me the mayor was there too?"

"No, the chief was quoting him."

"I can see the mayor being upset, but why the press? One way or another they have a story. If we solve the case, we're heroes and Norfolk is saved. If we don't, they have a story of a mad killer on the loose. Makes for good reading, you must admit."

"Correction, it makes for good reading in a crime novel. In real life it's a tragedy and bad for the department."

Wharton contemplated the ash at the end of his cigarette.

"So where do we go from here, Matt?"

"We accelerate the investigation. The chief said if we don't come up with an arrest soon, he'll shut down the investigation. Said he's not going to waste the taxpayers' money on a case we can't solve."

"You suppose the Navy can help us out?"

"How?"

"Well, maybe they know more about Gallagher and Pike than what they told us. Maybe one of them has a criminal background. Maybe *both* do."

Hostetler laughed without mirth.

"Come on, Jake, you don't really believe that, do you? Hell, one's a decorated fighter pilot and Vietnam vet. The other's a hotshot naval officer with an unblemished service record. Do you actually think they could be where they are today if they both had a rap sheet?"

"Was just thinking out loud."

"If you have to think, think clearly, for God's sake!"

"Sorry, Matt, I just don't know what else to suggest."

"All right, let's start from the beginning again. There's only two witnesses to the murder—the victim and the killer. For now, Gallagher and Pike are the only suspects we have. Pike claims he was out with his girlfriend that night."

"That's what they both claim. They were at a country bar in Portsmouth. The Gunslinger, I think they called it."

"Did the owner of the club verify that they'd had been there that night?"

"Yeah, twice," said Wharton, staring at his notes. "He said he knows for sure because the girl works there full-time as a barmaid. It happened to be her night off."

"All right, so that brings us to Gallagher. According to him, Marlene Pike dropped him off at the airport at quarter to seven, where he left for San Diego a half hour later."

"Which was verified by the airline company and his commanding officer, Steve what's-his-name."

"Watson."

"Yeah. Anyway, I called Oceana to verify that Gallagher arrived in San Diego and when he returned."

"So the only part of his story that could be bogus is the part about the car." Hostetler stared across the desk. "Are you with me, Jake?"

"Yeah. You're thinking that Gallagher went to her apartment earlier in the day, strangled her, and then took a taxi to the airport. His story that she had dropped him off there was a fabrication to cover his tracks."

"Now you're talking, Jake. Get on the horn and call the taxi companies to see if they have any record of a pickup in the vicinity of the girl's apartment that night."

"And if they don't?"

"In that case, we're back to square one."

*   *   *

But they got nowhere with that idea. Both Yellow Cab and the Black-and-White taxi service had no customer pickups that night within a ten-block radius of the murder scene.

While Hostetler and Wharton were making their inquiries, Bill Gallagher was making good time along Interstate-95. He saw the town of Fredericksburg in the foreground, knowing he was approximately one-third of the way home.

He had the convertible top down, though it did little to improve his disposition. He still couldn't believe Marlene was gone from his life. Why had she been murdered? What had been the killer's motive?

For most of the trip, his mind kept flashing back to the many wonderful times they had shared, particularly the tender moments during their final week together. Not once, not twice, but three times he was forced to pull off the road when the tears came pouring out. He arrived in Oceana a half hour later than planned.

He had supper at the officers' mess with his roommate, Chet Greaves. Afterward Greaves talked him into leaving the base and they ended up at a boardwalk café on the Virginia Beach oceanfront near Atlantic and Fifth. It was a beautiful summer evening, yet neither seemed interested in the crashing sounds of the black ocean, the serene southwesterly breeze, or the constant flow of tourists strolling along the boardwalk. It was a very good night to drink.

"I love this place," Greaves was saying. "When I get out of the navy next year, I think I'll settle down here. Maybe even get a place near the waterfront." He chuckled, adding, "No more Boston for me. It's too cold up there."

"You're lucky," said Gallagher, speaking to his beer. "There's no way I could live here, not after what's happened."

"So what now? Have you talked to Steve?"

"Yeah."

"And?"

"I asked him for a transfer."

"You're not thinking of going back to 'Nam again?"

"Don't know. Maybe they'll ship me overseas to Europe this time. The problem is I can't leave until the murder case is wrapped up."

"What if the police don't find the killer?"

"I know who killed her, Chet. I met him today."

"Bill, come on, you can't get involved in this. You got no proof that Pike killed her, and neither do the police."

"He did it, Chet, I know it! You should have been there today. It was pathetic. He called Marlene a tramp and tried to convince me that *he* was the good guy during their marriage. I swear to you, I wanted to put a dent in his face right then and there."

Greaves nodded for no special reason and saw a young couple, teenagers, strolling along the boardwalk arm-in-arm. Both had dirty-looking shoulder-length dark hair and wore peace chains around their necks. It was impossible to tell which sex was which.

"So what happens now, Bill?"

"I got an appointment with the police in the morning. I have to be there at ten."

"What do you think will happen?"

"God knows. But I'm going to tell them about my meeting with Pike today. That might light a fire under them."

"So you really think he killed her?"

"I'm *telling* you he killed her. According to Marlene, he knew about us and threatened to kill her. There's no doubt in my mind he killed her out of jealousy. That was his motive."

"All right, maybe it was his motive, but you still need proof he did it."

Gallagher nodded with reluctance, but said nothing in return as he reached for his beer.

Greaves went on, "What about Pike's girlfriend? You said the police told you that she was with him at the time of the murder. You think she was lying?"

"Maybe."

"Well, if it's true, and if Pike did kill his wife, that sort of makes her an accessory to the murder, doesn't it?"

"Yeah, I suppose it does."

"Gee, Bill, if you're right and the police are wrong, how are you going to prove he did it?"

"Don't know, but I'll think of something."

"It still seems like a dead end to me."

"Maybe you're right, Chet, but there must be a way to find out the truth. There *must* be."

Greaves finished his beer and ordered another. When the waitress had gone, he reached closer and dropped a comforting hand on his friend's shoulder.

"Bill, I have to tell you that you're reacting out of pure hate for this guy. It's clouding your judgment. If you keep it up, you'll become a prime candidate for the funny farm. Get your life back, for cryin' out loud. You must stop grieving. Eventually you'll find another girl."

"I don't want another girl, Chet. There will never be another girl for me. I loved her—I wanted to marry her. All I want now is to see the killer pay for his crime. I swear to you, if it's the last thing I do, I'm going to prove that…that *gentleman* did it, one way or another."

They left the boardwalk four beers later. Gallagher fell asleep that night stoned drunk. It was the sixth day in a row he had accomplished the feat.

CHAPTER 7

Gallagher arrived at the Norfolk police station at 9:52 on Wednesday morning and was ushered into Hostetler's office six minutes later by Jake Wharton. He made himself comfortable in the chair provided, was offered a cup of coffee, which he accepted, and sampled the brew as Wharton took his usual place next to the file cabinet. Three minutes later the homicide inspector appeared in the room, Gallagher stood, and the two men shook hands.

"Thanks for coming in, Lieutenant." Hostetler went behind his desk, opened the top drawer and yanked out a manila folder stuffed with notes. "This won't take long, I promise."

Bill sipped and waited as Hostetler took his seat. Watching him, Wharton tucked a filter cigarette between his lips and produced a note pad and pen from his shirt pocket.

Hostetler said to him, "All right, Jake, begin."

"Right." Wharton lit the cigarette with a lighter and said to the marine, "Lieutenant, we'd like to review your original testimony starting with the night of the murder. It's important that you recall everything that happened."

"I understand."

"Good, please proceed."

Gallagher told his story again, starting when he and Marlene parted company at the airport and ending in the present. Wharton shot a glance at his boss, who nodded in return, a signal that he was satisfied with what he had heard.

"Thank you, Lieutenant." Hostetler's grin was short-lived. "I only have a few questions for you."

"I'm all ears, Inspector."

"About your car. Exactly why did you leave it with her that night?"

"Well, like I told you the first time, I had asked her to look after it while I was away. We had spent the previous night together, and it saved me the trouble of leaving the car at the base and taking a bus to the airport."

"And she agreed to pick you up at the airport when you arrived back from California?"

"Yes."

Hostetler went on, "At our first meeting you said that you didn't know what she planned to do after she dropped you off at the airport. Correct?"

"That's right. If she told me, I don't remember."

Hostetler scratched the itch behind his ear.

"One last question. Did she ever confide in you the names of other boyfriends she dated before she met you?"

"No."

"Are you sure?"

"Yes, I'm sure."

"Thank you." Hostetler turned. "You have any questions for the lieutenant, Jake?"

"No, Matt."

Nodding, Hostetler said to Gallagher, "Well, that about wraps it up."

Bill stared at him, his pale face a picture of confusion.

"But what happens now, Inspector?" There was something close to desperation in his voice. "You're not closing the case, are you?"

"No. Officially, the investigation remains open until we solve the case. Unofficially, there's not much else we can do right now. We've got no leads."

"You're saying the murderer may never be found?"

It was Wharton who answered, "Unfortunately, yes. It's happened before."

Gallagher said to Hostetler. "What about Pike?"

"Commander Pike will be coming in tomorrow for more questioning," was the cop's answer.

"He was at the funeral," Bill told him, as if speaking to himself.

"Interesting," muttered Wharton.

Hostetler added nothing, and Gallagher went on, "The bastard did it! You should have seen him yesterday. I actually was surprised he had the guts to show up at his wife's funeral. The ugly things he said about her—"

Hostetler cut him off.

"Lieutenant, we know how you feel about him."

"No, Inspector, you don't know how I feel. I lost the woman who was going to be my wife. She was the most important person in my life. I loved her! It was the first time I had ever really cared about another woman."

"We know that." Hostetler produced a postcard from the folder, the one Gallagher had mailed from San Diego on the night of the murder. He leaned across the desk and gave it to the marine. "We believe your story."

Bill stared at the postcard with the picture of the Golden Gate Bridge on the front side and flipped it over. He read:

Marlene, I miss you already. I'll count the hours until we meet again. Be ready to celebrate when I return. Love, Bill.

He raised his head slowly, blinking fiercely. Watching him, Hostetler expected a flood of tears to erupt at any moment. He exchanged glances with his partner, seemingly at a loss to continue. Gallagher ended the silence.

"You both probably think I'm crazy. But Pike killed her—I know it! I can't shake the feeling."

"Unfortunately, the only thing that holds up in a court of law is proof that he did it," said Hostetler. "Until we get the proof, Pike is a free man."

"But you're closing the investigation."

"No, not officially," Hostetler corrected him. "Like I said before, it doesn't end until we solve the case."

"But you said the case may never be solved."

"Unfortunately, that does seem to be the case here," said Wharton, butting in. "We have no leads. As police, there's just so much we can do. We run on a strict budget."

Hostetler added, "I'm sorry, Lieutenant."

"Okay." Gallagher let loose a tired sigh. "Is there anything else, Inspector?"

"No, you're free to go."

After he had gone, Hostetler produced a pack of cigarettes,

shook one out and took his time lighting it with a match. He glanced at Wharton as he exhaled the first puff.

"Glad that's over with," he said unnecessarily.

"You know, Matt, I feel sorry for that man. If the same thing had happened to one of us, we probably would've reacted the same way."

"Yep, you're right. But what else can we do?"

"There's still Pike."

"Come on, Jake, you know what'll happen tomorrow. He'll tell us exactly what he told us the first time he was here. No, we won't get any new information out of him. Let's face it, we're licked. No clues, no witnesses, no nothing. Whoever committed the crime is out there somewhere enjoying himself. Who knows, maybe it's the same bastard who murdered Gloria Hingston."

"Well, if it is, it eliminates Pike as a suspect. He was at sea the day she was murdered. I've already checked on it. And Gallagher was on leave at the time visiting his family in Florida. So that rules him out too." He shook his head, adding, "'Fraid you're right, Matt, we *are* licked."

"Yep, it's enough to make you weep and want to go back and pound the beat again."

Gallagher did not return to Oceana after leaving the police station. Instead, he drove out to Marlene's apartment and parked in the lot where he usually did when visiting her.

The neighborhood was oddly quiet for a weekday. He caught a glimpse of a Greyhound bus cruising along Bayview Boulevard in the rearview mirror, then shut his eyes and saw Marlene's face smiling back at him in his mind. So long ago, he thought, so very long ago. No, he would never see her again, never be able to touch her or hold her in his arms; never be able to kiss her the way she liked or make love to her; never be able to tell her how much he cared about her and of his dreams to make her happy for the rest of their lives…

He started the car and leaned on the accelerator pedal, unsure where he was going; nor did he care. It was as if the power inside him had been switched off. How did it happen? One moment she was there, then suddenly she was not.

The police were stumped, yes, but he knew who had done the evil deed. He knew exactly what the murderer looked like, how he talked, what brand of cigarette he smoked, and how he dressed at funerals. Yes, Charles Pike had nerves of steel, but he had done the crime. There were no other possibilities, no other suspects. "There's not much else we can do right now," Hostetler had told him. Yes, the killer was a free man, free to walk among the innocent and decent people of the world…

Bill cleared his thoughts. He was behaving like a fool. If he continued this way, he would surely go crazy, as Greaves had warned him. It was time to get on with his life, pick up the pieces and figure out what he would do. Maybe he could find another girl and…

He swerved off the road and stopped the car as Marlene's lovely smile popped into his mind again. He reached inside his shirt pocket, yanked out the postcard and reread the last sentence:

Be ready to celebrate when I return.

He swore angrily and ripped the card in half.

Later that night he got drunk at the officers' lounge. It was not a celebration.

The murder investigation was put to mothballs the following

Tuesday by Fuzzy Hostetler on the advice of the chief of police. Jake Wharton telephoned Oceana Naval Air Station and informed Gallagher of the news. The detective conveyed his regrets that nothing more could be done, thanked him again for his cooperation, and added that he hoped the killer would someday be brought to justice. His words did little to soothe Bill's conscience.

Later in the afternoon he visited the NAS training center to have a word with his boss. Steve Watson, who had been working on junior officers' fitness reports, was showing the effects of a long day but smiled when his protégé stepped into the office.

"Good to see you, Bill." He waited as Gallagher sat in the chair next to the window. "Been thinking about you."

"Hope you don't mind me stopping by, sir?"

"Not at all. Actually it saves me the trouble of finding you. We need to talk."

"Oh?"

"It's about your future, Bill. I talked to the CO about the murder case and—"

"The police suspended the investigation this morning," interjected the marine, speaking to the floor. "I got the call an hour ago."

"I see."

"No leads, no witnesses, no suspects, they said."

"But they'll keep looking, won't they?"

"Well, sort of, but they're not optimistic. They said there was a similar case a few months ago that's still unresolved." Watson saw anger in his eyes. "Dammit, Steve, are the police stupid or are criminals getting smarter?"

Watson ignored the comment and lit a cigarette.

"So what now, Bill? What are you thinking?"

"What do you mean?"

"Well, what I mean is, how do you feel about it?"

"I know who killed her, Steve. I met the man. I told the police he did it, but they need proof to arrest him."

"Naturally."

"I'm telling you, Steve, the way they talked, it's almost as if Marlene had been killed by the invisible man from outer space." He shook his head sadly, adding, "But Pike did it. I know the bastard did it!"

Watson frowned at him, not liking the sound of that.

"Bill, this is not like you. The police are right. You can't say he did it without proof. Your feelings for this man won't solve a blessed thing."

"I just wish there was something I could do to help solve the case. I feel responsible somehow."

"Would that make you sleep better?"

"Sir, I've not had a good night's sleep since I got back from California. Most of the time—"

"You sit at the bar drowning in sorrow," Watson finished for him. Gallagher scowled at him.

"Yes, I've been drinking a lot. So what? You would, too, Steve, if it'd happened to your wife."

Watson stood out of his chair.

"Bill, I had a chat with Chet Greaves earlier. He said he's worried about you. Said you drink until you're almost too drunk to walk home at night."

"My personal affairs are none of his business."

"No, but it's my business. More importantly, it's the Navy's business. I can't have one of my officers stumbling around the base stoned all the time. Sooner or later it'll catch up with you. And I won't like that, not one damned bit."

"All right, so I'll stop drinking."

"I'm afraid it's not that easy."

"What do you mean?"

Watson started a pacing routine, hands clasped behind him. The mood on his face was cold, determined, as if carved from stone.

"Bill, I want you to go to Portsmouth Naval Hospital next week."

"Hospital? Why? What for?"

"You're to see a specialist. His name is Dr. Chandler. He's the fleet medical psychiatrist."

"Psychiatrist?" Bill squinted. "What's this all about, sir?"

"It's about your health."

"But I'm fine. There's nothing wrong with me."

"Bill, you're not fine—and you know it. Your head's in a cloud, twisted into a thousand knots. Greaves was right. You drink yourself silly to alleviate the pain of your girlfriend's death. You're no good to the service right now. More importantly, you're no good to me. And I need you back on the job. I need a clear-headed officer who's in total command of his faculties."

"So *that's* why you wanted to see me?"

"Well, that's part of it."

"All right, surprise me, what's the other part?"

"It's about your future. I spoke with the CO yesterday regarding your transfer request. He said he would arrange it, but only on the condition that you're given a clean bill of health by Dr. Chandler. If not, he said you'll have to resign your commission."

Gallagher turned pale.

"And you agreed with him?"

"Bill, I'm just a lowly commander in charge of flight training on this base. A navy captain is a monarch. He reports to no one. When he gives an order, it's final."

"Tell you the truth, Steve, I've been thinking about quitting the service and latching on to one of those cushy airline jobs. Those pilots live a pretty good life, you know. I wouldn't starve, that's for sure."

"But you don't want to leave the service, is that it?"

"That's right. I joined the Corps with the intention of making it a career. I love this life! I want to be a squadron commander someday. Perhaps even command a fighter wing."

"And you can be all those things, Bill—I know it. Who knows, maybe you'll wind up a general someday. I like a man with ambition. It shows me he's confident in himself, and his career."

"But my future rests in the hands of a head shrink, right?"

"I'm afraid so. No transfer unless you go to Portsmouth next week."

"And if I don't go, I'm a civilian again."

Watson stepped around the desk.

"Bill, all you have to do is go to the hospital and answer a few questions. I'm sure you'll pass with flying colors."

"I'll think about it, Steve."

"Okay, but I'll need an answer soon. The CO wants you back on active duty." Watson clapped him on the shoulder, smiling. "I need the old Bill Gallagher back."

While Gallagher and Watson were discussing the former's future, Fuzzy Hostetler and Jake Wharton were sharing a pizza lunch at A Taste of Roma, a popular downtown restaurant.

"I really shouldn't be eating this stuff," said the elder Hostetler. "I usually get heartburn. Drives my wife crazy."

"You know, Matt, I've been thinking a lot about the murder case."

"Thinking too much gets us nowhere, Jake. We need clues,

witnesses, suspects."

"I know, but it can't hurt to hypothesize."

"So what's your theory?"

"Well, suppose Gallagher's hunch about Pike is correct."

"Jake, the guy had an alibi. He was with his girlfriend that night at The Gunslinger. He said so and so did the girl. And it was verified by the owner of the nightclub. Besides, Pike and his wife were getting a divorce. But even if he did have a motive to kill her, what was it? Jealousy because his soon-to-be ex-wife was shacked up with another man?" He shook his head. "No, I can't buy it, not for a minute."

"But maybe there's more to it. Maybe he didn't want to pay alimony."

"But even if the court ordered him to pay alimony, I'm sure a small setback like that wouldn't have put much of a dent in his budget. Pike's an officer. I'm sure he'd have had enough money left to get by on."

"Yeah, I suppose you're right. Still, there's something about this case that bothers me. I just think Gallagher might have something. Those death threats, for instance. He just might know a lot more than we give him credit for."

"Maybe, but it's still not enough to continue the investigation. It's one man's word against another's."

"You're right again, Matt. Still, I got a funny feeling about this case and it won't go away."

Hostetler swallowed a mouthful of pizza and chased it with a sip of ice tea.

"Well, there's nothing more we can do about it for now. So do me a favor, will you, Jake?"

"What's that?"

"Pass the cheese."

CHAPTER 8

The beautiful dark-haired woman in the green silk negligé sipped her champagne gratefully and smiled at the strapping blond-haired, blue-eyed man lying in bed beside her.

"You've still not told me," she said. "Why are we celebrating?"

"Because I feel like it, that's why," was his answer. He grabbed the champagne bottle on the night table and refilled her flute glass. "Any objections?"

She purred as he snuggled closer, his free hand gliding across the smooth sloping curve of her inner thigh.

"You're naughty," she told him.

"That's because I'm in a naughty mood." He reached closer and nibbled her earlobe, enjoying the tantalizing scent of her European perfume.

She said, "Shall I turn off the TV? You know I don't like

distractions when we make love."

He looked over his shoulder at the portable television and watched the program, chuckling when the adorable young actress in the white nun's outfit was swept off the ground by the wind and magically began to fly.

"No, leave it on," he said. "I like this show."

"But it's ridiculous."

"Of course it's ridiculous. But Sally Field is cute. I've always had a crush on her."

"Cuter than I?"

Smiling, he leaned closer and gently kissed her on the lips.

"Does that answer your question?"

"Mmm! You do have a way about you, I must admit." She sipped her drink, placed the glass on the night table and inched closer, running her fingers lightly across his chest. "Now, how can I please you, darling?"

"Not now, Mary."

"Why not? I'm in the mood and so are you."

"Yes, but first we need to talk."

"All right." She stared at him curiously, her sapphire blue eyes twinkling like stars. "What about?"

"Us," he said. "Let's get married."

"*Married?*" Her voice was horrified. "You can't be serious?"

"Of course I'm serious. I love you, baby!"

"I love you too. But why do you want to spoil everything? I thought we were happy."

"But that's exactly my point. Happy people like us *should* get married." He raked his fingers through her long jet-black hair, ending up at the space between her shoulder blades. "So what do you say?"

"Impossible! I...I'm not ready. And I don't think you're ready either. It's just too soon since—"

"My wife's death?" He laughed without mirth. "That's got nothing to do with it."

"But I just don't want to rush into it," she said, her voice laden with obvious concern. "Marriage is a big step. We need to spend more time together, make sure it's right for us."

"It's right for me, I know that."

"How can you say that after the way your wife treated you all those years? How do you know I won't be like her?"

"You could never be like her," he said, stroking her chin with his lips. "Besides, I'm older and wiser now. I know what I want. You're perfect for me."

"Why, because we have terrific sex?"

"No, there's more to it than that."

"I'm still not ready," she said. "I must be a hundred percent sure. I don't want you to make another mistake like you did with your first marriage."

"Okay, maybe you're right. Maybe we shouldn't rush into it. But when I get back from sea, we'll discuss it again, all right?"

She didn't answer. Instead, she asked, "When are you leaving Norfolk? Have they told you yet?"

"Yes, the end of September," he said to the television.

"How long will you be gone?"

"About four months."

"But that's awful! What am I going to do all that time without you?"

"You're going to miss me," he said, smirking. *'That's* what you'll do."

"But I'll go out of my mind, I know it."

"Believe me, baby, it won't be easy for me either."

"Was thinking about that the other day. What do sailors do

when they're at sea so long? Don't you ever get horny?"

"Of course. I just try not to think about sex. I try to keep my mind on my job."

"Chief engineering officer," she said matter-of-factly, as if speaking to herself. "Must be a very important job."

"Nuclear engineering," he corrected her.

She shivered from the sound of that, as if a gust of winter wind had entered the bedroom.

"That's scary," she said. "Aren't you ever afraid the engine might blow up by accident?"

"No, not really. The radiation is well contained. It's very safe, actually. Now take submarines. They use atomic power and can stay submerged for weeks at a time. Now *that's* scary."

"It still sounds dangerous."

"Well, if you don't know what you're doing, it can be. We're constantly being trained on safety and how to prevent accidents at sea, like fires. But American sailors are the best firemen in the world."

"That's not very comforting, but tell me more."

He rambled on about his duties aboard the *U.S.S. Roosevelt* for several minutes. When he had finished, she slipped out of the bed and switched off the television. When she turned back, she stared at him in that devilish way he adored as she reached up and yanked on the ribbon holding her negligé in place. He watched with a grateful smile as it fell to the floor without a sound.

"Commander Pike, are you still in the mood?"

Bill Gallagher spent most of Thursday the fourteenth playing pool at the officers' lounge. At six o'clock he settled in front of the television to watch the evening news. It contained the usual: student protests at an Ivy League college in New York, followed by film footage of incomprehensible jungle fighting in Vietnam. There was also a special report on last month's lunar expedition.

He spent the following day at the beach trying to put his mind back in order; but it wasn't easy. He was still a train wreck, hardly in command of himself. "This is not like you," Watson had told him. Yes, Marlene was dead and there was nothing more to be done about it. Not now, perhaps never. The best thing he could do for himself was relax and try to forget.

But what about his future? Was it time to leave the marines and try something else? Perhaps he *could* find work as a commercial airline pilot. It would be a challenge learning how to fly those jumbo airbuses and get well paid in the process. He could buy a house, live almost anywhere he chose, perhaps even go back to college and try for his master's, which indubitably would mean even more opportunities down the road. The possibilities suddenly seemed endless.

But he had to make a decision, and soon. Watson had given him a polite ultimatum. To remain in the Corps meant a visit to the fleet medical psychiatrist. If he refused, he would be compelled to resign his commission and exit the service. He shook his head. Somehow it just didn't seem fair.

By Sunday noon he had made his decision when he received a surprise telephone call from Jake Wharton.

"What can I do for you, Mr. Wharton?"

"Sorry to bother you on Sunday, Lieutenant, but I was hoping to have a word with you."

"Sure, fire away."

"I'd prefer not to discuss it over the phone," Wharton told him. "Was hoping we could meet somewhere. Is there a chance you could get away from the base?"

"I suppose so. What's it all about?"

"I'll explain when we meet."

Bill thought, wondering what the secrecy was all about.

"We could meet at the beach," he suggested.

"What time?"

"How's two o'clock sound? I'll meet you on the boardwalk at Nineteenth Street."

"Fine."

Gallagher arrived at the Virginia Beach boardwalk a few minutes before their scheduled rendezvous wearing blue shorts, a sleeveless gray sweat shirt, sandals and a New York Yankees baseball cap he had purchased in Fort Lauderdale while on leave in February.

It was a gorgeous afternoon on the oceanfront. The beach was crowded, the warm air humid, a green sea shimmering in the background. He located an empty bench nearby, sat and observed a school of silver dolphins leapfrogging the whitecaps about a hundred yards out from the coastline.

Not long thereafter his memory kicked in. He remembered it was on a similar day not far from where he was sitting when he had first met Marlene. He and his friend Roger Morrison had come to the beach that June afternoon for a day's relaxation, which included flirting with the opposite sex. "Two-legged deer hunting," Morrison called it. Then, when he spotted Marlene, he was sure his heart skipped a beat. She was the most inspiring sight on the beach that day: straight shoulder-length blond hair that was meant for a man to run his fingers through; the perfect hourglass figure barely contained in that inviting red bikini.

He remembered when Roger beat him to the punch and asked her for a date, but was relieved when she politely declined. "I'd like to know more about you," she told him when they were alone. They talked for a while, then later strolled along the beach holding hands while playing tag with the ocean tide. When he had finally mustered up the courage to ask her out, he was not surprised when she readily accepted. He knew then that she was the girl he had been waiting for all his life.

He cleared his thoughts and sighed. So long ago, so very long ago, he thought bitterly. That wonderful moment in time was now but a memory, a blur in his mind. The most beautiful, desirable girl he had ever met was gone forever. He shook his head, feeling the anguish boiling inside him.

He composed himself in a hurry when he saw Jake Wharton approaching. The homicide detective was sporting a bright yellow tee shirt, sunglasses, white shorts and sneakers, as if prepared to do some serious jogging. Gallagher stood and they shook hands.

"Thanks for taking the time to meet me, Lieutenant."

"No problem. By the way, just call me Bill."

"All right, as long as you call me Jake."

"Agreed."

Wharton waited for Gallagher to reclaim his seat, then sat beside him and lit a cigarette.

"A beautiful day, huh?"

"Yeah, sure can't complain about the weather. So what can I do for you, Jake?"

"Actually, I thought I could to do something for you, Bill."

"Oh?"

"I've been thinking a lot lately about the murder case."

"I thought the investigation was more or less kaput?"

"Yeah, well, as you know, we don't have any leads. And our budget is tight, like most police departments these days, which is a crime in itself. Still, that doesn't mean we close the file and forget about it." A quick puff from his cigarette. "Anyway, like I said, I've been thinking about it a lot."

"Of what in particular?"

"For instance, take the night of the murder. There was no forced entry of her apartment. The place was not ransacked or burgled. And she wasn't raped according to the coroner's report."

"In other words, what you're trying to say is that the murderer had only one purpose in being there—to kill her."

"Yeah."

Gallagher's face puckered into a frown of confusion.

"What makes you so sure, Jake?"

"Well, as you know, Marlene was found naked in her bed, which leads me to conclude that that's where the struggle took place. My guess is that she never heard him enter the apartment, which means she had little time to react when he attacked her. I think she might have been asleep at the time."

"But how did he get in?"

"Two possibilities. One, he could have had a key. The other…"

"Go on."

"Well, it's possible her door was unlocked."

Gallagher went pale, his eyes stilettos.

"Are you trying to tell me that she was expecting him?" He shook his head with emphasis. "No, I can't buy that, not for a minute."

"I know how you feel, Bill, but in my line of work one has to consider all possibilities. Remember, no one in the apartment building heard any suspicious noises that night."

"That's because people don't want to get involved with other people's problems."

Wharton continued, "Anyway, I believe her husband killed her, like you do."

"But what was his motive?"

"Jealousy, I think," answered the policeman. "And jealousy is a very powerful emotion. It can make even a sane person do crazy things, including murder."

"But you have to prove he did it, and so far you've got no evidence. Hell, anybody could have killed her, like a burglar."

"No, I don't think so. Burglars are thieves, not killers. Still, even if it was a burglar, why didn't he steal something? From what we found in her apartment, she had over two hundred dollars in her purse, not to mention the jewelry she owned."

"Maybe he was in a hurry to get out."

"I think that's a given."

Gallagher stared out at the ocean, his mind racing at top speed.

"What does Hostetler think about your theory, Jake?"

"He disagrees with me. He doesn't believe Pike's the kind of man who would kill his wife in cold blood. He thinks there's someone else involved. He also believes we'll never solve the case."

"So why did you want this meeting today?"

"Well, there's nothing more we can do for now, and that's a fact. But there's something you can do, Bill, and I thought I might be able to help you."

"Explain."

"Well, I was thinking you could hire a private detective to hunt down the murderer."

"You're not serious?"

"Oh, but I am. It's rarely done in these circumstances, but it's an option for you to consider."

"But that means money out of my pocket, Jake. I don't think I can afford it."

"Yeah, well, that's your business. However, like I said, it's an option to consider. Who knows, maybe he can find a lead that'll help us solve the case."

"And if he finds nothing, I'm minus a lot of cash."

"Like I said, it's an option to consider. Take it for what it's worth. I just thought you'd want to know." Wharton inhaled through the cigarette for the last time and flicked the butt aside.

Gallagher thought as he stared at the human congestion on the beach. Finally he said, "Tell me, Jake, how much does a private eye cost?"

"Depends on who you get, I suppose."

"Is there anyone you can recommend?"

"As a matter of fact, there is." Wharton reached inside his hip pocket, yanked out a crumpled piece of paper and handed it across. On it were a name and telephone number.

Gallagher read, "Timothy Davis."

"Yeah, Tim's a good friend of mine. I worked with him for two years when I was in vice. He used to work for the Chesapeake police before he became a private dick. He still lives there but has an office in Norfolk just two blocks from city hall. Mention my name and he might give you a break on his fee."

"I appreciate this, Jake."

"Of course Fuzzy and I will continue to investigate when time permits. Would you like me to call Tim and tell him to expect a call from you?"

"Yes, would you? I've got an appointment in Portsmouth on Tuesday morning. I could drop by his office afterwards."

Nodding, Wharton climbed off the bench.

"That's about as much as I can do for you, Bill."

"Thanks for the suggestion, Jake." He stood and they shook hands. "I appreciate it."

"Good luck, Bill, whatever you decide to do."

THE SPY

CHAPTER 9

The Portsmouth Naval Hospital is the largest military facility of its kind in the United States. Built in 1922, the great medical center is tucked away in the northeast corner of the city. On the map, Portsmouth looks like a fetus in the womb of Tidewater. The rural, less populous town of Suffolk is southwest of her. To the southeast is the rapidly developing town of Chesapeake. Across the Elizabeth River to the northeast is her more celebrated sister city, Norfolk. From Oceana Naval Air Station in Virginia Beach to the Portsmouth Naval Hospital, it is an uncomplicated twenty-mile drive along the main freeway and through the downtown tunnel which serves as the umbilical artery linking the two venerable cities.

As he exited the tunnel on the Portsmouth side of the river, Lieutenant William Francis Gallagher took a deep breath and eased up on the gas pedal, prepared for a busy day ahead. First on the agenda was his morning appointment with the fleet medical psychiatrist. In the afternoon he would return to Norfolk and meet with the private investigator, Timothy Davis, whom Jake Wharton had recommended.

Captain Rockwell Burton Chandler was a middle-aged New Englander of salt-and-pepper hair who sported a pencil-point mustache of the same color and a larger-than-normal midsection, the latter a consequence of his Georgia wife's rich southern recipes. Following an exchange of pleasantries, Chandler offered the marine the lone chair at the front of his wide navy-gray metallic desk. As Gallagher obliged him, the career navy healer circled behind the desk, sat and opened a folder.

"Been reading over your record, Lieutenant."

"This is the first time I've been in a hospital since I joined the service," Bill told him. Then corrected himself, "That is, except for a routine dental checkup."

"I know. But I wasn't referring to your medical record. It's your service record I've been reading. Commander Watson was kind enough to send a copy over yesterday so I could review it before we talked."

Gallagher nodded, as if only for something to do, and the clinician continued, "From what I've read, you've put together quite an impressive record during your four years in the marines. Some might even call it colorful. Officer training in Quantico. Flight school in Pensacola. Tour in Vietnam. Then a year in Japan. And now you're working in Oceana as a classroom flight instructor." He grinned, adding, "Commander Watson speaks very highly of you."

Gallagher smiled in gratitude of the compliment but said nothing in return. Hands folded across his lap, he watched as Chandler leaned back in his brown leather chair and took a moment to caress his moustache with forefinger and thumb.

"Your girlfriend's death two weeks ago must have been quite a shock for you."

"To say the least, sir. I'm still having a hard time adjusting."

"It's always difficult to lose a loved one, whether it be an immediate family member, or in your case a girlfriend. But more so, I think, when it happens in such a sadistic way. Commander Watson said you were planning to marry her."

"Yes, sir."

"But she was already married, was she not?"

"Yes, but legally separated from her husband."

"Who, I understand, is a naval officer." Chandler stroked his moustache again, as if to verify it was still there.

He continued, "I've been following the newspaper's account of the murder investigation in bits and pieces. From what I read, the police have no leads in the case."

"Yes, sir. In fact, they've more or less given up looking for the murderer."

"And how do you feel about that?"

"I'm not happy. Like any sane human being who believes in law and order, I want to see the killer brought to justice and pay for his crime."

"Commander Watson said you're convinced her husband was the murderer."

"That's right."

Chandler paused for a breath of air, but then leaned forward in his chair, elbows on the desk, hands locked together as if in prayer.

"Tell me, Lieutenant, what are your plans for the future? Do you intend to stay in the Corps?"

"To be honest, I'm not sure. Originally I had wanted to make it a career. But I'm not so sure anymore."

"If you decide to leave, have you thought about how you're going to make a living?"

"Well, I thought about applying for a job with the airline companies. I'm also thinking about grad school."

Chandler nodded, then startled Gallagher when he said, "How often do you drink?"

"Lately, frequently—I don't deny it. But considering the circumstances—"

"Do you smoke?"

"No, sir."

"Let me rephrase that. Have you ever experimented with marijuana?"

"No, sir."

"But you drink a lot?"

"Yes, but I can stop anytime I want. I've been drinking because I've got a lot of free time on my hands."

"Alcohol is a drug, Lieutenant. Casual drinking can be tolerated in the service. However, when a man begins to drink excessively, particularly someone with your responsibilities, it becomes a concern for everyone involved. There's too much at stake in the military. Loss of life and property damage, for instance. I must also point out that the airline companies have high standards for their pilots. Let's face it, driving one of those passenger planes, one needs to keep a clear head."

"I beg your pardon, sir, but I'm not a drunk." Bill's words were terse. "As soon as I'm back on active duty, I'll be fine. Like I said, I can stop drinking anytime I want."

"Yes, but sometimes that's easier said than done." Chandler glanced at Gallagher's service record, then changed the subject.

"So tell me about your job at Oceana. Do you like it?"

"Yes and no."

"Explain."

"Well, I like the area, I like my boss, but I don't like my duties as an instructor. I feel I can best serve my country as a flyer. It's what I love most. Since I was a kid, it's all I've ever wanted to do."

"According to your record, you've done an outstanding job as a pilot. In my opinion, you could almost name your own job if you decided to leave the Corps."

Gallagher said nothing in return, sat ramrod straight in the chair, wishing the interview would soon end.

"I've only a few more questions, Lieutenant."

"Yes, sir?"

"I'd like to know your opinion of the war, both as an officer and personally."

Bill thought, staring at the folded hands on his lap. How would he answer? What significance would it play in Chandler's evaluation of him?

He said, "Militarily, the war can't be won. Personally speaking, I think it's a disgrace to the nation."

"Go on."

"When it's over, many questions will need to be answered by the hawks in Congress and the Pentagon big shots."

"Despite your feelings about the war, you're proud to serve your country as an officer and flyer?"

"Yes, sir. I joined the marines because I wanted to fly, to do what I had always dreamed of doing."

Chandler closed the folder.

"Just one last question. Have you ever wanted to kill a human being?"

"I beg your pardon?"

"You heard me, Lieutenant. Have you ever thought of killing someone?"

"Yes," Bill heard himself say.

"Your girlfriend's husband, perhaps?"

"Yes, sir, but…I could never do it."

"Neither do I."

Chandler closed the folder and rose from his seat. As Gallagher followed suit, he stepped around the desk and offered a smile.

"Thank you for coming in, Lieutenant."

"You mean that's all?"

"Yes."

"So what happens now?"

"I'll submit my recommendation to your base commander, Captain Russo."

"And what will you tell him? Am I okay? Am I normal?"

Chandler threw back his head and chuckled.

"Don't worry, Lieutenant, you're fine. In fact, I'm very much impressed with you. You're a bright, honest, mature officer. A credit to the service. I'll recommend that you be reassigned to active duty." They shook hands. "Good luck."

Gallagher left the hospital after having lunch in the officers' galley and returned to Norfolk to honor his one o'clock appointment with the private detective.

The writing on the frosted glass door of Timothy Davis' third-floor office on Union Street read: *Robert Jennings, Jr. and Associates.* Bill knocked but there was no answer. He knocked again without results and tried the doorknob. It moved, and moments later he was closing the door from the inside.

The walls were bare and dingy white, the desk in front of the man sitting behind it covered with folders, newspaper clippings, camera equipment, boxes of Kodak film and other assorted notes, papers and documents. The room was stuffy despite the fact that both windows were open, allowing for an occasional zephyr of city air to sneak in.

The man behind the desk, a thin, frail-looking sort with steel-rimmed reading glasses and a shrinking brown hairline, was speaking to the telephone in his hand. He gestured Gallagher with his free hand to take the empty seat at the side of the desk. Bill did so and waited. Finally Davis ended the conversation, hung up and stared across the desk, flashing a grin at the same time.

"So," he said, "you're Gallagher." He reached across the desk and they shook hands.

"At first I thought I might be in the wrong place," Bill told him.

"I take it you're referring to the name on the door?"

"Yeah."

"My good friend Bob Jennings started the business," explained Davis. "I was the 'Associates'. When he retired last year, I took over the business."

"Jake Wharton said you used to work for the Chesapeake police."

"That's right. I worked vice the last nine years I was there. It gave me a lot of valuable experience for my present line of work." He produced a note pad and pencil from the top drawer. "Shall we begin, Lieutenant?"

"Fine."

"I spoke with Jake yesterday and he filled me in on the murder case. From what he told me, he and Fuzzy Hostetler have reached a dead end. Without leads, there's not much else they can do."

"You think you can help?"

"I honestly don't know," answered Davis. "First of all, we need to get a few things out in the open. Jake tells me you believe the deceased's husband was the killer."

"That's right—he did it! I'm convinced of that."

Davis frowned at the marine, not liking the intensity in his voice. He cleared the gravel from his throat.

"I'm sure I don't need to tell you, Mr. Gallagher, that what you or I or anyone else thinks means absolute diddly-squat. We can speculate all we want from beer to breakfast, but all it'll give us is a bad headache. Detectives follow leads and clues. We need solid, substantiated evidence to make an arrest. It's the law."

"Naturally."

Davis continued, "I know from experience that Fuzzy and Jake are two of the most thorough homicide detectives in the business. In my opinion, they're two of the best. If they're stumped, what makes you think I can help you?"

"I don't. I'm just following Jake's recommendation. He seems to think very highly of you."

"Jake and I go back many years. We're very good friends. He's referred business to Bob and me before. But after what he told me, I don't know."

"But Wharton believes Pike killed her too."

"Yes, but that's just his gut feeling. He's been wrong before."

"The bastard did it!" Bill spouted through clenched teeth. "Before she was murdered, Marlene told me he had threatened to kill her several times. She was frightened of him."

"Yes, Jake mentioned that. But death threats don't convict a man of murder. Nevertheless, it's something to think about. Might even be a starting point for me."

"Does that mean you'll take the case?"

"I'm always interested in new business, Lieutenant."

"All right, so what's your fee?"

"First of all, I want to make it perfectly clear that you could spend a lot of money on this case and get little or nothing in return. What I mean is, I could snoop around for weeks and come up with absolutely nothing."

"I thought about that," Bill said to the floor. "But if you're trying to scare me, you can't, Mr. Davis. I'd be willing to pay you for the rest of my life if you found the evidence to convict that bastard."

"But that's exactly my point. I may find nothing and you'd still have to pay me."

"I'm willing to take a chance. I'll borrow money from the bank if I have to."

Davis shook his head. He got out of the chair and stepped over to the file cabinet. He opened the bottom drawer, reached in and produced a small portable fan. He placed it on top of the cabinet, plugged in the cord and switched it on.

"Look, Mr. Gallagher, I don't want to give you any false hopes. I know what your take-home pay is. I've had many servicemen as clients. In fact my last job was for a navy warrant officer. He suspected his wife was cheating on him, and he hired me to get the proof."

"Did you?"

"Absolutely. I got some pretty good snapshots of the old lady and her secret lover. Anyway, to make a long story short, the man who hired me is still paying me."

"I can afford it, Mr. Davis."

"Very well. My fee is forty dollars a day, excluding expenses. If I need to work weekends, that's two hundred and eighty dollars a week. Now, can you *still* afford it?"

"I can manage."

"Well, I admire your grit." Davis stroked his chin, as if it would help him make a decision. Finally he said, "All right, Lieutenant, I'll take the job."

"Fine. When can you start?"

"Right away," was the PI's answer. "I'll talk to Jake again and ask him for a list of all the people involved in the case. I'll need to read the transcripts of the police interrogations, including Pike's testimony. It'll save me a lot of time from the jump. Hopefully I'll find a new lead and maybe some hard evidence."

"If you do, then what happens?"

"Well, I can't make an arrest, if that's what you mean. I can only pass on what I find to the police. They'll take it from there."

Davis stepped around the desk and leaned against it with legs crossed, arms folded together.

"Lieutenant, real detective work is not like those private eye TV programs. It's hard work. At times it's frustrating. A good percentage of it is being in the right place at the right time. I'll do my best for you, but if I decide I'm beating my head up against the wall, I'll tell you straight away so I don't waste your time and money."

"I appreciate that," Bill told him. Then quickly added, "If there's anything I can do to help, please let me know. And keep me informed of anything you find."

"That I'll do, I promise."

Later that evening Gallagher and his roommate were engaged in conversation at the officers' club. Greaves sat in front of a half empty mug of beer, his friend fondling a tall glass of ginger ale.

"I got to hand it to you, old buddy, you really mean business."

"I owe it to Marlene, Chet."

"You sure you can afford this private eye fellow? Forty dollars a day ain't exactly chicken feed."

"I'll manage. I got some savings."

"But what happens when the cash runs out?"

"Don't know. Guess I'll get a loan from the bank."

Greaves picked up his mug and slurped, wiping the foam from his lips with his fingers.

He said, "But what if Davis finds nothing, then what?"

"Then it's all over, I suppose."

"Have you told Watson yet?"

"No. And I don't want you telling him either."

"Okay, okay." Greaves drank some more beer, then said, "Bill, we're pretty good friends, right? Can I give you a little advice?"

"Chet, I know what you're going to tell me. That I'm wasting my time, right?"

"No, that's none of my business. I just wanted to say that whatever happens, even if Davis finds out that Pike killed Marlene, nothing will bring her back. You're never going to see her again. What I mean is, will you sleep better knowing that he killed her?"

"I don't know. Maybe, maybe not."

"You know what I think? I think you're doing this just to prove that you're right and the police are wrong. You have so much hate for Pike, you're not just looking for justice, you want vengeance."

"Okay, maybe I do."

"But did you ever give Pike the benefit of the doubt? He said his wife was unfaithful. How do you know it wasn't true? You've only considered this from her point of view."

"Then who killed her, Chet?"

"God knows. Maybe this is a job for the FBI...or Sherlock Holmes."

Gallagher laughed, in spite of himself.

"Very funny, man." He slid off the stool. "I'm going to bed. See you in the morning."

CHAPTER 10

K arl-Heinz Brandt was an unpretentious hard-working man. Born and raised in Stuttgart, Germany, he had inherited the family tavern when his father fell one wintry morning and never got up again. The old man was found too late by his wife and died of the heart seizure just moments before the ambulance arrived at the hospital. The date on the death certificate was 30 December 1923.

With help from his twin brother and spinster sister, Brandt continued the business with dedicated vigor. He matured faster because of his new responsibilities and took a wife after the first year his bookkeeping showed a profit margin. Most of his customers were regulars from the metal foundries which honeycombed the Baden-Württemberg capital. Many were army veterans like his father who had experienced the holocaust at the western front during the Great War. Whatever their trade or military background, his patrons had one thing in common. They were devout Communists, as was Karl-Heinz Brandt.

By the end of the decade, Europe was locked in the jaws of the Great Depression. Hardest hit was the working man of Germany. Unemployment was rampant, while paper currency was good only for trips to the toilet. Worse, the feeble Weimar Republic had lost control, allowing the seeds of revolution to sprout on every street corner. Most famous of the soapbox revolutionists was a former Viennese derelict who had served with distinction in the war and reshaped an obscure political organization in his own image. The group called itself the National Socialist German Workers' Party, or Nazi party. His name was Adolf Hitler.

The main opposition to Hitler's rise to power was the Communist party. To neutralize the Reds, the self-proclaimed *Führer* created his own paramilitary of ruffians and misfits known as *Sturmabteilungen*, or SA. This legion of storm troops with the ugly brown uniforms battled the *Bolsheviks* for control of the streets. The majority of the bullies were recruited from the ranks of the unemployed, of whom many were ex-servicemen who felt they had been betrayed during the war by the Kaiser and his faction of back-stabbing Jewish financiers. It was the latter, the Nazis proclaimed, who had brought the country to its knees by covertly destabilizing the nation's war industry and once powerful economy.

Many died in the daily street brawls between the Nazis and Reds. Ironically, the Nazis prevailed in the end not by brute force, but by the vote of the people. In January 1933, Hitler assumed power from the ailing Hindenburg, the Weimar democracy was abolished—again lawfully—and retribution became the order of the day. Among those singled out for punishment were political extremists, Jews, left-wing intellectuals and diehard Communists.

The Brownshirts came for Karl-Heinz Brandt in the middle of the night of 9 September 1934. He was dragged from his home and beaten to a bloody pulp by three hooligans whose faces he never recognized. The brutes let him live long enough to see his wife raped three times in succession. The tavern was then razed to the ground as the final insult, ending the family business of four generations.

Elsa Brandt buried her husband and left Stuttgart, relocating with her aunt and uncle in Munich, where she managed to make a modest living as a seamstress for her uncle, a tailor, who owned a small shop on the city's east side. Despite her hatred of Hitler and the Nazis, she survived the brutal war years that followed.

In June of '45, just one month following the Nazi surrender to the Allies, she met and fell in love with a lonely American soldier, a military policeman named Charlie O'Neal from Hartford, Connecticut. At the time, Elsa Brandt was thirty-eight years old, O'Neal six years her junior. The affair never worked out, and when he left Germany for reassignment in the States, she found herself five months pregnant with his child.

She considered making a formal protest to the American occupying authorities, but there was too much red tape involved and she backed down. She considered having an abortion but was talked into keeping the soon-to-be newborn by her relatives. The baby girl, whom she named Maria Theresa, arrived in the world on the afternoon of 10 March 1946.

Despite her loathing of everything America stood for, Elsa Brandt learned to love her daughter. The girl grew up fast and bright. By her twelfth birthday, she had been told of the irresponsible GI who had jilted her mother and the Brownshirts who had murdered her parent's only husband. Like her mother, Maria was drawn to politics like a magnet to metal and took the opinion that Communism was the only way that would lead the working class to freedom. Then, in the spring of '61, tragedy struck the Brandt family again.

Elsa Brandt was killed by a drunk driver while crossing the street on her way to the market. After several weeks of mourning, her surviving offspring made the most consequential decision of her life. She packed her lone suitcase with her favorite dresses and the modest sum her mother had left behind in her bank account and moved to East Berlin a month before the Wall went up. Juggling school with a night job as a hostel waitress, Maria Brandt was never happier. This was where she belonged, among the working class of the German Democratic Republic, of whom many believed that world socialism would someday prevail and cleanse the earth of the decadent capitalist West.

By the time she was eighteen, Maria Brandt was a beautiful streetwise woman. A handsome Red Army officer introduced himself one day at the hostel while he was on furlough and they talked when she had the time. His name was Yuri Chislenko, and before his leave was up, he had fallen in love with her. He pleaded with her to come back to Moscow with him but was desolated when she politely declined. Despite that, they stayed in touch through monthly correspondence and he visited her whenever the opportunity arose. In her letters, Chislenko learned of her hatred of Western ideals and one day mentioned it to his boss, who in turn passed it on to a friend who worked for Soviet Intelligence, the *Komitet gosudarstvennoy bezopasnosti,* or KGB.

Maria Brandt never expected that one day she would become a Soviet spy. Although she spoke fluent English, albeit with a German accent, the idea of leaving her beloved fatherland to live among the spoiled masses of money-hungry America was revolting, even if it were for the ultimate betterment of the

Marxist-Leninist world movement. Following her recruitment in 1965, she spent the next two years in Russia training to become an undercover operative. She learned to speak American without an accent. She learned about Wall Street, rock 'n roll, "Gunsmoke" and Gregory Peck. She learned how to "shake a tail," send coded messages, and how to make contact with a fellow agent despite being surrounded by the opposition. She also perfected the art of murder, whether it be with a handgun, switchblade or poisonous cocktail.

Yet her greatest weapon was herself. She was not only attractive, but scrumptiously desirable, could entice any man into wanting her. She sported long black hair, sensuous lips that begged to be kissed, and a shapely hourglass figure that could put most of Hugh Hefner's *Playboy* models out to pasture. While in training, she had numerous affairs to hone her skills as a man-eating siren, skills she would employ in the coming years to benefit both herself and the cause of which she was devoutly subservient.

By January '67 she was ready. She was given an alias—Mary Young—and slipped across the American border by way of Toronto, Canada. Within a week she had made contact with the man who would run her during her expected lengthy stay in the United States. His name was Yevgeny Kozlov, a KGB officer who was deputy to the military attaché at the Soviet embassy in Washington, D.C. Her mission would be uncomplicated and easy, he told Maria. "A piece of cake," was the natives' phrase.

Her first year in the New World was the most difficult. Although Kozlov had found work for her as a secretary for an obscure Montana senator—a married man she despised sleeping with who belonged to the Senate Armed Services Committee—she missed her beloved homeland. Eventually she got used to being what she was supposed to be and was able to pilfer from the gullible Republican classified documents which included military spending and procurement. Their association ended in the fall of '68 when the congressman was booted out of office by the voters, leaving his "faithful" Mary behind to return to his ranch and homely wife.

How long ago that seemed, thought Maria as she drew the bedroom curtains and waited for her lover to arrive. Oh well. She was more than content with her new job as a lover for the muscular, good-looking sailor. They enjoyed fantastic sex, quite unlike her association with the ex-senator. More importantly, the military information she had been able to squeeze out of him was "good stuff," as Kozlov had told her.

She saw the blue Chevrolet turn the corner and park on the opposite side of the street. She waited until he climbed out of the car before she closed the curtains and went back to bed. Five minutes later she heard the key rattle in the lock, then his voice call out, "I'm home!"

She saw the light go on in the living room, then his tall silhouette standing at the door. She couldn't see the mood on his face but knew he was smiling. He always smiled a lot when he was with her.

"What kept you, darling?" she said, pretending to sound upset.

"Sorry, baby, I got hung up at the base."

He stepped over to the bed and sat beside her. She reached up and wrapped a hand around his head, pulled herself closer and kissed him fiercely on the mouth.

"You've been smoking," she said, the disappointment obvious in her voice.

"I'll brush my teeth," he told her.

Another kiss before he reached under the sheets and caressed her warm silky-smooth body, feeling himself becoming aroused.

When he ran his hand lightly across her bosom, she purred with delight.

"You're a tease," she told him.

"I know, but I can't help it. You're irresistible, my sweet." He slipped off the bed with reluctance. "Now don't go away, I'll be back."

He turned away and moments later the light went on in the bathroom. She listened as he brushed his teeth, gargled, but waited until she heard the sound of the shower door closing before sliding out of bed. She went to the living room and found his briefcase next to the sideboard, like always. She knew it was locked, but would take care of that problem later. Like taking candy from a baby, she thought with a sinister grin.

She went to the kitchen and made two martinis. Back in the bedroom, she put one on the night stand at his side of the bed. She sipped her drink—it was watered down just the way she liked it—and placed it on the night stand at her side of the queen-sized bed. Five minutes later her lover reappeared, a blue cotton towel locked around his waist, promoting his washboard abdomen. He grabbed his martini, sipped, swallowed and smiled.

"Perfect," he said. "Just what the doctor ordered."

"Thought you might want one."

He put the drink down, unbuckled the towel, letting it fall to the floor, peeled back the sheets and slipped in beside her. She came to him instantly.

"Your hair's damp," she scolded. "Aren't you going to shut off the bathroom light?"

"No, leave it on. I can't see your gorgeous body in the dark when we make love. You know how that excites me."

"Am I the most exciting woman you've ever known?"

"You make it sound as if I sleep around."

"Sorry, darling, but I must know. Am I the most desirable woman you've ever been with?"

"Of course."

"Even more desirable than—"

"Yes," he interjected, knowing she was referring to his late wife. He rubbed his hand across her stomach, feeling her twitch, and ended up between her legs.

"No, you don't!" She grabbed his hand. "Tonight's my turn." She pushed him away and maneuvered on top.

"I love it when you spoil me," he said, closing his eyes.

"That's better," she said, and kissed him again. "Now relax, Commander Pike, and enjoy."

Later, after the lovemaking ended, she watched him as he slept. After a while she slipped out of the bed without a sound, rummaged through the pockets of his khaki slacks, which he had deposited on the chair next to the bathroom door, found what she wanted and tiptoed into the living room. She grabbed the briefcase, carried it into the kitchen and switched on the overhead light. She opened the briefcase with the key, removed the documents and smiled.

"Time to go to work," she told herself.

She opened the cabinet next to the refrigerator and reached for the small camera hidden behind the box of Rice Krispies on the top shelf. Six minutes later Maria Brandt was back in bed beside her lover, sleeping like a newborn.

On Thursday the twenty-first, Bill Gallagher arrived at the NAS training center for a meeting with his boss.

"Been reading over the doctor's report," Watson told him, looking up from the open folder. "Looks good."

"All it says is that I'm not crazy."

"Don't get the Irish up, Bill. I had no choice in the matter. It was the CO's decision to send you to the hospital."

"I know, sorry, sir."

Watson stared down at the typewritten report and said, "According to this, Dr. Chandler sees no reason why you shouldn't return to active duty."

"Back to training lectures again?" Gallagher's words were spiked with obvious bitterness. He turned and gazed through the window, adding, "You know I don't want that, Steve."

"Bill, I talked to the CO again about your transfer request. He told me he'll look into it as soon as he can."

"Did he say where I might go?"

"No." Watson frowned, seemed annoyed by the question. "Bill, what do you want from me? You know these things take time. You'll have to be patient. In the meantime—"

"I can't leave," said Gallagher, cutting him off. There was something close to desperation in his voice. "I have to stay in Tidewater. Just get me out of this wretched classroom work. I'm not a bookworm."

"But I thought you wanted to get away from the area. Why the sudden change of heart?"

"I have my reasons," was Gallagher's cryptic response. "I just need to stay in Virginia a while longer, preferably right here in Oceana."

"But what happens if the CO can't accommodate you? What if the Navy transfers you overseas?"

"Then I'll resign my commission."

Watson's jaw dropped. He leaned forward in his seat, both eyes wary.

"What is it, Bill? What are you thinking about?"

"What do you mean?"

"Come on, buddy boy, I know you too well. Why the change of attitude? Does it really matter *where* they send you?"

"It does now."

"And what's that supposed to mean? Does this have anything to do with your girlfriend's death?"

"That's right. I haven't given up looking for the killer. I've hired a private detective to investigate."

"You've done *what?*"

"You heard me, Steve. I hired a private eye. The police may have given up, but I haven't."

"Do the police know about this?"

"No, why should they? This is my business. This has nothing to do with them, or the Navy, or anyone else."

"I…can't believe you're doing this," said Watson, the grim tone in his voice in harmony with his words. "How much is this costing you?"

"With all due respect, sir, it's none of your business. I can handle the cost."

"When did you decide to do this?" was Watson's next question.

"Last week."

"But do you honestly believe a private eye can do what the police couldn't?"

"God knows. Maybe he can find a new lead or maybe some hard evidence. The police are human. They don't have all the answers, you know."

"So that's why you want to stay here?"

"That's right."

"Well, I must admit, you got a lot of John Wayne in you." A thoughtful pause before he continued, "So you still believe Pike murdered your girlfriend?"

"Yeah, that's right. And I'm going to prove it, one way or another."

"Even if you go bankrupt?" When there was no response, Watson stood out of his chair and began to pace back and forth in a straight line, hands clasped behind him.

"Bill, you've changed, despite what the doctor wrote in his report. Even if you were ordered back to active duty, I couldn't use you, not in your present condition."

"So *you* think I'm crazy?"

"No, I just think you're not yourself. You're obsessed with the murder case. It's got you twisted around like a pretzel. Logic means nothing to you anymore. You're working out of pure hate for this man. I tell you, it's going to hurt you in the end, more than you realize."

"No, you're wrong, sir, I can handle it. I can handle anything. Yes, I hate Pike—I admit it. But after I met him in the cemetery, I hated him even more. But it's different now. It's not vengeance I'm looking for. I want justice for Marlene's sake, if nothing else."

"But she'll never know."

"No, but I will. I have to live with my conscience."

Watson stopped pacing, said, "I'll tell the captain you'd like to stay in Tidewater a little while longer." A tired sigh. "Okay?"

"Okay. Thanks, Steve."

CHAPTER 11

Bill Gallagher met with Timothy Davis the following Monday in the PI's Norfolk office.

It was sticky hot in the city. Both men were in shirtsleeves and noticeably uncomfortable, beads of perspiration dotting their foreheads. Davis had the portable fan working, though it did little to improve matters.

"I've reviewed the police transcripts several times," Davis was saying. "I also interviewed the people who knew Mrs. Pike privately." He stared at the list on his note pad. "Lisa D'Angelo. Raymond Johnston, the apartment landlord. J. Paul Wainwright, her boss at the Little Creek commissary. Olga Sandberg, another co-worker, and a few others I found on my own." He shook his head, adding, "Unfortunately, they told me exactly what they told the police."

"In other words, you struck out?"

"I'm afraid so." Davis flipped a page. "I also looked up this Larry Phillips guy you told me about."

"And?"

"Well, the Navy told me he was transferred to Groton, Connecticut, four months ago. He's in the submarine service, went there for advanced training."

"Well, that rules him out."

Davis mopped the moisture from his brow with a handkerchief and carried on, "Now, as far as her parents are concerned—"

"No!" The word had whipped out of Bill's mouth like a pistol shot. "Don't bother them. Leave them be."

"But why? They might give us a lead or two. Don't you think it best we try?"

"But they live in Baltimore. What are you going to do, fly up there and interrogate them?"

"No, I'll drive up there. I'll interview them and get what I need in one day. If it makes you feel better, I won't even charge you for the trip."

"I don't know. Let's hold that thought for now."

"Look, Bill, a visit to her parents might yield some valuable information. They might know someone their daughter may have been involved with that no one else knew about. Like a former boyfriend, for instance. See what I mean?"

"Yeah, but I still don't think they'll tell you much more than what they told the police."

"Look, the police are human. They make mistakes like the rest of us. Besides, if you're really serious about this, you'll have to give me a free hand and trust my instincts."

Gallagher pursed his lips and thought about it. When he spoke, remorse accented his words, as if he was reproaching himself for challenging the detective.

"Okay, Tim, we'll do it your way." An impatient sigh. "Now, what about Commander Pike?"

"Well, that's going to be a little tricky."

"How do you mean?"

"Well, I just can't go over to the naval base and ask him if he murdered his wife, can I? My guess is that he'll want to see my ID. If he finds out you hired me, he'll clam up and refer me to his lawyer."

"Yeah, he's too smart to cooperate with a private detective." Another thoughtful pause. "So what are you going to do?"

"I'll use one of my undercover plans."

"What's that?"

"My reporter gig," Davis told him. "You see, I know this guy who works for the *Virginian-Pilot* on occasion. His name is Jeremy Sharp. He's a freelance writer and I have a copy of his press card. I'll go through proper channels to get an interview with Pike, flash Jeremy's press card in his face when I see him, and tell him I'm doing research for a story about the recent crime wave. Which, of course, includes the murder of his wife."

"Isn't that a bit obvious posing as a newspaper reporter?" challenged the marine. "What if Pike calls the newspaper to verify who you are?"

"If he does, the *Pilot* will tell him exactly what I told you—that Sharp only works for them part-time."

"It still sounds dangerous to me. Pike is no fool."

"Don't worry, Bill, I've done this gig before." Davis offered an encouraging smile. "It'll work, trust me."

"What about Pike's girlfriend? What do you know about her so far?"

"Only what Jake told me." Davis stared at his notes. "Her name is Mary Young. She works nights at a country nightclub in

Portsmouth called The Gunslinger."

"Yeah, I've heard of it. Marlene told me she and her husband used to go there a lot before they broke up. You know where it is?"

"Yeah, Victory Boulevard." Davis took another swipe with the handkerchief. "Jake showed me a picture of the girl. Dark hair, terrific figure. A real looker. She works at the club as a barmaid, or so she told the police. It was where she met Pike."

"Marlene said they were living together."

"According to Jake, six months."

"In other words, they've been together almost from the time him and Marlene split up?"

Davis nodded thoughtfully, expecting to hear more. When nothing happened, he leaned forward in his chair, elbows on the desk, eyes begging for more information.

"Go on," he urged.

"Come on, you know what I'm thinking, Tim. I think she's the reason Pike killed his wife. His motivation, so to speak."

"An interesting hypothesis. In a case such as this one, there's usually another woman involved. Yes, you could have something there. I mean, considering this was a clear-cut murder."

"So you agree with me that Pike was the killer?"

"Let's just say he's my prime suspect. Let's face it, Marlene's apartment was not burgled or ransacked on the night of the murder. Like Jake said, the man, whoever he was, walked into the place to do his evil work, and then walked out as if he'd gone to the bank to make a deposit. He, the killer, is the only witness we have. And for now, Pike is our only suspect."

"So what are you going to do about Miss Young?"

"I'll interview her too."

"As a reporter?"

"No, *that* would be obvious, for she'll tell her boyfriend about me and he'll put two and two together. No, for her I'll have to think of something else. I might even have to wear a disguise when I see her. In fact, now that I think of it, I'll use another scheme that works fairly well. I'll pose as an employee of the Census Bureau."

"Sounds like you could make a good living as a spy, Tim."

"You're right," laughed Davis. "That's basically what I am."

Gallagher returned to the BOQ following the meeting and found a note taped to the refrigerator door. Greaves had written: *Call RM!* Below the words was a telephone number. Bill dialed the number, and two rings later a female voice spoke to him.

"Norfolk Airport. May I help you?"

"Hello, my name is Bill Gallagher. I'd like to speak to Mr. Roger Morrison, airline traffic control."

"One moment, please."

Gallagher waited for the connection, wondering what it was all about. He had not talked to his old navy buddy in over three months. The last time happened on the day Morrison left the service. Finally a bass drum voice came on the line, the muted sounds of human chatter in the background.

"Is that you, Bill, for cryin' out loud?"

"You bet, Roger. Just got your message from Chet. How the hell are you?"

"Fine," was Morrison's reply. "Greaves told me you're on some sort of special leave. Thought we might be able to get together tonight."

"Sounds good. What do you got in mind?"

"Thought maybe we could have dinner together, then do some drinking and carousing, like old times."

"That suits me fine. Where and when?"

"I'll be done here in an hour and we can meet anywhere you want. You pick the spot."

Gallagher pondered. Finally he said, "I got it. How about that restaurant on Military Highway we used to go to?"

"The Steak Pit?"

"Yeah."

Gallagher met his friend at the Steak Pit at half past six. Having arrived first, Morrison had reserved a booth and grinned hugely when his buddy walked in. They shook hands warmly.

"Good to see you again, Bill." Morrison waved a hand over his head, snaring the eyes of a loitering waitress. "And don't worry, everything's on me tonight," he added.

Morrison was wearing gray suit pants, the sleeves of his white shirt rolled up to the elbows, proof that he'd had a busy day on the job. His black-and-red-striped tie hung loose from an open collar, and the wavy brown mane covering his scalp was all over the place, unlike the last time Gallagher had seen him when his hair was cropped in the classic military style. Bill thought he seemed overly happy.

They ordered a pitcher of beer when the waitress appeared. As she turned to leave, Gallagher said, "You look fit and content with life, Roger. What's the occasion?"

"Actually I had been thinking of calling you for several days but kept putting it off. Anyway, I had lunch today with a TWA pilot on layover and he told me about his navy days when he was stationed at Oceana. I told him about us, and afterwards I decided to call you. Chet said you were in Norfolk at the time."

"Yeah. What else did that character tell you?"

"Not much, actually. Said you were still working for Steve Watson and that you'd applied for a transfer."

The waitress reappeared with the beer and two frosted mugs and asked for their dinner orders. Both ordered a porterhouse steak with a side order of fries. Salad came with the meal, she told them, and they nodded with reluctance. Neither was a lover of the green stuff.

She left, and Morrison said, "So, buddy, how's the military treating you these days?"

"Okay," replied the marine, hoisting the glass to his lips. The insincere tone which had accompanied his words was obvious to his friend.

Morrison said, "Seems so long ago since we last saw each other, doesn't it?"

"Still living in Hampton?"

"Yeah, got a small pad there, but I'm thinking of moving back to the south side. Don't like commuting through that damned tunnel everyday. Maybe I'll get a place in Norfolk or somewhere near the Beach. But I'm not in any hurry. Got plenty of time to think about it."

"How's the job?"

"I love it, Bill. Technically, I'm still in training, but it won't be long till I'm on my own."

"Sounds great, Roger."

"It *is* great. No orders, no saluting, no crazy duty hours. Just do your job and get paid." A brief chuckle before he went on, "We're union, you know. If we go on strike, the airport shuts down. But that'll never happen."

"Sounds tempting," Gallagher said to his beer.

"Yeah, but not for you. You're a career jarhead."

"You always could read my mind."

More laughter from the ex-sailor. He swigged some beer, licking the residue of foam from his lips.

He said, "Chet told me you're pretty adamant about that transfer. Finally tired of the classroom, huh?"

"Yeah."

"You're not thinking of going back to 'Nam, are you?"

"Don't know. Maybe."

Morrison drank some beer, hesitated, but then shook his head with emphasis.

"For God's sake, Bill, don't do it. Those gooks aren't worth fighting for."

Gallagher said nothing in return. Instead, he glanced away as an elderly couple strolled by their table, smiling at him. When he looked back, he found Morrison studying him closely.

"What's on your mind, Roger?"

"Bill, I...I have tell you that I've been following the murder case in the newspaper. When I first read about it, I went into shock. I thought about calling you but held back. I figured you wouldn't want to talk about it."

"It shocked the hell out of me too." Bill's voice was barely audible. He cleared the frog from his throat. "That girl was special to me."

"From what I read, the police have no leads. Have they already given up looking for the killer?"

"Yeah, but I haven't."

"What does that mean?"

Gallagher told him what he meant.

"My God!" was Morrison's reaction. "Whatever gave you the idea to hire a private eye?"

"Actually it was a recommendation from one of the police detectives assigned to the case."

"So the police *have* given up searching for the killer?"

"Yeah, it's a simple matter of finances, they said. They've got no leads, so they can't devote anymore time looking."

Morrison pondered, or so it seemed.

"So what does this private eye think, Bill? Does he believe her husband was the murderer, like you do?"

"No."

"But you're convinced, aren't you?"

"He did it, Roger. He and Marlene had a turbulent marriage. He had even threatened to kill her several times—she told me so. The last time scared the hell out of her."

"So just because he threatened her, you think he killed her?"

"Yeah, but there's more to it than that. I met Pike. He's smart, he's arrogant, he's—"

"A hot-shot navy commander," Morrison finished for him. Gallagher glared at his friend.

"What's that got to do with it, man? Do you believe that all navy officers are clean-cut and virtuous? Don't you think it's possible he killed her in a moment of rage…or jealousy?"

"You're right, anything's possible." Morrison reached for his glass, sipped and continued, "So what's your private eye going to do?"

"He's investigating Pike and his girlfriend."

"What's his girlfriend got to do with it?"

"Who knows? Maybe she's the reason he killed Marlene. His motivation, so to speak."

"What's her story?"

"All we know so far is that they're shacked up together. She works in Portsmouth at a place called The Gunslinger."

"Yeah, I've heard of it. It's a country nightclub on Victory Boulevard. I've seen ads for it in the newspaper and magazines. Supposed to be a jumping place."

"Yeah, if you like that kind of music."

"Hey, I got an idea. Why don't we go over there after dinner and check the place out? Maybe we'll run into her, do a little undercover work of our own."

"Are you nuts?"

"No, I'm serious. She's never seen you before, right?"

"Not that I know of."

"Well then, let's do it. Might be fun."

"Could also be dangerous. I mean, what if Pike shows up? Remember, he knows me."

"That's negative thinking, buddy boy." Morrison smiled at his friend. "Come on, let's do it. What do you say?"

They arrived at The Gunslinger a little after eight o'clock. They were obliged to pay a one-dollar cover charge at the door, strolled in and found the only vacant table available two rows back from the dance floor.

The club was unusually crowded for a Monday night, a blanket of cigarette smoke hovering in the air like an early morning fog. Participants on the dance floor, which was encircled by a corral-like fence, moved about in a circle to the beat of the country band on stage. The lead singer of the group, a mustached middle-aged man wearing a denim vest and black leather saddle pants, was singing a Hank Williams' tune in a dubious Dixie twang that was laughable.

"Do you believe this place?" said Morrison, glancing about. "I'll bet you ten to one that most of those jerks on the dance floor wearing cowboy hats have never been out west or seen a horse in their life. Except maybe on 'Bonanza'."

"Yeah, it's pretty funny, ain't it?"

"But that's the way life is," rambled on Morrison. "Most people these days want to be something other than what they are."

"You're right. Look at all the hippies running around loose. A few years from now they'll all be married with a house full of kids and bills to pay." He shook his head, adding, "It's a crazy world we live in."

"Any sign of Pike's girlfriend?"

"Not sure, man. I don't see anyone who fits her description. This place is so crowded, we might never see her."

"Yeah, she may not even be working tonight."

The music stopped suddenly, but then restarted, this time in a slower, sad tempo, dance partners clutching each other in the traditional hug and shuffle routine. Not long thereafter Morrison nudged his friend on the elbow, gesturing toward the bar.

"What about her, Bill?"

Gallagher turned and saw a wall of men sitting at the bar, chatting with the barmaid as she made her rounds along the horseshoe-shaped bar, refilling their drinks. She was slim, dark-haired, attractive, an ample bosom emphasizing her scrumptious figure. She wore a sleeveless denim blouse, a white cowboy hat tiled back on her head, exposing her bangs, red lipstick and a scarf tied at the throat that matched the color of her mouth. Bill painted a picture in his mind of her and Pike as a couple.

"Yeah, that could be her," he said matter-of-factly.

"She's a doll, no question about it," added the gawking Morrison. "Hell, she could ride in my saddle anytime. Wonder if she's wearing those cute shorts and cowboy boots all the other waitresses have on."

"Well, there's only one way to find out."

They sauntered over to the bar, Morrison leading the way. Gallagher commandeered the only vacant stool available, his friend standing beside him. Morrison reached into his wallet, yanked out a ten dollar bill and slapped it on the bar, snatching the girl's attention. She stepped closer, grinning at them, much to the dismay of the other patrons.

"Howdy, boys!" she said cordially, looking them over. "You must be new here. Haven't seen you before."

"Yeah, we just rode in from the range, honey," said Morrison, suppressing the urge to laugh. "Been driving the cattle to market."

"Sure, partner, in a white shirt and tie." She winked at him, then switched her attention to Gallagher. "And what's your story, good-lookin'? And don't tell me your name is Tex or Wyatt Earp. You got navy written all over you."

"Gee, is it that obvious?" She giggled.

"So what'll it be, gents?"

"Two cold ones from the keg," Morrison told her.

"Any particular brand?"

"No, surprise us, honey."

She gave him a sexy smile and promptly turned away to fill the order. Morrison poked his friend in the ribs.

"So what do you think, Bill?"

"Don't know, man. How do we find out if she's Pike's girlfriend? We just can't ask her."

"Sure we can. We'll be subtle about it. Women love to talk, especially about themselves. You'll see."

She returned with two Budweisers. She grabbed the money, stepped over to the cash register, returned and stacked seven one-dollar bills in front of him, smiling. Morrison returned the smile.

"Thanks, honey."

"You're welcome, cowboy."

"Is this place always so dern crowded?"

"You think it's crowded now, you should be here Saturday nights. It's wall-to-wall people."

"I'll bet it's all because of you, darlin'. By the way, what's your name?"

"Mary."

"Mary what?"

"Mary Young," she said. Then quickly added, "But don't waste your time, partner. I'm already spoken for."

"But I don't see no ring on your finger." Morrison turned. "Do you, Tex?"

Gallagher shook his head, barely containing the laughter.

"Nope, sure don't, Wyatt."

She burst into laughter.

"You gents must be stoned. You been smokin' too much happy grass?"

"Nope, we never touch the stuff," Morrison told her. "It's bad for the constitution."

Grinning, she glanced away and noticed three glasses that needed refilling at the far end of the bar.

"Excuse me, boys."

When she was out of earshot, Gallagher whispered to his friend, "Nice work, man, it's her—Mary Young. That's her name."

"You know, Bill, I like this undercover work. It's exciting, don't you think?"

"It's dangerous. Hell, what if Pike shows up and sees me?"

"So what? It's a free country. We got a right to be here like anyone else."

Young finished her barmaiding and started back toward them. Bill watched her every step, enjoying the suggestive swagger of her hips and mouth-watering lips. Certainly not the girl who lived next door, he thought. She parked herself in front of them, hands on the bar, and gave her attention to Morrison.

"So where do you boys hail from?"

"Texas—where else?" A confirmed bachelor, Morrison was an

expert at patronizing the opposite sex.

She said, "Yeah, and the war is not really happening." Lips pursed, she folded her arms together: a picture of impatience.

"Come on, boys, tell the truth. Where do you hail from?"

It was Morrison who answered, "My buddy Will is from Florida, and I'm a Hoosier from the great state of Indiana. Went to school at Purdue."

"Impressive," she said. "Is that what you always say to pick up the smart girls?"

"It never fails," he replied, chuckling between words. She turned.

"What about you, darlin'? What ship are you stationed on?"

"What makes you think I'm in the navy?"

"Because every guy your age who's not in the service has his hair down to his shoulders. Hell, half the guys in this club are sailors, can't you tell?"

"Well, I'm not a sailor. I'm just passing through."

She seemed skeptical, but had no time to respond when she was beckoned away by a new customer.

Gallagher waited until she was gone before he said to his friend, "Let's get out of here."

"Why?"

"'Cause I think she suspects something. Did you see the way she looked at me?"

"Ah, come on, just keep humoring her. Who knows, we might find out something about her boyfriend."

"No, I don't think we should underestimate her."

"Yeah, you might have a point. She's smart as a whip."

They waited five more minutes, but she never returned, was too busy tending the needs of her clientele. Gallagher's jaw went south when Morrison left a five-dollar tip on the bar for her. It was quarter past ten when they finally left the club.

They returned to Norfolk and stopped at an all-night restaurant on West Tidewater Drive. Morrison, a big man with a twenty-four-hour appetite, ordered coffee and a slice of blueberry pie. Gallagher ordered cappuccino.

"Quite a night, huh, Bill?"

Gallagher sipped his drink, nodded and said, "Yeah, you can say that again."

"So now that you got a closer look, what do you think of her?"

"Not sure, man. She seemed harmless enough."

"She was absolutely gorgeous! If we hadn't known who she was, I might have gone after her tonight."

"You haven't changed a bit, buddy. You're still a ladies' man. In fact, I think she liked you. I think she enjoyed flirting with you."

"Maybe, but she's spoken for, remember? Weren't those her exact words?"

"Still, there's something about her that bothers me."

"What's that?"

"Don't know exactly, can't put my finger on it. She just didn't seem to belong in that place."

"Why, because she didn't speak like Annie Oakley?"

"No, it's not that. I just can't see Pike getting involved with a common barmaid."

"I wouldn't call her common, buddy. She had a body to kill for."

"That's for sure," seconded Gallagher. "Still, there's something about her that makes me nervous."

"By the way, Bill, is there anything I can do to help? I mean, this private eye thing must be costing you a fortune. If you need some extra bread, I've got a few bucks stashed away."

"Thanks, but no thanks, Roger. I can handle it on my own."

"Well, if you get a little tight, don't be afraid to ask. What's a friend for if he can't help his old buddy?"

"Thanks, man." Bill clapped him on the shoulder. "I appreciate it."

CHAPTER 12

Tim Davis dialed Pike's home phone number the following evening but there was no answer after seven rings. The next morning he telephoned the Norfolk Naval Station and informed the base duty officer that he was a freelance reporter and would Commander Pike please return his call "as soon as it's convenient for him." It was later in the day when the *U.S.S. Roosevelt's* chief nuclear engineering officer finally returned his call and agreed to do the interview at seven o'clock the following evening. "My girlfriend will be working, so we'll have the place to ourselves."

Davis arrived at the fifth-floor Granby Street apartment per schedule and was ushered into the place by the broad-shouldered sailor, who was dressed in khaki uniform and smoking a cigarette.

The apartment suite was austere, Davis would tell Gallagher at their next meeting. The furniture was Early American, an army of porcelain animal knickknacks scattered throughout the place. Hanging from the wall above the sideboard was an authentic-looking oil painting of Thomas Jefferson that gave emphasis to the surrounding décor. Davis was offered the love seat directly opposite the couch and sat. The wide screen RCA television set in the corner to his left was not on.

"I suspect you'll want to see my press card," said Davis as Pike plopped down on the couch.

"No, not really," said the sailor.

Davis produced the copy of Jeremy Sharp's press card anyway and handed it across. He waited as Pike glanced at it, then reclaimed it when it was offered back.

"I appreciate your time, Commander. I'll try to make this as painless as possible."

"It's all right, Mr. Sharp, I wasn't doing anything important, just reading the sports page." Pike grabbed the newspaper spread out across the coffee table, folded it together and tossed it on the end of the couch.

"Looks like the Chicago Cubs are going to win the pennant this year," said Davis conversationally. "They got, what, a ten game lead over the Mets?"

"Yes, but the Orioles have the best team in the majors," countered Pike. "Look at that powerful lineup they have. Frank Robinson. Brooks Robinson. Boog Powell. And with that great pitching staff, they'll be tough to beat."

"Sounds like you're a baseball fan, sir."

"I follow the daily box scores. But football's my favorite game. Played linebacker at Annapolis for three years, was on the same team with Roger Staubach when he won the Heisman trophy in '63." The ex-letterman flaunted a proud smile.

"How long have you been in the navy, sir?"

"Ten years."

"Do you like it?"

"Yes, there's nothing I'd rather do," was the sailor's answer. "I'm sort of following in my father's footsteps. He was a career officer. During the war he served at Midway, Savo Island and Leyte Gulf. Retired a fleet admiral a couple of years ago." He paused for a breath of air, eyes twinkling like stars. "A brilliant man," he added.

Strangely enough, Davis found himself nodding in agreement. He reached inside his shirt pocket and pulled out a note pad and pen.

Watching him, Pike said, "So how can I help you, Mr. Sharp?"

"Well, as I mentioned on the phone yesterday, I'm preparing an article based on the recent crime wave. The *Pilot's* editorial staff has received a ton of mail from residents who are fed up with the police department's inability to solve two brutal murders the past six months."

"Including my wife's, of course?"

"Yes."

Pike took a puff from his cigarette, showing no signs of emotion, and Davis went on, "The article is not intended to discredit or ridicule the police in any way. Guess what I'm really trying to accomplish is to bring awareness to the community that the police are undermanned when it comes to combating violent crime."

"Is that what you've uncovered so far?"

"Well, I've got a lot more research to do, but yes. I honestly believe the police need more help. And by that, I mean, financial help. More money means more police officers, not to mention new and better crime-fighting equipment."

Pike deliberated, or so it seemed. Davis cleared his throat.

"Anyway," he said, "I'm hoping the article will light a fire under the mayor and his administration. Maybe they'll get off their lazy behinds and find new ways to increase the police budget, perhaps even lobby Richmond for financial assistance. I've mentioned the idea to the police commissioner and several members of the city council. They like what I'm doing."

"Well, I'm all for it too," said Pike, nodding. "And so will any clearheaded law-abiding citizen." He grinned, showing a collection of pearl-white teeth. "So how can I help you, Mr. Sharp?"

"Well, sir, if you don't mind telling me, I'd like to know your impression of the police investigation of your wife's murder."

"All I can tell you is that they interviewed me twice."

"They also interviewed your girlfriend, correct?"

"Yes, they did."

Davis continued, "Tell me about the time when you and your wife broke up."

"What would you like to know?"

"Was it amicable?"

"No."

"Explain."

"We had many disagreements while we were married, Mr. Sharp. After I filed for divorce, we went our separate ways. We rarely spoke to one another. It was the way she wanted it."

"So you didn't know much about her personal life during the period of separation?"

"That's right." Pike jabbed the cigarette between his lips and inhaled calmly.

Davis continued, "I've worked with the Norfolk police many times during my career. I've written several articles about crimes they solved and some they didn't. I know for a fact that when they reach a point when they believe a case becomes unsolvable, they put it away in a pending file, on the back burner, so to speak. It's a matter of economics, they tell me. I guess it's like that with all police departments."

"In other words, they only work on a case as long as their budget permits?"

"Precisely. Unfortunately, they've now reached that point in the investigation of your wife's murder. They have no leads to justify the costs to continue the investigation. Meanwhile the murderer remains free to come and go as he pleases. Thus the locals get restless. I tell you, crime in this city's getting so bad, I'm almost afraid to go out at night."

Pike nodded as he inhaled more cigarette.

Davis carried on, "So tell me, Commander, if you don't mind me asking, as a concerned citizen who believes in law and order, how do you feel about the fact that the police have, more or less, swept the case under the rug?"

"Considering what you just told me, Mr. Sharp, I feel somewhat embittered. However, in my opinion, simply handing the police a blank check won't solve violent crime in this city. The bigger issue here is how they utilize the money. For me, training would be the key. You can spend all the money in the bank, but if your training methods are second rate, you'd only be wasting your time."

"Sounds like you've had some experience along those lines, Commander."

"That's how it is in the service, Mr. Sharp. Sailors come and go all the time. You wouldn't believe the amount of time we spend on training and retraining. But it's all necessary, believe me. Too many lives are at stake."

"A good point." Davis scribbled on his notepad.

Watching him, Pike inhaled another drag before he said, "By

the way, is there anything I can offer you, Mr. Sharp? Coffee? A drink?"

"No, thank you." Davis flipped a page in the notepad and returned to the main topic.

"Mr. Pike, could you please tell me when you found out that your wife had been murdered?"

"The Tuesday after the fact," was the reply. "The twenty-ninth of July, I believe it was."

"How did you find out?"

"The police. They called the apartment that morning but I wasn't here. My girlfriend took the call."

"I take it you were working at the time?"

"Yes, I was at the naval base. The police interviewed me later that morning."

"Did they ever say that you were a suspect?"

"No, they just wanted to know about my relationship with my wife, the last time I had seen her, and where I was on the night of the murder. Things like that." Davis jotted it down.

"Sir, do you know of anyone who might have had a motive to kill your wife, such as an angry ex-boyfriend or coworker?"

Pike corkscrewed his head and frowned, as if puzzled by the question. Finally he said, "I wouldn't know."

Davis watched as he stubbed out the cigarette butt in the ashtray on the coffee table. Pike then reached for the pack of Camels next to it and held it up.

"Cigarette, Mr. Sharp?"

"No, thank you." Davis waited as Pike helped himself to another cigarette. "So you have no idea who might've had a motive for killing your wife?"

"Like I said, Marlene and I didn't see much of each other after we split up."

"Did you know she had a boyfriend?"

"Yes, his name is Bill Gallagher."

"He's also in the military, I understand."

"That's right," verified the poker-faced sailor. "Do you intend to interview him too?"

"Yes."

"Well, if it means anything, I can tell you for a fact that he thinks *I* killed my wife."

"You mean to say you've met this man?"

"Yes, at my wife's funeral. Not an amicable encounter, I might add."

"Interesting." Davis stared down at his notes, knowing he had to refrain from asking anymore personal questions about the case without arousing suspicion. The big man sitting on the couch was obviously no fool.

"I believe that's all I need to ask you, Commander." He rose from the chair and Pike quickly followed suit. "Again I want to thank you for sparing the time tonight. Hope it wasn't too much of an inconvenience."

"Not at all, sir. I just hope I was able to help you out. Good luck with your project."

Davis smiled. He turned to leave, but then stopped suddenly to admire the Jefferson portrait.

"Is there anything wrong, Mr. Sharp?"

"No, I was just wondering about that painting."

"It was a birthday gift from my father," Pike told him. "You do recognize him, of course?"

"Yes, Thomas Jefferson."

"An idol of mine," said Pike with obvious pride in his voice. "In my opinion, the greatest American who ever lived. In fact, you might remember that during his presidency he was responsible for the Louisiana Purchase, perhaps the most significant achievement in our country's history."

"No, I wasn't aware of that."

"Patrick Henry is another favorite of mine," rambled on Pike. "Someday I'm hoping to acquire his portrait too."

"Are you a Virginian, sir?"

"Yes, born in Arlington."

Smiling, Davis held out his hand.

"Thanks again for your time, Commander."

"You're welcome," said Pike, and they shook hands.

It was 1:35 a.m. when Mary Young returned to the apartment after a tedious night of playing barmaid at The Gunslinger. To her surprise, she found her boyfriend sitting on the couch reading a book.

"Darling, what are you doing up so late?"

He smelled the scent of stale cigarette smoke in her hair as she leaned over and pecked him on the cheek with a kiss.

"Couldn't sleep," he said, and closed the book. "Why don't you make us a drink? Maybe it'll help me doze off."

An inviting smile, another quick kiss before she hustled off to the kitchen. Several minutes later she reappeared toting two martinis. She gave him one and sat beside him, making herself comfortable.

"How was your night?" he asked.

"Oh, the usual. About a dozen men asked me to go home with them."

"The whole world is horny." He sipped his drink. "Why don't you quit that crummy job?"

"And become a housewife like you want me to?" She shook her head. "I need to be busy, you know that."

"Had a visitor," he said, curling his arm around her shoulders.

"Who?" she urged.

"A reporter."

"Reporter? You mean a newspaper reporter?" Her voice was anxious.

"Yeah, claimed he was a freelance writer. Said he's working on an article about the recent city crime wave. Wanted to talk to me about my wife's murder."

"Did it bother you?"

"No."

She was suddenly angry and proved it with her next statement.

"The nerve of him! First the police, then a nosy reporter. You just can't get any privacy anymore. It's not fair."

"You're right. Next time it'll probably be the FBI knocking on the door. Maybe even J. Edgar Hoover himself." He laughed and she snuggled closer.

"Let's take a shower together," she said. "Are you in a frisky mood?"

"No, but if we take a shower together, I will be."

Later, after they had made love, Maria Brandt waited until her boyfriend was asleep before slipping out of the bed and tiptoeing into the living room. She grabbed his briefcase, carried it into the kitchen and switched on the light.

She unlocked the briefcase, removed the documents inside that looked important, opened the cabinet and grabbed the camera. Seven minutes later she was back in bed beside him and fell asleep with her head resting comfortably on his shoulder.

On Wednesday the twenty-seventh, Davis phoned Norfolk police headquarters and asked to talk to his friend who worked there.

"Sorry to bother you, Jake. You free to talk?"

"Sure, Fuzzy's in court. I'm here all by my lonesome." Wharton chuckled. "So what's up, buddy?"

"Need to talk to you about the Pike murder case."

"Shoot."

"I saw Commander Pike last night."

"Interesting. What was your impression?"

"Not sure, but I have a theory." Davis hesitated.

"Go on," urged Wharton.

"Well, I don't think he's the murderer."

"Is this another one of your talented hunches, Tim, or do you have something to back it up with?"

"No, guess it's just a gut feeling."

"I know what you mean."

"He's the all-American boy, Jake. Son of a war hero. Head of his class at Annapolis. Even if he *were* the jealous type, I don't think he'd be stupid enough to kill his wife in cold blood."

"So what are you going to do?"

"Not sure. Was going to see his girlfriend next, but first I'll have a chat with Gallagher before I do. I'm going to lay it on the line and tell him he's wasting his time."

"And give up that easy money?" Davis heard another chuckle. "You're getting soft in your old age, Tim."

Davis arranged a meeting with Gallagher that same evening. The former was munching on an egg salad sandwich when the marine walked into the office.

"Good of you to come, Lieutenant. Grab a seat."

Gallagher sat in the chair opposite and waited as Davis put the sandwich aside and wiped his mouth with a napkin. They had chatted briefly on the phone earlier, but Davis had preferred not to divulge what he wanted to discuss. Bill suspected it was not good news.

"You were very mysterious on the phone, Mr. Davis."

"Sorry about that, but I prefer to talk business with my clients face to face."

Gallagher watched as Davis stared at the notes in front of him, as if gathering the right amount of verbal ammunition needed to say what he had to say.

"I saw Pike last night," he said finally. "He invited me up to his apartment and we chatted for almost an hour. He was most cooperative."

"You interviewed him as a reporter?"

"Yes." Davis paused, seemed hesitant to go on, but then climbed on his feet. "I'll be frank with you, Mr. Gallagher. I think you're wasting your time and money on this case."

"So you don't think he's the murderer?"

"That's right. I checked and rechecked the affidavits, read and reread the police reports, interviewed everyone except Pike's girlfriend. After meeting with him, I'm convinced he's innocent."

"What makes you say that?"

"Well, you're not going to like the answer, but it's a feeling I have."

"*Feeling?*"

"Yes, or call it experience." Davis slowly stepped around the desk, arms folded together. "I've been involved in detective work most of my working life, Bill. After a while you begin to understand how the criminal mind operates. You notice certain things about suspects in lineups, learn how they react during interrogations. You can pretty much tell if they're guilty or not by the sound of their voice, their facial expressions and body movements. I know that doesn't sound very modern or scientific, but that's the way it is."

Gallagher sighed heavily, seeming bemused.

"So what now, Tim?"

"Well, like I said, I think you're wasting your time. I could keep digging around, but I know I'll end up on a dead-end street. Sorry, but I don't think we'll ever find the killer."

"What about Pike's girlfriend? Another waste of time?"

"Probably."

"I saw her the other night," Gallagher told him, speaking to the desk. "I was out with a friend and we talked a lot about the case. Anyway, we decided to visit that nightclub she works at. We were curious to know what she was like."

"Did she know who you were?"

"No."

"So what happened?"

"Not much, really. We just flirted with her. But it was a busy night. She had to take care of a lot of customers."

"Mostly men, I take it?"

"Naturally."

"So what was your impression of her?"

"She seemed normal, if that's what you mean."

"Anything at all about her that may have suggested she was not what she seemed to be, such as the belligerent type?"

"I don't follow you?"

"Well, what I mean is, did she seem like the type who could commit murder?"

"Anyone is capable of murder, Mr. Davis."

"Yes, but I must remind you that Mrs. Pike was strangled to death presumably by a man. But that doesn't mean a woman couldn't have done it. You saw her, Lieutenant. Do you think she's capable of killing a woman the size of Marlene?"

"No, I don't. She's petite, smaller than Marlene. I don't think she'd be strong enough to strangle her, let alone anybody."

"So, for the sake of argument, if Miss Young had planned the murder, she obviously hired someone to do it, with or without Pike's knowledge."

The mood on Gallagher's face seemed to come alive.

"Yeah, that's a real possibility. So you think she might've been the brains behind the murder?"

"Just chalk it up as a theory," was the PI's answer.

"Tim, I appreciate all you've done so far, but I want you to do one more thing before we call it quits."

"You want me to interview the girl, right?"

"Yeah. Maybe you can find out something about her that the police couldn't. Personally, I still believe Pike was the killer. And maybe Mary Young had a hand in it too."

"And if I *don't* find anything?"

"Then I guess it's over."

CHAPTER 13

Davis altered his schedule on Friday morning to accommodate Gallagher's request. As he had told the marine the night before, he would interview Mary Young as a representative of the Census Bureau. Before leaving the house, he donned a fake moustache that complemented his brown hair and sideburns. "You look ten years older," his wife told him.

He left his car in the parking lot across the street from the eight-story high rise. Wearing a gray suit, fake reading glasses and toting a black briefcase, he looked like the prototypical door-to-door salesman. It was 10:03 when he rang the doorbell of Pike's fifth-floor suite.

No reply.

He knocked.

More silence.

After a failed third attempt, he returned to the car, deciding to try again next week.

It was drizzling on the Tuesday after the Labor Day holiday. Davis parked his Ford Falcon and headed for the Granby Street apartment building wearing the same ensemble as the week previous, including the phony moustache and glasses.

A taxicab, its motor idling in neutral, was parked in front of the entrance of the luxury high rise. As he stood on the corner waiting for the traffic light to change, Mary Young emerged from the building. She was outfitted in a chic black beret that highlighted her beige raincoat, a black belt tied snugly at the waist. The light changed, Davis started across, but stopped when she stepped toward the taxi and ducked into the back seat.

He hustled back to his car and started the engine. He glanced at his wristwatch, his mind racing at full throttle. Where was she going at 9:30 in the morning? His instincts told him to follow.

The taxi was easy to chase. It started north on Granby, then east onto Little Creek Road. The cabbie turned south when he reached Military Highway, then made a left-hand turn at the Norview Avenue exit. His destination: the city airport.

Motor traffic was light outside the passenger terminal. Davis stopped the Ford three car lengths behind the cab, which had parked along the front curb of the terminal, and waited.

Mary Young emerged from the taxi a half minute later. She fumbled with her purse, eventually found what she needed, reached through the open window, paid the driver and started toward the terminal. Before reaching the door, she removed the beret, briefly glanced around, turned again and walked into the building.

Davis leaned on the accelerator pedal and parked in the short-term lot across the way. He removed the disguise and followed in after her. The time was 9:51.

Pedestrian traffic inside the terminal was light. He had expected to find her with little trouble but was surprised when he didn't see her. He made a thorough search of the concourse without success. Back in the main lobby, he purchased a copy of the *Virginian-Pilot* at the newsstand, deciding to hang around for a while.

He located a vacant seat along the wall, sat and deliberated. Where had she gone? Was she leaving on a business trip, or perhaps a vacation? No, she didn't have any luggage with her. He opened the newspaper and scanned the lobby.

A Pan Am flight from Philadelphia had just arrived at Gate 2, announced the public address speaker. Davis gave his attention to the editorial page, wondering if he should leave. When he looked up again, he saw her.

She had just left the women's rest room, which was located at the opposite side of the lobby. The raincoat folded neatly over her left arm, she was clad in a pastel green blouse and white miniskirt, her mouth wearing a fresh coat of red lipstick, her hair smartly arranged at shoulder length. She picked up her momentum, ignoring the admiring stares of three sailors loitering near the newsstand. Davis rose from his seat, took a deep breath and followed.

She made the obligatory turn into the concourse, heading in the direction of Gate 2. Was she taking that plane to its next destination, or was she meeting someone from Philadelphia? Davis swore privately, convinced he was wasting his time, but decided to stay longer for the sake of curiosity.

He spotted an empty corner nearby, took up position there and watched her closely, the newspaper open between his hands. The information board on the wall behind the departure counter told him that the plane's next destination would be Atlanta, Georgia.

Departure was scheduled for 10:45.

He watched as the passengers from Philadelphia began funneling through the exit ramp doors and spilling into the waiting area. Davis lost sight of her as a group of eight happy people— obviously family members who had been apart for sometime— gathered in the universal reunion ritual of hugging and kissing. Davis fidgeted as he glanced at the newspaper. When he looked up, the family had dispersed and he saw Young about to shake hands with a man who had appeared in the waiting area.

The newcomer was bald-headed, middle-aged and stocky, had an ordinary face, gray moustache and neatly-trimmed sideburns of the same color. He sported a light blue pinstriped suit and brown shoes, carried a heavy-looking tan briefcase.

They chatted for several minutes and then started down the concourse runway. Following at a discreet distance, Davis surmised that their next stop would be the luggage carousel; only it didn't happen. Instead, the two made a casual beeline for the coffee lounge, which was situated in the terminal not far from the front-street exit.

Davis watched as Young and baldy sat together at a corner table by the window, heads together in conversation. Davis scanned the lobby and found a vacant seat outside the café and sat, the newspaper open in front of him. Working vice nine years for the police and another four years as a private investigator had prepared him well for moments like these. Spying on people without being conspicuous was his specialty.

He glanced at his wristwatch: 10:15. He studied the flight schedule on the wall above the information booth. The Pan Am to Atlanta would be leaving in thirty minutes. A United Airlines flight to Kansas City would be departing from Gate 1 at 11:00. Another flight, a shuttle to Washington, D.C., was scheduled to leave Gate

3 at 11:30. Davis switched his attention to the lounge. Young and baldy were being served coffee by the waitress.

Davis noticed three other people in the place: a young couple, a man and a woman; the other, a bespectacled middle-aged gentleman seated in the corner three tables away from Miss Young and her out-of-town friend. The couple, wearing bright-colored clothes, looked like the prototypical summer tourists. The man with the glasses wore a gray business suit and was reading a paperback book. Someone killing time waiting for a flight, thought Davis.

Suddenly, Mary Young turned away from her companion and glanced around, as if expecting someone to be there, but then looked back and resumed her chat with baldy. Davis considered leaving, but abandoned the idea when she reached into the pocket of her raincoat, which was draped across the empty chair beside her. She produced a yellow envelope and placed it on the table. Baldy glanced at the envelope, as if merely for something to do, grabbed his coffee cup and sipped. Young said something to him, smiled, rose from her seat, collected her raincoat, said something else, turned away and walked out of the lounge.

Davis buried his head behind the sports section and caught a whiff of her perfume as she strolled past him. When he looked up, she was heading for the women's rest room. He turned and found baldy staring out the window. The envelope was exactly where she had left it.

The girl emerged from the rest room seven minutes later wearing the raincoat and hat, exited the building and hailed a taxi. Moments later a cab pulled up alongside the curb. She climbed inside and the taxi departed. Davis closed the newspaper and sighed. Very strange.

At 11:09, after a second cup of coffee, baldy gestured for the waitress. He paid the check with cash and a smile, waited until she was gone, opened his briefcase with a key, shoved the envelope inside, locked the briefcase, stood and vacated the café at a leisurely pace. Neither the waitress, nor the tourists, nor the four-eyed man, who had abandoned his paperback in favor of a slice of chocolate cake, noticed.

Davis followed after baldy as he started toward the concourse. The stranger was heading in the direction of Gate 3, where the D.C. shuttle would be leaving in twenty minutes.

Baldy stood in line at the departure counter and patiently awaited his turn. Davis watched until he had boarded the plane before vacating the terminal and returning to his car.

The shuttle to Washington, D.C., left Norfolk Airport as scheduled. Had Davis stayed longer, he might have noticed the man with the glasses and gray suit leaving the coffee lounge at 11:35. He bought a pack of cigarettes from the vending machine around the corner, lit one and stepped into an unoccupied phone booth.

He pushed a dime through the coin slot, dialed zero for the operator and waited for the connection. Six minutes later he hung up the phone and walked out of the booth.

On the drive back to the office, Davis reviewed the events at the airport, step by step. No, none of it made sense. In fact the whole thing had been bizarre: a welcoming handshake; coffee for two; a brief conversation; a yellow envelope; the D.C. shuttle. He shook his head. Very, very strange.

On Wednesday morning, he donned the moustache and glasses again and revisited the Pike residence. He arrived in the parking lot across the street from the high-rise at 9:25 but waited in the car until half past ten. The elevator delivered him to the fifth floor nine minutes later. He tried the doorbell: no answer. After two more fruitless attempts, he knocked with his fist and the door creaked open.

Mary Young peered out at him wearing a wrinkled frown of curiosity, eyes blinking nonstop. She was dressed in a blue cotton bathrobe and orange slippers, the ends of her long hair scattered across her shoulders in disarray. Someone who had just climbed out of bed, thought Davis.

"Yes?"

"Good morning," he said to her, pretending to sound cheerful. "Are you the lady of the house?"

"Yes."

"My name is Henderson," he said. He produced the bogus identity card and showed it to her. "As you can see, I'm with the Census Bureau."

"What can I do for you?"

"I need some of your time, ma'am. May I come in?"

"It's very early," she said. "Can you come back another time?"

"Sorry for the inconvenience, but it won't take long."

She seemed annoyed, reluctant to comply, but then nodded politely and opened the door wider. Davis smiled gratefully and stepped into the apartment.

The place looked exactly the way it'd had when he had interviewed her boyfriend the week before. He exchanged glances with the placid-faced Tom Jefferson as he followed her into the living room.

"Please be seated," she told him.

He thanked her with a nod and sat down on the love seat next to the record player.

"What can I do for you, Mister..."

"Henderson," he said, "John Henderson."

She stepped over to the window behind the couch and opened the Venetian blinds, bringing sunlight to the room. She returned to the couch and sat down, rubbing her eyes with care.

"Forgive me for receiving you like this, Mr. Henderson, but I work nights and usually don't get up before noon."

"I stopped by yesterday morning and rang the doorbell, but you didn't answer."

"That's because I wasn't here. You see, I do volunteer work at the library on Tuesdays. I'm...a reading tutor for pre-kindergarten children."

You're also a liar, lady.

He said, "Doesn't that mess up your sleep habits?"

"Somewhat." She faked a grin, adding, "Like I said, it's only on Tuesdays."

"Well, it's a good thing I came over today." He punctuated his statement with a bogus smile of his own.

She watched uninterestedly as he opened his briefcase and took out a note pad and pencil. He cleared his throat.

"I'm doing a special audit of the Hampton Roads area," he told her. "As you may know, the Bureau does a nationwide census every ten years." A brief pause. "Your name, please?"

"Mary Young."

"Do you live here alone?"

"No, I share it with my boyfriend."

"His name, please?"

"Charles Pike."

Davis continued the charade for another ten minutes. When he had finished, he thanked her for her time and left, deciding to pay Jake Wharton a visit at the police station. Luckily for him, he found the homicide detective seated behind his desk, poring over a small mountain of paperwork while munching on a jelly doughnut.

"Well, look what the cat dragged in," said Wharton, chuckling between words. "What can I do for you, old buddy?"

"Just happened to be in the neighborhood," Davis told him. He was still wearing the disguise and Wharton saw the connection.

"Don't tell me, let me guess. You've been using that old census gig again." He smirked. "So who was it this time?"

Davis peeled off the moustache and grinned hugely.

"Went over to see Mary Young," was his answer.

"You mean that gorgeous piece of skirt shacked up with Commander Pike?"

"Yeah."

"So you're still working for Gallagher, huh?"

"Yeah, but not for much longer. I've hit a roadblock."

Davis claimed the chair opposite the desk, Wharton offered him a doughnut, but he politely declined. Wharton took a bite out of the one he was holding, chewed and swallowed.

"Have you told Gallagher yet, Tim?"

"No, but I will later. Thought I'd drop by to see you before I did."

"Go on."

"There's something strange about this whole business, Jake. I told Gallagher the other day that I was wasting my time, but he told me to keep digging around."

"And what did you find?"

"Not sure. Logic says I should stop, but my instincts tell me to keep plugging. Something very strange happened yesterday."

Wharton was fascinated and showed it on his face.

"Explain."

Davis told him about yesterday's episode at the airport and of the details of his meeting with Mary Young earlier. When he had finished, Wharton turned pensive.

"So she lied about her meeting at the airport with the bald-headed man."

"Yeah. I tell you, Jake, if I were working vice again, I'd have thought it was just an ordinary dope exchange or payoff of some kind, yet something inside me tells me a different story. Know what I mean?"

"Yeah." Wharton scratched the itch under his chin. "Let's assume for the sake of argument that it was a payoff. For instance, a payment for the murder of Marlene Pike."

"I thought about that, Jake. But why would a hit man from Philadelphia pick up his fee for a job that was done over a month ago, then leave on a plane to D.C.?" He shook his head. "No, it's too bizarre. Besides, baldy didn't look like the type to be a killer."

"Exactly what type *did* he look like?"

"God knows. Perhaps a used car salesman, or maybe a college professor. But not a murderer—I'm sure of that."

"So what's your conclusion?"

"Don't have one," replied the head-shaking Davis.

Wharton finished eating and wiped the residue from his mouth with a napkin.

"What about your interview with the girl, Tim? Did you notice anything that seemed strange or suspicious?"

"No, nothing I can put my finger on. However, she seemed overly defensive when answering questions about her past. She seemed to take her time about it before giving me an answer. Know what I mean?"

"So you think she was lying about everything? As if to say she wasn't who she was supposed to be?"

"Yeah. I tell you, Jake, I'm beginning to believe that if she *did* have something to do with the murder, I doubt Pike knew about it. She's shifty, that girl, very shifty."

"So what are you going to tell Gallagher?"

"Not sure yet. In the meantime I'm going to check out this Mary Young. Maybe I can find something about her that'll make sense."

"What about baldy? Think you could recognize him again if you saw him?"

"Yeah, but I doubt you have him on file."

"But maybe he's on file in Philly…or maybe D.C."

"Yeah, maybe."

"Tim, why don't you look through our files just for the sake of argument? Can't do any harm."

But that yielded nothing.

Back in his office later, Davis telephoned Gallagher and they agreed to a meeting on Friday morning to discuss the new turn of events.

"A yellow envelope, huh?" Gallagher had muttered the words as if speaking to himself. "Anything else?"

"No, nothing."

"So then the man from Philadelphia hops on another plane to Washington." He shook his head with emphasis, adding, "Sounds like something you'd read in a Mickey Spillane novel."

"Or Ian Fleming," said Davis, referring to the late British author who had made James Bond a household name.

"So what are you planning to do next, Tim?"

"Not sure. That's why I wanted to see you, Bill. If Mary Young has anything to do with the murder, she's clever and not about to make mistakes. Say, for instance, the man from Philly's involved. We'd still need evidence to link them together. In other words, it could get very complicated."

"You mean expensive for me, don't you?" Davis did not

respond, and Gallagher continued, "What about Pike? You think he's involved in this?"

"God knows. Look, Bill, all of this talk is pure speculation. That meeting at the airport on Tuesday might've been just a friendly get together. It might've had a lot to do about nothing."

"Or something to do about everything," countered the marine.

"Look, Bill, I've tried to be up front with you from the beginning. At this point we would need a busload of detectives to continue. Right now I'm a blind man walking down a dark alley without a cane."

"In other words, you want to drop the case altogether, like you did the other day?"

"Yes. Granted, this whole thing gets more fascinating by the minute. But for you, that dark alley could turn into a financial disaster."

"Let me worry about the costs, okay?"

"Bill, why don't you think about what I've told you before you make a decision to proceed or not? Sleep on it, take all weekend if you have to, and then get back to me. What do you say?"

Gallagher stared at Davis at length, as if reluctant to give in, but then nodded in agreement.

"All right, Tim."

That weekend Gallagher did nothing else. It was a beautiful weekend, warm and sunny, a great time to visit the beach, and yet he never left that base. He spent most of his time at the officers' lounge watching television, reading and thinking. Mostly thinking.

On one hand, he agreed with Davis. Perhaps they *were* heading down a dark alley. But there was so much about the episode at the airport that gnawed at him. Who was the mysterious man from Philadelphia? Why had he come to Norfolk to visit Mary Young and then leave on a plane for Washington? And what was in the envelope? Davis had said that Mary Young did volunteer tutoring every Tuesday, but that obviously had been a lie. Maybe she was involved in some kind of black market activity with the man from Philadelphia. If so, how did that involve Pike? Or did it?

Yes, Davis was right—the possibilities were endless. If Pike had hired baldy to kill his wife and the price was exorbitant, it seemed logical that he would have to pay the man in installments. Perhaps Young paid baldy every Tuesday morning. If so, it was neat, a clever arrangement. Still, would it be enough to implicate Pike as the mastermind behind the murder?

By nine o'clock on Sunday night Gallagher had made his decision. He reached for the telephone.

"Hi, Tim, it's me. Sorry to bother you at home, but I have to see you first thing in the morning."

There was a brief moment of silence before Davis replied.

"Yeah, ten is fine. Thanks, Tim."

CHAPTER 14

"We're going to the airport tomorrow," was the first thing Gallagher said when he marched into the PI's office the next day.

Davis had not moved, was still standing by the open door, hand clutching the doorknob. For a few seconds longer he stared at the marine, his Monday morning face a mask of incredulity.

"So," he said, "you're not giving up?"

"That's right." Gallagher sat in the chair by the desk, making himself comfortable. "I'm convinced that Miss Young is the key player in this affair. I believe she's the mastermind behind it all."

"You think she hired a hit man to kill Marlene?"

"Yes…or maybe Pike did. But it really doesn't matter now who did. They're both in this together."

Davis closed the door and returned to his seat behind the desk.

"So what will going to the airport prove?"

"Well, we both know that Young lied when she told you she does volunteer work every Tuesday. I believe she'll go to the airport tomorrow to make contact with the man from Philadelphia again."

"Who, you believe, is the hit man or errand boy who collects payments for the killer?"

A rhetorical question, but Gallagher nodded anyway.

Davis went on, "But what do you propose to do, Bill, just walk up to him when she hands over another envelope and accuse him of murdering Marlene?" Davis embellished his sarcasm with a sarcastic chuckle, to which Gallagher took exception.

"Look, Tim, if you don't want to help me anymore, that's fine. But I'm not giving up. Maybe I'll hire another detective, or maybe I'll just do it myself. If you want to quit, just tell me what I owe you and I'll write you a check and be on my way."

"Sorry, Bill. It's just that I hate to see you waste a lot of time and money for nothing. Sure, I could tell you I'll keep working for you and take your money. Hell, a lot of private dicks I know would say I'd be a fool *not* to. But you have to face facts. The more I investigate this, the more complicated it gets. I'm not Joe Friday. This is real life with real people, not 'Dragnet'."

"Pike killed Marlene, Tim, and I'm going to prove it one way or another. And if Mary Young's involved, I'm going to nail her to the wall too."

"All right. Let's assume for a moment that Pike hired an out-of-town hit man to kill his wife. The fee was enormous and he's been paying him back in weekly installments. Obviously the killer doesn't have a legitimate mailing address, thus the reason for the Tuesday meetings at the airport."

"Right."

"But what about the D.C. connection? Why would the man from Philadelphia fly to Norfolk to collect an alleged payment and then leave for Washington?"

"God knows. Maybe he likes to do some sight-seeing before he goes back to Philly."

Davis scowled, proof that he was not amused by the marine's sardonic humor. He took a moment to scratch the mosquito itch behind his ear, the same which had been pestering him all morning.

Gallagher heard him say, "So what's the next step?"

"I told you, we're going to the airport tomorrow and—"

"Wait a minute, hold the phone!" Davis cut him off. "What do you mean 'we'?"

"I'm going with you."

"No, you're not, I work alone," Davis corrected him. "If I need help, I'll find someone who knows what he's doing. Besides, Mary Young saw you before. At the night club, remember?"

"She knows you too."

"She only knows me when I'm wearing my phony moustache and glasses. Not being recognized is part of my profession. I'll wear something she's never seen before." Davis stared across the desk, eyes daggers. "I'm a pro and you're not," he added.

"I'll wear a disguise too."

"No, you won't, because you're not going. If I take you along tomorrow and you screw things up, we'll never find out who killed Marlene."

Gallagher sighed heavily, looking tired, defeated. He thought for a moment, pressuring his brain to work harder, but then nodded reluctantly, giving in to the PI's logic.

"All right, Tim, maybe you're right."

"I *am* right. Now, when I get to the airport tomorrow, exactly what do you want me to do?"

"I want you to follow baldy to Washington, or Philly...or wherever he goes."

"But what if he flies to Alaska or South America? You want me to follow him then?"

"Well..."

"Look, Bill, for the sake of argument, what if Miss Young and her bald-headed friend don't meet tomorrow? What if their weekly rendezvous takes place on another day? Maybe they're meeting at this very moment, or maybe they won't meet at all. Maybe it's a monthly meeting, or maybe the fee has already been paid in full and there won't be anymore meetings. Have you thought about that?"

"It's a chance we'll have to take. Besides, what do we got to lose?"

Davis pondered, or so it seemed. Finally he said, "Okay, let's say they meet at the airport tomorrow and baldy hops on the Washington shuttle. Exactly what do you think I'll find when I get there?"

"Who knows? Just follow him anywhere he goes. Eventually you'll find out where he lives."

"And then what?"

"Well, you said he might have a record on file there."

"By that, you mean, I should pay a visit to police headquarters to see if he has a rap sheet. Is that it?"

"It's a start, isn't it?"

"Start to what, Bill?" Davis shook his head: an obvious show of frustration. "I'm telling you, you could be sending me on a wild goose chase."

"Look, Tim, are you going to help me or not?"

"Yes, I want to help. But so did Jake Wharton and Fuzzy

Hostetler. And you know what happened there."

"You think I'm a fool, don't you?"

"No, I don't. I just think you're not thinking clearly. Hell, the possibilities here are too many to contemplate. I'm a one-man operation. I don't have a dozen PIs working for me. That's what this investigation will take now."

Gallagher said nothing in return. Instead, he turned away and stared at the picture of downtown Norfolk in the window.

Davis continued, "Bill, you have so much hate for Pike bottled up inside you, you could sell some of it and still have plenty left over."

"Yes, I hate him. I hate his guts!"

"Look at you, for God's sake. You're becoming paranoid. And all because you *think* he killed Marlene."

"No, Tim, he killed her. Maybe not by his own hands, but he arranged it. And maybe with Mary Young's help."

"Come on, Bill, you don't even know this guy. All you know is what Marlene told you. Did you ever think for a moment that she was only telling you things about him that *she* wanted you to hear, things that would make her shine in a favorable light? Hell, it's natural for a woman to hate her spouse during a divorce, especially when things get nasty. Believe me, I know from experience. More than half my clients hire me because they're looking for revenge. Is that what you want too?"

"Yes, I want revenge."

"But that won't bring Marlene back."

"No, but maybe I'll be able to live with myself again."

"But what if we find out that Pike's not who you think he is? What if he *is* the all-American, spit-and-polish officer and gentleman and not the murderer you suspect him of being? What then, Lieutenant? Will you be able to live with yourself then?"

"Don't know, Tim, but I have to find out one way or the other. By doing nothing makes me a coward. I *must* know the truth."

Silence entered the room. It was Davis who ended it.

"Sorry, Bill. I just wanted you to know what you're getting into. I don't want you to throw away your money and get nothing in return."

"I appreciate that, Tim."

"All right. Tomorrow I'll tail baldy and see where he leads me. If he has a record on file, I'll find it, that much I promise you."

"Good. By the way, something just occurred to me. Could you get copies of the passenger manifests of last Tuesday? You know, the incoming Philly plane and the Washington shuttle?"

"Yes, I see what you mean. Baldy may have used the same surname on both flights. I could check on that today."

"What do you mean 'may have used'?"

"Well, if this is an elaborate murder plot like you think it is, it's possible he uses a false name when traveling from city to city. If he works in the underworld, it goes without saying."

"Check on it anyway, Tim. Who knows, maybe he's not that clever and you'll have a name to go on."

But Davis found nothing when he made his inquiries. Baldy, whoever he was, had used different names during his Philadelphia-to-Norfolk-to-Washington excursion.

Back at the BOQ later that day, Gallagher received a surprise visit from Steve Watson.

"Working overtime?" Bill asked jokingly as he ushered him in.

"Yeah, something like that," replied Watson.

They made themselves comfortable on the couch in front of the television, where a "Batman" rerun was in progress.

Watson said, "You like that crazy show?"

"It's a diversion," Bill told him. "It's so stupid, it's funny." He smiled. "Can I get you something, Steve? Coffee? A Coke?"

"No, thanks. Just came by to tell you I'm putting you back on active duty."

"My new orders came through?"

"No, the CO is still working on that. In the meantime the Navy's giving you back to me."

Gallagher frowned at him, seemed anxious.

"You're not putting me back in the classroom again?"

"And if I did, you wouldn't like that, would you?"

"Sir, that's not much of an answer."

"All right. You're not going back to the classroom. But you're still working for me. Mundane work, I'm afraid—revising training manuals."

"Training manuals?" Bill glared at him. "What kind of work is that for a human being?"

"It's mundane, like I said. But it's a job that needs to be done. Anyway, you need something to do. You must be going crazy by now."

"How long is this going to last, Steve?"

"Just until your transfer's approved."

"But that could take forever."

"Or it could be as early as next week. You know how the Navy operates."

Gallagher got on his feet. He stepped across the room and switched off the television, then started pacing back and forth, hands buried in his pockets, eyes fixed on what was ahead.

"What's wrong, Bill? What are you thinking about?"

"I *must* stay in Virginia, Steve. The Navy can't transfer me out of Tidewater."

"The CO knows what you want. He's doing his best to arrange it."

Gallagher stopped pacing and told Watson about Tim Davis and what the PI had learned. Through it all, Watson listened attentively, absorbing every detail. When Gallagher had finished, he took a slow, deep breath, as if for added strength.

"Why didn't you tell me this before, Bill?"

"Why, would that have changed anything?"

Watson ignored him. "So what does this private eye think?"

"He thinks I'm wasting my time."

"But you don't?"

"If I did, you think I'd spend my money on something like this? No, I'm not wasting my time. What we've learned so far is just the tip of the iceberg."

"But you and this private eye fellow haven't learned a thing. What if the bald-headed man and the girl don't meet at the airport tomorrow? What then?"

"Don't know, but I'll think of something."

"Bill, you better start thinking about your career."

"You think I'm a fool, don't you?"

"No, I just think you're getting in over your head. This isn't a murder investigation anymore, it's some sort of private vendetta. It's as plain as the hair on your head."

"Pike killed Marlene, Steve. He did it, he did it, *he did it!*"

"Bill, stop torturing yourself and face reality. The police have no evidence to convict Pike. Even Davis told you to forget it. Doesn't that tell you anything? Don't you trust anyone anymore?"

"I'll only believe it when I'm convinced he didn't do it."

"Why, to prove to the world you're right and the police are incompetent?"

"Don't you understand, Steve, I can't stop now. Marlene was

special to me. I have to do it, for her sake."

"If she was that special, you'll let her rest in peace. Get on with your life, Bill. You owe it to yourself and your career."

Gallagher reclaimed his seat on the couch, fumbling with his hands.

Watson said, "Who else knows about this?"

"Just Greaves. But I told him to keep his big trap shut."

"I see." Watson stood off the couch and waited for his friend to do the same. "Bill, you're to report to me first thing Monday morning."

"Training manuals?"

"Yeah, that's right. And you're going to do a four-oh job for me, right, Lieutenant?"

"Yes, sir."

When Watson had gone, Bill showered, shaved, read the newspaper until his eyes ached, and then went to bed. Yes, Watson was annoyed with him, but he didn't care. Nothing mattered anymore. He was in too deep now to give up. Davis would have to find something, or else. If not…

No, he didn't care about anything other than finding out who killed Marlene. His career was shot to pieces. The Navy had been clever to the point of being diabolical. His meeting with the fleet psychiatrist was recorded fact, a stain on his once unblemished record and reputation. He would never regain what he'd had; of that he was certain. The Navy would never let him fly again; would never give him a duty assignment that *he* wanted…

"Training manuals, Lieutenant Gallagher," he heard himself say. "They've got you exactly where they want you. Your career ended the day Marlene was killed."

He swore, rolled over and cried himself to sleep.

CHAPTER 15

Norfolk, Virginia, dawned overcast and sticky warm on Tuesday. Rain had pummeled the city the night before, and it was still spitting drizzle as Tim Davis leaned on the brake pedal, stopping the Ford two blocks from the Granby Street high-rise.

"Why are you parking here, Tim?"

"So I won't miss her when she comes out," he answered his wife.

A fairly attractive petite woman, Janet Davis was outfitted in a sleeveless green blouse and white shorts. She wore very little makeup, and her dubious auburn hair was tied back in a comely ponytail not uncommon among others of her trade. They called themselves housewives.

Her husband stared through the windshield, eyes locked on the apartment building. Although convinced he was wasting his time, he had decided to ignore his better judgment and continue the investigation. After all, a job was a job, and Gallagher's money was as good as any other client's.

A quick glance at his wristwatch: 9:13. He sighed nervously. Was Mary Young preparing for another trip to the airport? He shook his head. No, a thousand-to-one long shot.

He scanned the street: no taxi. Another anxious sigh as he stared at the dirty gray sky, wondering if the sun would ever make an appearance.

He heard, "Are you sure you have everything, dear?"

"I'm sure," was his answer.

She reached for the olive green gym bag at her feet and opened the zipper. Stuffed inside were a camera, boxes of film, two note pads and as many pens; a striped summer shirt, three changes of underwear, an extra pair of black socks, shaving kit, deodorant spray, toothbrush and toothpaste.

"You should have packed more clothes," she said as if scolding a youngster for misbehavior. "What if you need them?"

"I won't be gone that long."

"How do you know?"

"I just do." He leaned over and planted a kiss on her cheek, provoking a grin from her. "Don't worry, honey, I'll call you when I get there, okay?"

"You better or I'll never forgive you."

He would not be away long, he was sure. But if the bald-headed man from Philadelphia left Norfolk for a destination other than Washington, he might need to purchase some extra things along the way. It was all part of being a private detective.

He wondered about the money Gallagher was using to pay for his services. The fact he was an officer suggested that he made a better-than-average wage. And he lived on base, meaning his meals and lodging were included. Yes, he had the money all right, no doubt about it. Still, why squander it on an investigation that was going nowhere?

A taxicab pulled up in front of the high-rise, snaring his attention. Soon thereafter an elderly white-haired gentleman in gray trench coat and low-cut rubber boots appeared outside the building and climbed into the backseat of the idling cab. Less than a minute later the cab drove off, leaving a cloud of blue-gray exhaust in its wake.

"Look at all that horrible pollution!" said Janet, the disgust in her voice obvious. "You'd think the taxi companies in this city would have better cars than that."

"Yeah."

"Speaking of cars, dear, when are you going to get rid of this old clunker?"

"Why, what's wrong with it? We've only had it a few years. Besides, it's paid off. Look at all the money we're saving."

"But that's my point. We can afford a new one."

He ignored her, keeping his mind focused on the task at hand. He glanced at his wristwatch: 9:22.

She said, "I'm taking Debbie to the dentist tomorrow."

"You told me that last night."

"The doctor said she's going to need braces. Think we can afford *that?*"

"We'll manage." He scanned the street. "Where is she, for cryin' out loud? It's almost nine-thirty."

"Maybe she's not going to the airport today."

"It's possible."

"What if she doesn't go, Tim?"

"Don't know, honey. Maybe that'll end it. Maybe Gallagher will come to his senses and realize the whole thing is a waste of time."

"I admire him," she said, her words surprising him.

"Why?" he urged.

"Because he refuses to give up looking for his girlfriend's murderer. That takes a lot of determination."

"Stubbornness, you mean."

"Call it what you like, dear, but I still admire him."

He grinned at her in the loving husband style, making her blush, started to respond, but decided against it when Mary Young appeared outside the apartment building.

She was dressed in a beige raincoat and black beret: the same ensemble she had worn the previous week. He watched as she stepped up to the curb, casually reached inside her left-hand pocket, yanked out a pack of cigarettes and lit one, exhaling the first puff skyward.

"There she is, honey."

Janet stared through the windshield and looked her over: one woman appraising another. Her facial expression reminded him of a similar look he had seen many times when she was undecided which dress to buy at the boutique.

"Very attractive," she said, but with little enthusiasm.

"That she is," he seconded. "But it's her out-of-town friend I'll be chasing today, not her."

"Yes, the mysterious man from Philadelphia." She giggled. "The man with no hair."

He ignored her, keeping his eyes fixed on Young's scrumptious figure. He scanned both ends of the street: still no taxi. He looked back and watched as Pike's girlfriend calmly smoked her cigarette as she loitered near the curb.

The taxicab arrived three minutes later.

Davis turned the ignition key as Young ducked inside the back seat. A half minute later the taxi accelerated and he let in the clutch.

"Here we go, Jan."

Traffic was light, and Davis had no trouble following the cab, maintaining at least two bus lengths behind at all times. The route was the same as the week previous: Granby Street to Little Creek Road to Military Highway to Norview Avenue.

At the airport, the taxi driver stopped in front of the terminal entrance and discharged his cargo. Davis waited until Mary Young was inside the building before pulling up alongside the curb.

He left the motor running in neutral, grabbed the gym bag from his wife, climbed out, and waited as she slid behind the steering wheel. Smiling, he leaned down and gave her another peck on the cheek.

"Remember, call me when you get to wherever it is you're going," she told him.

"I will, I promise."

He waited as she put the car in gear and drove off. He took a deep breath and marched into the terminal.

People traffic inside was moderate. Davis purchased a copy of the *Pilot* at the newsstand, found an empty spot to stand in, and reviewed the information flight board across the way.

The Pan Am from Philadelphia was due at ten o'clock at Gate 2 and would leave Norfolk for Atlanta forty-five minuets later. The D.C. shuttle was scheduled to depart from Gate 3 at 11:30. Exactly like last week's schedule. He scanned the lobby but there was no sign of Miss Young. He picked up his momentum and headed for the concourse. His destination: Gate 2.

He found her there loitering in the waiting area wearing a light blue chiffon dress and smoking a cigarette, the raincoat hanging from her left arm.

Was there an envelope inside?

Davis parked himself next to a candy vending machine, the newspaper open in front of him. He saw only a handful of people in the waiting area, but there was a herd of others quickly approaching. Mary Young turned suddenly and glanced in his direction, forcing him to bury his face behind the paper.

The Pan Am from Philadelphia arrived on schedule.

Baldy was the fourth passenger to appear through the exit ramp doors. Young greeted him with a cordial smile and handshake and offered him a cigarette. Baldy shook his head, and several minutes later they were sitting together at a window table in the coffee lounge, Davis watching them closely.

At 10:20, the public address speaker announced the first call for the 10:45 flight to Atlanta. Neither baldy nor Young appeared interested in the news. No doubt they were waiting for the announcement for the Washington shuttle, thought Davis.

He left the lobby and made his way back through the concourse, ending up at Gate 3, where he purchased a standby ticket for the Washington shuttle. The day before he had inquired about available tickets for the flight and was informed that there would be plenty of seats available. "It's normally only half-booked," the reservationist had told him.

Ticket in hand, Davis returned to the main lobby and resumed his surveillance outside the café. Mary Young and baldy were still there, both with a cup of coffee stationed in front of them. No envelope yet, he observed. A glance at his wristwatch: 10:31. The first call for the D.C. shuttle would soon be forthcoming.

When it happened at 11:09, Young rose from her seat. Davis watched over the brim of the newspaper as she pulled out a yellow envelope from her raincoat pocket, said a few parting words to her chum, and then vacated the lounge with raincoat and hat in hand, heading in the direction of the women's rest room.

She reappeared six minutes later wearing the rain gear and started for the exit. Exactly two minutes after she had gone, baldy reached for the envelope and stuffed it inside his briefcase. He hailed the waitress, paid her in cash with a broad smile and promptly left the café. Davis folded the newspaper together, took a deep breath and went after him.

The shuttle to Washington, D.C., left Norfolk Airport at exactly 11:32 with thirty-two people aboard, including Davis and Mary Young's associate.

At 11:37, a bespectacled man sporting a gray suit, fake mustache, real sideburns and a gray slouch hat sauntered out of the café, where he had just finished devouring a slice of coconut custard pie. He stepped into a vacant telephone booth, deposited a dime into the machine and dialed the operator. When she came on the line, he told her the number he wanted and patiently waited for the connection.

"Yes?" said a voice at last.

"It's me," said the man with the glasses. "It's a beautiful day in Tidewater."

"Thank you."

"By the way," said the gray suit, "please transfer me to Mr. Dawson."

Tim Davis hated flying. Despite airline boasts that flying was the safest form of mass travel, he felt uncomfortable during the trip. Sitting trapped with a safety belt across his lap was a feeling of helplessness, of being unable to determine his fate should something go wrong. He preferred trains instead for long distance travel. At least they were always on the ground. For most of the flight he kept his eyes buried in the newspaper, trying to keep himself from worrying about it. Fortunately for him, the journey took less than forty-five minutes.

His seat was several rows in front of baldy, making it impossible for him to do any surveillance of the man. When the plane had touched down and taxied to a stop at National Airport, Davis waited for him to pass him in the aisle, hurriedly grabbed his gear from the overhead compartment and followed after him.

Outside the terminal, baldy was picked up by a waiting midnight-black Mercedes sedan. Davis hailed a taxicab in full stride, climbed in when it stopped and told the driver to follow it.

"Get no closer than three car lengths," he added.

"You chasin' someone, buddy?"

"Yeah, but if you lose him, no tip. Understand?"

"Got it," said the driver.

The Mercedes led them north along Route 1, then east across the Potomac River via the Theodore Roosevelt Bridge. It exited at Constitution Avenue, and Davis saw the Lincoln Memorial slide by on his right. A quarter mile later he caught a glimpse of the White House on his left. To his immediate right was the missile-like obelisk of the Washington Monument: a steel gray shadow towering above the capital like a gigantic sundial.

At the Pennsylvania Avenue intersection, the black car was forced to submit to a crawl with the rest of the traffic due to road work. Eventually the Mercedes left the construction site behind, turned left onto Louisiana, took the next left at New Jersey, and then another left at Massachusetts.

Davis heard the cabbie say, "I think this fellow's lost. He's backtracking."

Davis kept his eyes focused on the black car, straining to read the numbers on the license plate. At 16th Street, the cabbie was obliged to take another left-hand turn to keep pace with the

Mercedes. His first visit ever to the capital, Davis was lost, had stopped trying to memorize the sign posts. The cab driver almost lost sight of the Mercedes when he was stopped by a red traffic signal. He accelerated when the light changed and was soon back on baldy's tail. A minute later the Mercedes stopped at the entrance gate of a three-story, brick-faced mansion, its mansard roof crowned with a spider web of antennae. Davis ordered the driver to pull over and park.

The ironwork security fence surrounding the mansion was at least ten feet high, Davis estimated. He produced the camera from the gym bag and took a snapshot of the license plate, then another of the mansion. Not long thereafter the gate was opened by a broad-shouldered security guard in green uniform. He beckoned the Mercedes with his hand and the driver accelerated into the compound driveway, eventually disappearing behind a wall of rhododendrons.

"Holy mackerel, would you look at that?" spouted the cabbie. "Ya know what that place is, buddy?"

"Yeah," muttered Davis, staring at the red flag with the gold hammer and sickle fluttering outside the building's middle, second-story window.

The mansion, originally called the Pullman House, contained sixty-four rooms. It was designed by the famous architect Nathan Wyeth and completed in 1910 for Hattie Sanger Pullman, widow of the Chicago sleeping car magnate who sold the place three years later to the Russian government for $350,000. In 1922, the United States broke diplomatic ties with Russia and the mansion remained empty until 1933 when President Franklin Roosevelt recognized, despite steep criticism to the contrary, the Stalinist régime of the new Russia, formally known to the world as the Union of Soviet Socialist Republics.

"Wow!" spoke the driver. He peeked at Davis through the rearview mirror. "Who you chasin', buddy, a Commie spy?"

Davis ignored him. He watched and waited, the wheels in his brain spinning furiously. Finally the whole thing made sense. It was like being hit by a sledgehammer without feeling the pain. He noted the time on his watch, took another snapshot of the embassy and made a decision.

"Take me to the train station, driver."

"Train station?" The cabbie scratched his head. "You sure, buddy?"

"Yeah, *buddy,* I'm sure."

Yevgeny Kozlov walked into the plush office on the second floor of the Soviet embassy, shut the door behind him and stepped over to the pristine mahogany writing desk. His nose wrinkled from the smell of furniture polish as he dropped his briefcase at the side of the desk. A bearded Karl Marx, imprisoned in a gold picture frame on the opposite wall, observed him as he slipped behind the desk and sat in the comfortable red-leather chair.

The Russian sighed. He was tired, having slept little the night previous. He loathed that Philadelphia hotel he always stayed in near the naval base. Tomorrow he would instruct his secretary to find another for next week, or else.

He lit a Marlboro cigarette, his favorite American brand, reached for the briefcase and opened it with his key. He pulled out Maria Brandt's envelope and the folder Pavel had given him in the hotel elevator less than twenty-four hours earlier. He extracted the contents of the envelope, separating the undeveloped roll of film from her coded paperwork, reached for the telephone and rang the duty clerk in the basement cryptographic room.

"Da?" he heard.

Kozlov explained the reason for his call.

"I'll be up immediately, Comrade Major."

"No, that won't be necessary," Kozlov told him. "I'll be down after I have my tea."

When Tim Davis arrived at Union Station, he arranged for a seat on the 3:10 express to Newport News. He located a coffee shop nearby, had an overpriced chicken sandwich and coffee for lunch, left, found an empty telephone booth and called his wife.

"I'm coming home," he told her.

"So soon?" Her voice was anxious.

"Yes. Pick me up at the train station at five. And try not to be late."

"Why aren't you flying home, Tim?"

"Because I hate planes, you know that."

"But why so soon? Is there something wrong?"

"Look, honey, just meet me at the station, okay?"

"All right, whatever you say."

She said goodbye and he heard the click as she hung up. He replaced the receiver on its cradle, his hand trembling.

"Holy Jesus, Mary and Joseph," he heard himself say, "as if I don't have enough problems on my plate."

Sean McCormack peered through the window of his spartan third-floor office in Langley to admire the lush Virginia acreage and cursed. The memorandum he had received an hour earlier had ruined his afternoon. What it was all about was still a mystery, but the man who was due in the office shortly would shed more light on the subject.

A tall man with the physique of a sumo wrestler and a rock face that could frighten the bejesus out of the devil, McCormack turned away from the window and waddled back to his seat behind the desk. He picked out the last "nail" from his silver cigarette case, lit it with his lighter and coughed when he exhaled, knowing the dirty vice was not in his best interest. "Your lungs are like the inside of a coal mine," the doctor had told him during his last check up. "Keep smoking and you'll never make retirement."

McCormack laughed without mirth. He was due for retirement in seven years, only what would he do if or when that day finally happened? Fishing every morning? Golf with his drinking buddies at the country club in the afternoon? He laughed again. Sure, why not? At least it would keep him away from his nagging wife.

He stared at the quivering cigarette in his hand, took another long drag and exhaled slowly, this time without coughing. No, he would never give up smoking, not for his wife's sake nor that damned Jewish quack.

Frank Sean McCormack was born in Newark, New Jersey, on the second day of December 1910, the day after the man who had sired him succumbed to his six-year battle with emphysema. His mother never remarried, and Sean grew up poor, not atypical of most children in the predominantly Irish neighborhood. When he was fifteen, his mother, who was slowly dying of stomach cancer, decided to relieve the pain forever by sampling a bottle of rat poison. Despondent and nearly suicidal himself, he dropped out of school and was taken in by his only relative, his uncle, whom he had been named after and who let him work in the small bakery shop he owned on the city's east side.

It was in late October '29, while he was cleaning up the shop after a long day's work of kneading and baking, when his uncle heard the news of the stock market crash from the radio. Sixteen weeks later Uncle Frank was out of business. Not long thereafter he was without a roof over his head when the bank showed no mercy and foreclosed on his property. Homeless, unemployed, undereducated, and with nary a penny to his name, Sean McCormack drifted from here to there like a common hobo, riding the rickety boxcars up and down the state and stopping to work menial jobs for the privilege of a day's meal. But all that changed when a funny-looking man with an even funnier-looking mustache decided to shake up the world by ordering his armies to invade Poland, a place Sean had never even heard of. The date on the calendar was 1 September 1939. Twenty-eight-year-old Sean McCormack couldn't get to the nearest army recruiting station fast enough to enlist.

Following basic training at Fort Dix, New Jersey, he applied for mess duty as a pastry chef. Unluckily for him, the army had a surplus of culinarians and he ended up working in the mail room as a file clerk. In spite of it, he was happy with his new life. He had a warm place to sleep, plenty of new friends, and three "squares" a day. Most importantly, he had a chance to succeed and be something.

During those tedious months in the mail room Sean became a ravenous reader of the miles of letters and other documentation that passed through his hands, something he had never had much patience for in high school. Then, one day, a "confidential" letter addressed to his commanding officer caught his eye. Unbeknownst to him, the contents of the letter would change his life forever.

It was an ordinary memorandum regarding personnel recruitment of a new unit that was being formed. The unit was called the Office of Strategic Services, or OSS. The job was intelligence work. After the official posting went up on the bulletin board, Sean told his boss he was interested in applying. The lieutenant reluctantly agreed, he passed the required battery tests, and not long thereafter Private McCormack was on an express train heading for OSS training in Quantico, Virginia.

Five months later Pearl Harbor happened. The United States was locked in a global shootout with the Axis Powers. In late 1943, Sergeant McCormack, now a skilled radio technician and cipher expert, was shipped off to East Anglia in southern England to participate in a top secret project that, he was told, would help win the war without a single shot being fired. The job involved feeding false information to the enemy by way of radio and Morse signal traffic: the art of deception and disinformation.

The idea was to dupe the Nazi High Command into believing that the Allied invasion of France, which was scheduled for the spring of '44, would take place at the Pas-de-Calais, far from the actual spearhead that would land to the southwest on the beaches of Normandy. As it turned out, the ruse was one of the most successful coups of the war. The German panzers at Calais never reacted to the June 6th attack and remained where they were during the critical stage of the battle, defending a tranquil coastline of surf and sand.

Following the operation he was promoted to lieutenant and applied for a more visible role in day-to-day counterespionage work. His request was granted, and he soon found himself in charge of twenty-four newly-trained agents operating in occupied Europe: an elite group of saboteurs whose accomplishments in covert activities would earn him high praise, but of whom more than half would never see the celebration of V-E Day.

After the atomic bombs obliterated the Japanese cities of Hiroshima and Nagasaki in August 1945, ending the great global conflict once and for all, McCormack remained in Europe at the behest of his employer. The reason: the Cold War had begun. The new threat to the Free World was the Soviet Red Army. Following several years of running agents behind the Iron Curtain in East

Germany and Czechoslovakia, he returned to the States to work as a training advisor for the Central Intelligence Agency. (It had succeeded the disbanded OSS in 1947.) Now, at the age of fifty-eight, Frank Sean McCormack, plump, multi-skilled and proud owner of a split-level rancher in nearby Alexandria, managed his own disinformation operation in the CIA, a network which included over two hundred agents and administrative personnel worldwide.

Not bad for a high school dropout.

The intercom buzzed, ruining his train of thought. He reached across the desk and flipped the toggle switch.

"Yes?"

"Sir, John Wilcox is here."

"Good, send him in, Carol." Wilcox marched into the room ten seconds later.

He was a tall man of dark hair and trim physique and fifteen years younger than the white-haired spymaster. He carried a black leather briefcase and placed it on his lap as he sat in the chair angled at the side of the desk. He opened the briefcase and produced a photograph.

"What do you got?" McCormack asked him.

"A private detective," replied Wilcox. He closed the briefcase, dropped it on the hunter-green rug, leaned forward and handed his boss the black-and-white photograph of Timothy Davis.

McCormack studied the photo. The man's face was ordinary, had a straight nose, thick eyebrows, neatly clipped sideburns, determined eyes and a receding hairline. He wore a loose-fitting striped shirt and was holding a large gym bag. McCormack noted the eyes with interest.

Cop eyes.

"Name?"

"Davis," said Wilcox. "Timothy Davis."

"Go on, John."

"We caught him tailing Kozlov."

"Where is he now?"

"On a train to Newport News."

"Deductions?"

"None. At least not yet."

McCormack puffed. "All right, John, let's get to the meat and potatoes. Start from the beginning."

"Joe Renner spotted him at the Norfolk Airport this morning. He left on the same plane as Kozlov."

"Joe's our man watching the Brandt girl, right?"

"Right," nodded Wilcox. "Joe called me after the plane left Norfolk, like he always does. He described the man in the picture and I had Bill Bates take that snapshot as he got off the plane at Washington National. Davis hailed a taxi and followed Kozlov to the embassy, then left suddenly and hopped on the train at Union Station."

"What do we know about him?" was McCormack's next question.

"Only that he's a private dick. He lives in Chesapeake but has an office in downtown Norfolk. I got the library clerks searching for more details on him right now. It shouldn't take long."

"Strange," McCormack said to his cigarette.

Wilcox continued, "Joe also said he was sure he had seen Davis the week before."

"Why didn't he report it then?"

"He didn't say."

McCormack took one last puff and rubbed out the cigarette, adding it to the pile of butts in the glass ashtray in front of him.

"What are you going to do, Sean?"

"Not sure, but this project is too important to jeopardize at this point. For now, let's wait till we get a complete dossier on Davis, then we'll move. But I'm not going to waste time on this. Tell Renner to keep his other eye on Davis."

"Right." Wilcox got off the chair, started to leave, but McCormack called him back.

"One more thing, Mr. Dawson."

"Yeah, Sean?"

"Got any smokes?" McCormack showed the empty cigarette case and grinned hopefully. "I'm fresh out."

THE HERO

CHAPTER 16

A contemplative Timothy Davis was greeted by his anxious wife as he stepped off the commuter express in Newport News.

Before leaving the station, he located an unoccupied phone booth, dialed Gallagher's number at the BOQ, but received a busy signal for his effort. A second try produced the same result.

At his home later he telephoned again, this time making contact with the marine, and recommended that they meet first thing in the morning to discuss the new turn of events. "I'll be there," Bill told him.

Gallagher arrived in the PI's office at precisely 8:30 on Wednesday morning in short-sleeve khaki uniform and side cap. It was warm and stuffy in the room. Davis had the fan working at full speed, though it did little to help the situation. There were bags under his bloodshot eyes, which Gallagher interpreted as a bad night's sleep.

Davis did not waste time and told his client everything he had witnessed yesterday, starting when Mary Young arrived at the airport and ending at the Soviet embassy.

"Incredible!" was Gallagher's reaction.

"That's an understatement, if I ever heard one," added Davis unnecessarily.

"So Miss Young leads a double life, is not as harmless as we thought she was."

"Yeah, it appears so. In fact, I'll stake everything I own that she's a Russian spy." Davis shook his head, as if to disbelieve what he had said.

He went on, "I've done a lot of undercover work in my career, Bill, but this beats the whole kit and caboodle. I never expected anything like this to happen."

"You can say that again. It…it's so incredible."

"Yeah, watching a spy movie is one thing, but this is the real world, not Hollywood."

"What about Pike, Tim? You think he's involved?"

"God knows. But if he is, he's in a world of trouble."

"Yeah, he could get the firing squad if he's found out to be working with the girl."

"And if he's not involved?"

"He'd still be in trouble. But that's beside the point. The question is what are we going to do about this?"

"But isn't it obvious? We need to report this at once."

"You're right again, Tim. We must get the Navy to stop her from doing what she's doing, whether Pike's involved or not. Let's face it, she could have almost anything stashed in those envelopes. Like blueprints of the latest carrier design."

"We could be jumping the gun here."

"What do you mean?"

"Well, what if we're wrong about this? What if the mysterious Miss Young and baldy are just friends who meet every Tuesday for coffee and conversation?"

Bill scowled at him, was not amused by his flippant remark.

"No, don't kid yourself, Tim."

"But what if we tell the Navy and they investigate and find that there's nothing suspicious or unusual going on? Hell, *we* could end up on the hot seat."

"So what? At this point we can't afford *not* to report this. Remember, we're at war with the Russians. Maybe it's just a Cold War for now, but it's a war nonetheless." Bill's eyes were volcanic marbles, as though about to explode from his head. "No, we *must* report this!"

"But to whom? The FBI? CIA?"

"No, first I'll tell my boss." Gallagher flashed a hopeful grin. "Can you come back with me to Oceana?"

"I suppose so. But why do you need me?"

"Because you're the key to it all, my friend. You're the one who witnessed everything. In fact, if this thing is what we think it is, you could make history. Who knows, maybe you've uncovered a Russian spy ring."

"Lieutenant, I think you've been reading too many spy novels. Besides, I don't want to be famous. I just want to make an honest living so I can pay for my daughter's braces and maybe buy a new car for my wife someday."

Gallagher rushed to his feet. His face was alive, not pale, the eyes alert, ready for action.

"Let's get started, Tim."

"One more thing, Bill."

"Yeah?"

"What about the murder investigation? What are you going to do, put it on hold?"

"Right now I don't know. Let's worry about that later."

Steve Watson stared across the desk at Gallagher for what seemed like an eternity, then shot a glance at the fidgety Davis. He had listened to their story with interest, making mental notes along the way.

He said, "You're both sure about this?"

"Of course we are!" spouted Gallagher. "You think I asked Mr. Davis to come all the way out here for his health?"

"At ease, Lieutenant, let's not get excited." Watson lit a cigarette, exhaling the first puff toward the ceiling. "These are serious accusations you're making here. We need to be absolutely sure of the facts before we proceed."

Davis said, "May I say something, Commander?"

"Please do, Mr. Davis."

"Thank you. You see, when I tailed baldy yesterday, we were hoping it would give us a new lead in the murder case. Then, when the chase ended at the Russian embassy…well, it seemed obvious to me what was happening."

Gallagher joined in, "The bald-headed man must be the girl's contact, Steve. They meet every Tuesday at the airport, she hands over an envelope, and then they part company. She then goes back to the apartment and he flies to Washington."

"How do you know they meet *every* Tuesday?" asked the dubious Watson.

"Actually, we don't know that for a fact," said Davis, chiming in. "However, they have met at the exact same time two weeks in a row. And I'll bet my mortgage they meet next week too."

"You said he always arrives from Philadelphia?"

"That's right."

"But doesn't that strike you as odd, Mr. Davis?"

It was Gallagher who answered, "Tim and I discussed that very point earlier, Steve. We've agreed on a theory about that."

"Go on?"

"Well, there's a naval base in Philly, right?"

"So?"

"Well, we believe that baldy might have another spy working there too. Maybe Tuesday is the day he collects information from them."

Watson chuckled. "You make it sound as if this could be some kind of elaborate spy operation."

"Anything's possible, sir."

"But it's just a theory," added Davis.

Watson pursed his lips as he studied the ash at the end of his cigarette. After a while he stood out of his chair, wandered over to the window and peered out at the airfield, watching a Skyhawk fighter shrinking in size as it rose from the runway and climbed above the horizon. When he looked back and spoke, his words were directed at Davis.

"What about Pike? You think he's mixed up in this caper?"

"No, I doubt it," was the PI's answer. "I've met the man and don't believe he's a traitor. I believe he's just an unwitting accomplice."

"Thank you." Watson turned. "What about you, Bill? Do you agree with Mr. Davis?"

"Steve, it doesn't matter what I think, one way or the other. Sure, I hate Pike—I hate his guts! I've made that plain more times than I probably should have. But this new episode is quite another matter. We're discussing national security here."

Davis asked of Watson, "What's the next step, sir?"

"This is the military, Mr. Davis, which means business gets done in a strict bureaucratic fashion. I'll take your story to the next level, our base commander. He'll decide the next step."

"And what might that be?" queried an anxious Gallagher.

"I would imagine Captain Russo will ask ONI to investigate."

"What's that?" urged Davis.

"Naval Intelligence," was the sailor's reply.

Davis shot a glance at Gallagher, who seemed locked in deep thought. Turning back, he asked of Watson, "Is there anything I can do to help?"

"Yes, for the time being you'll need to keep everything you know to yourself. You mustn't mention any of this to anyone, including your wife."

"I understand."

"I'd also like you to be available when I contact you again. After I tell the CO about this, he'll probably want to meet with all of us as soon as possible. In fact, it could be as early as tomorrow morning. Might even be tonight."

"Yes, sir," nodded Davis. "That's no problem."

Anthony Russo had seen both the good and the not-so good during his career in the navy. After graduating from Annapolis in 1944, he joined the submarine service. He didn't mind it at first, but there was something about being in a submerged vessel that eventually got to him and he applied for and was granted a transfer into naval aviation at the tail end of the Korean conflict. He served two years on the *Forrestal*, the attack carrier named after the former Secretary of the Navy, during which he experienced one of the most tragic peacetime accidents in naval history.

A Saber jet had made an emergency landing on the flight deck and plowed through two parked aircraft during a training exercise in the choppy Sea of Japan. Two sailors were incinerated in the resulting series of explosions, with a half dozen others receiving third-degree burns. Topside at the time, Russo broke his pelvis while trying to rescue one of the victims and spent the next twenty-one weeks in traction in a Yokohama hospital. It was in Japan where he met his future wife, a Red Cross nurse.

He married the angelic Hiroku the following year while on liberty and took her back to the States upon his transfer to Willow Grove Air Station in eastern Pennsylvania. He sired two children during the 'fifties while excelling as an administrator of aircraft personnel deployment, rising in rank as permitted by the Navy. His promotion to captain was the icing on his career as a professional sailor.

When Steve Watson arrived in his office later that afternoon and outlined the story which had been told to him earlier by Davis and Gallagher, Russo found himself at a loss for words. He scratched the top of his bristly gray crew cut, reached for his half empty coffee mug and drank.

"Have you mentioned this to anyone else, Steve?"

"No, sir, not a soul."

"Good, let's keep it that way." A thoughtful pause before he continued, "So all of this happened because of Gallagher's stubbornness in trying to find the man who murdered his girlfriend?"

"That's right, sir. It was a pure stroke of luck."

"I wonder."

"Sir?"

"Well, what I mean is, we just can't jump to conclusions, can we? All we have to go on is a theory. A man and a woman meet at the airport two weeks in a row, she hands him an envelope each time, and then he leaves and ends up at the Russian embassy." He shook his head. "Hell, Steve, those envelopes might contain almost anything. Perhaps two Hershey bars and a pack of cigarettes." He laughed without mirth.

Watson came back, "They might also contain military information the girl either acquired somehow or stole from her navy lover. The possibilities are staggering."

"You're right, Steve. On the other hand…" Russo stopped his voice and reached for his mug.

"Tony, what are you going to do about this?"

Russo ignored the question.

"What about this sailor who's shacked up with the girl, Steve? What was his name again?"

"Lieutenant-Commander Charles Pike. He's currently stationed aboard the *Roosevelt*. I was told that she sets sail at the end of the month. NATO maneuvers in the Mediterranean, or something or other."

Russo made no comment in return, and Watson squirmed.

"Sir, with all due respect, you *must* do something about this."

"And I will. I'll pass the information on to ONI. I'm sure they'll want to look into this matter. I've no idea what they'll recommend, but be ready for anything. My guess is that they'll want to have a chat with Gallagher and his private eye friend."

"I've asked Mr. Davis to make himself available," Watson told him.

"Good. I'd also like to have a representative of the Norfolk police on hand when ONI starts investigating. He might be able to shed more light on this."

"Yes, sir. I'll talk to Bill Gallagher about that."

"Gallagher's working for you again, right, Steve?"

"Yes, sir."

"All right, but don't be surprised if I have to place him on involuntary leave again. It might be necessary."

"Aye, aye, sir."

Watson received a phone call from Russo later in the day.

"Steve, I want to set up a meeting for Friday morning with you, Gallagher and that private eye fellow. By the way, were you able to contact the Norfolk police?"

"Yes, sir. I spoke with a Detective Sergeant Wharton. He was originally assigned to the murder case. Said he'd be willing to cooperate any time you say."

"Good, make the necessary arrangements."

"Tony, what about ONI?"

"They're sending over one of their people. I was told he's an expert in Soviet intelligence operations." Russo stared at his note pad. "His name is Bledsoe—Lieutenant-Commander James T. Bledsoe."

In Langley, Sean McCormack was in conference with his senior associate.

He looked up from the dossier in front of him. After a while he reached forward and opened the cigarette case, which was full again, picked one out and lit it with his lighter. Wilcox watched impatiently as he inhaled, coughed, inhaled again, and then shook his head with emphasis.

"It doesn't make sense, John."

"No, sir. Still, what are we going to do about it?"

"We'll have to find out what Davis was up to and why he has an interest in Miss Brandt."

"You think someone hired him?"

"That's usually the case, John. He's a private dick. He doesn't work for free."

"He's a one-man operation, used to work for a man called Robert Jennings. In fact, his office door still has Jennings' name on it."

"A former cop turned private dick who was hired by someone who's interested in Brandt and friend Kozlov." McCormack moaned thoughtfully. "Yes, we've got to move on this, and quick."

"What do you want me to do, Sean?"

"Nothing, for now. I've got an appointment with the DCI tomorrow morning. Afterwards you and I are flying to Norfolk."

"Shouldn't Joe Renner handle this?"

"No, this project is too important to be left to him. You and I will take charge down there."

"And Davis will be our first objective?"

"That's right." McCormack flicked ash from his cigarette, adding, "It's the logical place to start."

CHAPTER 17

Most Americans remember where they were and what they were doing at 1:30 p.m. New York time on 22 November 1963. For Jim Bledsoe, it was the darkest moment of his young life. He was involved in a spirited game of flag football with his dorm buddies at William and Mary College when his girlfriend suddenly appeared on the gridiron and told him with tears in her eyes that his hero, John Fitzgerald Kennedy, had been assassinated.

Jim Bledsoe cried when CBS news anchor Walter Cronkite confirmed the tragic news on television: the 35th President of the United States had been brutally gunned down in the streets of Dallas, Texas. Bledsoe had studied JFK's naval career with religious interest and subsequent rise to the White House following the handsome New England junior senator's stunning victory over Richard Milhous Nixon in the 1960 general election. The album of photographs and newspaper clippings of his hero, the same one he kept in his dorm room, was known to all of his friends. They teased him about it on occasion but he didn't care. Jack Kennedy, the man who had forced Nikita Khrushchev to his knees in a game of chess the print media called the Cuban Missile Crisis, the event which had brought the civilized world to the brink of nuclear Armageddon, would live forever in his mind as one of the great leaders of all time.

Jim Bledsoe remembered that black Friday in '63 as if it had happened yesterday. He remembered sitting in front of the television and watching through watery eyes the horse-drawn carriage bearing the president's casket; of France's Charles de Gaulle spearheading the legion of foreign dignitaries in its wake; and of the thousands of mourning citizens lining the streets of the capital while the never-ending drumroll echoed hauntingly in the background. He vividly recalled the burial ceremony at Arlington National Cemetery: the images of Jackie, Bobby and Ted; of John-John's farewell salute to his heroic father; and of the eternal flame at the great man's final resting place. For Jim Bledsoe, it was as if a part of him had died also.

Who had done the killing? Had it been a one-man hit job or an elaborate *coup d'état?* Privately, Bledsoe rejected the Warren Commission's conclusion that Lee Harvey Oswald was the lone sniper. He had convinced himself that the Communists had had something to do with it. Perhaps the killing had been Fidel Castro's brainchild, or that of an infiltrating KGB hit team. Even if it were Oswald working alone, had he not once been a Soviet citizen? For Jim Bledsoe, all clues led to the Kremlin.

After graduating in '64, Bledsoe, an ROTC student, joined the navy, just like his hero had before him. He served two years as a communications officer aboard a destroyer stationed out of Pearl

Harbor before returning stateside in the fall of '66. He liked the navy and his status as an officer, but never thought he'd make it his permanent vocation. He changed his mind later that year during an interview with the Office of Naval Intelligence after a conscientious personnel clerk discovered that he had studied Russian history in college and spoke the language fluently thanks to his maternal grandmother, a transplanted Muscovite.

He was offered a posting in March of '67, which he readily accepted, and was transferred to Great Lakes, Illinois, for advanced training. Eventually he ended up at the Norfolk Naval Station as an assistant to the Atlantic Fleet commander's intelligence staff, foreign section. Since then he had been twice promoted and was now responsible for investigating all Soviet intelligence activities in the Second Fleet district. Jim Bledsoe was doing something he had wanted ever since that dark 1963 November day: fighting back against the evil enemy that, he was sure, had helped destroy his country's greatest hero since Abraham Lincoln.

A baby-faced thirty-one-year-old man with pale blue eyes and dirty blond hair, Jim Bledsoe looked like a church minister whenever he wore his oval-shaped, wire-rimmed glasses. Sitting at the right-hand side of Tony Russo's desk, he adjusted the eyewear as he studied the four men seated side by side at the front of the desk.

To his immediate left sat navy Commander Steve Watson. Next to him was the young marine lieutenant, Bill Gallagher, whose girlfriend's murder had started the whole incredible affair. Next in line was the seemingly unflappable private investigator, Timothy Davis, a former cop who had caught Mary Young and her Russian comrade "in the act." On his left was Detective Sergeant Wharton of the Norfolk police, a reserved man who had yet to contribute much to the discussion.

Bledsoe looked them over again, one by one, knowing each of them by his name and title. Names and titles were easy for him, for Lieutenant-Commander James Thomas Bledsoe had a sharp photographic memory. He glanced at the other man in gray suit and glasses who was sitting calmly with legs crossed at the opposite end of the desk. His name was Michael Weintraub, an FBI special agent with whom Bledsoe had worked two times previous. Bledsoe took a deep breath and addressed Russo.

"Captain, how many others know about this?"

"No one," replied the Oceana base commander.

Weintraub said, "Before we get too involved with this, I'd like to ask Mr. Wharton a question." He faced the policeman. "Why did the Norfolk police discontinue the investigation of Mrs. Pike's murder?"

"Officially, we've not closed the case," Wharton told him.

"Officially, unofficially—what's the difference?"

"We had no leads or evidence, Mr. Weintraub. But the truth of the matter is, the chief of police made the decision to suspend the investigation. My boss, Inspector Hostetler, and I had no choice in the matter. You see, we take orders too."

Bledsoe regained the floor, his words directed at Gallagher.

"So, Lieutenant, you decided to take matters into your own hands and start your own investigation?"

"Yes, sir."

"Without authorization?"

"I don't understand."

"Well, did it ever occur to you to inform Commander Watson about this beforehand?"

"No, sir."

"Why not?"

"Well…"

"You're in the military," Bledsoe reminded him. "As an officer, your first duty is to the service. Didn't you think he had a right to know what you were up to?"

"No, sir, I didn't. Last I heard it's still a free country. My decision to hire Tim was my business—not his, not the Navy's, nor anyone else's."

"Point taken. Nevertheless—"

Watson interrupted, "Mr. Bledsoe, I'd like to point out something. Bill Gallagher is an outstanding officer. He's also a decorated fighter ace. He knows his duty better than most. When he told me he had hired Mr. Davis, I was surprised to say the least. However, I sympathized with him. He was convinced that Pike murdered his girlfriend. I probably would have done the same thing had it happened to me."

Davis said, "You must admit, gentlemen, if it hadn't been for Bill Gallagher, we wouldn't be talking about Russian spies right now."

"What he did, with your help," interjected Weintraub, "was inadvertently stumble upon the possibility—I repeat, possibility—that Miss Young is a Soviet agent."

"But you *must* investigate this!" Davis looked away from the stone-faced FBI agent and stared at Bledsoe hopefully. "Surely the Navy will?"

"Only if we determine it to be a threat to national security," Bledsoe told him. "I'm sure the FBI will concur. Mike?"

All eyes turned to Weintraub, who nodded in agreement, although it was obvious he was not thrilled about it.

Russo asked of Bledsoe, "What do you recommend we do next, Commander?"

"Before we proceed, Captain, we need to make a few

deductions. For instance, this Pike fellow. What do we know about him so far?"

"He's a lieutenant-commander stationed aboard the *Roosevelt*. His title is chief nuclear engineering officer."

"Impressive."

Russo continued, "According to his ship commander, whom I spoke with yesterday, he was top midshipman in his class at Annapolis. Grade point average four-point-oh. The awards he's accrued since joining the navy are mind-boggling."

"In other words, we're talking about some kind of wonder boy or genius?"

"Yes, it would appear so."

Davis intruded, "He might also be a traitor selling information to the Russians."

"Those are strong words, Mr. Private Detective!" countered the acid-tongued Weintraub. "To accuse a United States naval officer of being a modern-day Benedict Arnold—"

"I didn't say he was a traitor," Davis corrected him. "I said he *might* be one."

"We appreciate the distinction, Mr. Davis," said Bledsoe, regaining the floor. "However, I agree with Mike. To accuse or even speculate that an officer of Pike's caliber is a traitor is treading deep water. It's my experience that we must give him the benefit of the doubt despite what any of us may think of him."

Wharton said, "Inspector Hostetler and I interviewed him twice, Mr. Bledsoe. At first he didn't strike me as the type who would murder his wife, let alone anyone. But after what Bill told me, I changed my opinion."

"Exactly what did Lieutenant Gallagher say that changed your mind?"

It was Gallagher who answered, "I told Jake that Pike

threatened to kill his wife several times. That's why I hired Tim. I thought—"

"Gentlemen, please!" It was Weintraub again. "I'm a former cop myself. I've lived in Long Island most of my life and saw some of the worst crime imaginable. But what you're implying here is clearly hypothetical. Commander Pike may have been this, he might have done that. The law demands that we provide proof, not hearsay evidence or random speculation."

Bledsoe said, "Hold on, Mike. Let's forget about the murder case for the moment. My interest in this is whether or not Pike and his girlfriend are working for the Russians. What Mr. Davis discovered the other day is the primary issue here."

Watson said, "It seems to me that Pike is someone the Reds would be interested in, considering his rank and the job he holds. Let's face it, gentlemen, they wouldn't go after an ordinary second-class swab jockey."

"His motive was probably money, if indeed he *is* working for the Russians," suggested Weintraub.

Russo said, "Frankly, gentlemen, I find it nauseating that a naval officer, whoever he might be, would betray his country for money or any other reason for that matter."

"Agreed," nodded Bledsoe. "Still, it's happened before, is happening now, and will continue to happen in the future. Blame it, if you will, on the dark side of human nature. As Mike pointed out, money is usually the number one motivation for traitors. Others do it because they feel they've been betrayed in some way and want to retaliate against the government. Others simply enjoy the thrill of espionage work."

Watson said, "But what if Pike's *not* working for the Russians? What if Miss Young is just a clever bitch milking information out of him? We still need to do something about it."

"And what would you propose we do?" challenged Weintraub. "We just can't stampede in and make an arrest. If she's an American citizen, she has legal rights, like any other citizen."

"But isn't there a way you can interrogate her without violating her rights?" persisted Watson.

"Yes, but I would advise against it," replied the FBI agent.

Davis cut in, "Then we'll just have to catch her in the act, won't we?"

"Yes," nodded Bledsoe. "The girl is the key player in this affair. She's the link in the chain, the middle man, so to speak."

Russo said, "What about the Russian diplomat? Is it not true he has immunity from prosecution?"

"That's right, Captain," nodded Weintraub. "If he's found out and we move against him, the worst that can happen to him is that he'll be kicked out of the country."

Bledsoe added, "That's *if* we decide to move against him."

His comment brought immediate silence to the room. It was Gallagher who put a stop to it.

"Sir, what are you saying? Are you saying that you might not want to arrest these people?"

"That's right."

"But I don't get it. We're talking about an enemy spy working right under our noses who is, perhaps, collaborating with a traitor. Hell, sir, we *must* do something."

"And we will, Lieutenant. But first there's something we need to consider before we make an aggressive move against them."

"What's that?" urged Russo.

"Well, sir, I'm thinking that the worst thing we can do at this point is make a wholesale arrest. Like Mike said, their rights could be violated and then the Navy would be subjected to harsh legal recriminations. Which means, of course, bad publicity for the

Navy, especially if we're found to be in the wrong about these people.

"Secondly, as Mr. Davis pointed out, we'll need to catch them in the act before we consider taking action against them. And that might prove to be very difficult and time-consuming. It would take additional manpower and round-the-clock surveillance of everyone involved. And even if we do that and find the evidence that will incriminate them, it may be prudent on our part not to move against them."

"Why?" urged the bemused-sounding Russo.

It was Weintraub who answered, "Because they just might be pieces of a larger puzzle. Perhaps even part of a Soviet spy ring operating on the east coast."

Bledsoe added, "If that's the case, we'll need to proceed very carefully indeed. You see, gentlemen, if the Reds become aware that we're on to them, they'll disband and go into hiding. Which means we'll never find out what they're up to or how big their network might be. So, I repeat, we need to proceed carefully. If not, the results could be disastrous."

Weintraub said, "Jim, I think this should be a joint Navy and FBI project, especially since a member of the Russian embassy's involved."

Russo asked of Bledsoe, "When will you get started?"

"Right away, sir." Bledsoe turned to the marine. "Lieutenant, I want to make it crystal clear that this private investigation of yours terminates as of this moment. I'm sure you understand."

"Yes, sir."

"So what happens next?" asked Russo, addressing Bledsoe.

"Well, Captain, with the FBI's help, we'll start a surveillance of Pike and his girlfriend. I'll also arrange to have one of my staff stationed aboard the *Roosevelt* to see if he's doing anything abnormal, such as leaving the ship with classified material. But that'll be tricky."

"What about the Russian?"

It was Weintraub who answered, "Don't worry, Captain, we'll keep a close eye on him too. I guarantee you we'll know his name before the day's out."

Bledsoe glanced at his watch and said, "Gentlemen, I suggest we adjourn for lunch. We can pick up with this business this afternoon." To Russo he said, "Sir, would it be possible to have lunch served here?"

"Of course, I'll take care of it."

Russo pressed the intercom button and made the arrangements. When he had finished, Bledsoe got to his feet.

"Gentlemen, from this point on, no one must mention this to anyone outside this room. I'm sure most of you remember the old navy saying, 'Loose lips sink ships'." The group bobbed their heads in unison, prompting a grin from Bledsoe. "Very well, thank you for your cooperation."

The afternoon session ended at 4:15. After the civilian delegation had departed, Bledsoe turned his attention to Russo.

"Captain, with your permission, I'd like Lieutenant Gallagher transferred to my office in Norfolk. I've no idea how long this will last, but I'll need his assistance, at least for a while."

"Of course, I'll take care of the paperwork."

Later that night Gallagher telephoned Davis and thanked him for his hard work in trying to find Marlene's killer.

"I'll mail you a check tomorrow," he added. Davis thanked him, and he went on, "Kind of weird the way things turned out, huh? Guess we'll never find out who killed Marlene."

"You don't know that, Bill. Maybe Jake and Fuzzy Hostetler will find something later. Anything's possible in police work."

"Yeah, but not probable in this case."

"Well, you must admit, we did get something in return for our efforts. My God, it's still hard to believe that Russian spies could be living in my own backyard."

"You're right, Tim. Maybe we can do some damage to them."

"Hope so. By the way, Bill, whatever happens, good luck to you. I'm glad I got to know you. If I can ever help you again, don't be afraid to call me."

"I will."

Gallagher said goodbye and hung up. He stared at the phone for a long moment, then wandered into the kitchen, found a bottle of Coca Cola in the refrigerator and returned to the couch.

He was exhausted, both mentally and physically. It had been a long, trying day. He shut his eyes and thought of a happier time: his last moment with Marlene. It had happened on that rainy July night at the Norfolk Airport, prior to his trip to San Diego. He could still see her in his mind: the beautiful soft smile; that final tender kiss and embrace; and then the sight of her driving away after they had said goodbye for the last time...

He put the bottle aside, dropped his face in his hands and wept. He never finished the drink.

CHAPTER 18

Surveillance of Charles Pike's apartment officially started at six o'clock on Saturday morning.

FBI watchers, handpicked by Michael Weintraub, parked their gray Buick LeSabre in an obscure alley that was catty-corner to a Mom and Pop confectionary store, just two blocks south of the Granby Street high-rise. There would be two teams of two working ten-hour shifts. Whenever Mary Young was spotted leaving the building, the team would relay the news to Weintraub and then follow her to her destination.

In Washington, D.C., a similar stakeout had begun outside the Soviet embassy. The FBI watchers had instructions to observe the bald-headed man, who had been identified as Yevgeny Kozlov, deputy assistant to the Soviet military attaché. Unfortunately for them, it proved to be a fruitless assignment, for the Russian failed to appear outside the embassy mansion.

At the Norfolk Naval Station, Ensign Andrew Lewis, an unassuming young man with curly dark hair and glasses, reported to the captain's cabin aboard the *U.S.S. Roosevelt*. His orders to conduct research on the effects of radiation among the crew, the captain read, were as bogus as nine-dollar bills. In fact, Lewis, an ONI officer attached to Jim Bledsoe's staff, had explicit instructions to keep a close eye on the supercarrier's chief nuclear engineering officer and report back with any abnormalities. On a ship with more than three thousand men, the ensign was just another tree in a vast forest of sailors.

Not much happened that first day. Pike and his girlfriend left the apartment to lunch at a waterside café and grocery shop at the local market. Later in the afternoon, Young was seen leaving the apartment—she was picked up by a young woman driving a green Mercury sedan—and was followed to The Gunslinger, where she stayed tending bar until one o'clock closing.

Just after noon on Sunday, the two lovebirds left their Granby Street nest in Pike's Chevrolet and spent part of the afternoon enjoying the sand and surf of Virginia Beach. It was an unexpected treat for Weintraub's stakeout team, who enjoyed keeping a close watch on the scrumptious Miss Young, who wore a titillating hot-pink bikini.

Monday dawned partly cloudy as Pike was spotted leaving the apartment in khaki uniform. He arrived at the main gate of the naval base at ten minutes to six and reported for muster aboard the *Roosevelt*.

At 8:30, Gallagher and Weintraub met with Bledsoe in the latter's office. Tim Davis, who also had been asked to participate, arrived a few minutes later after having dropped his daughter off at elementary school. The focus of the meeting was to prepare for the anticipated airport rendezvous of Young and Kozlov the next day. Davis had the floor.

"The past two weeks Kozlov has arrived from Philadelphia on the same flight. The girl greets him in the waiting area, they visit the lounge for a cup of coffee, she hands over an envelope, and then they part company. She returns to the apartment and he leaves on the eleven o'clock shuttle to D.C."

"So far we haven't noticed anything suspicious about Pike or the girl," joined in Weintraub. "Whether she'll go to the airport tomorrow is anyone's guess."

Bledsoe said, "Are we clear on how we're going to handle this, Mike?"

"Everything's in place," replied the FBI special agent. "My men on Granby have orders to follow her everywhere she goes. Every step she takes will be monitored."

"What have you found out about her so far?" was Bledsoe's next question.

"We know that she moved to Norfolk sometime at the end of last year. She works full time at a night club in Portsmouth called The Gunslinger."

"It's probably where she met Pike," said Gallagher, injecting his opinion. "Marlene once told me that she and her husband used to go there on occasion when they were still living together. After they split up, Mary Young moved in with him."

Weintraub continued, "Before she moved to Norfolk, she lived in a studio apartment in the Georgetown section of Washington. She was employed as a secretary for a Montana Senator named Russell Brubaker."

"Never heard of him," commented Bledsoe.

"He only served one term, was voted out of office during last year's election." Weintraub chuckled. "It was a landslide victory for his opponent."

Bledsoe pondered, or so it seemed. He cleared the frog from his throat.

"Mike, does Miss Young have a record on file?"

"No, Jim."

"What about her background? Anything there?"

"I'm afraid not. It's almost as if she materialized out of thin air. We're trying to trace her work history through the IRS, but that'll take time."

"Her job with the senator, Mike. She obviously got clearance to work for him. Exactly what did she do?"

"She was just an ordinary office secretary."

"Ordinary is hardly the word I'd use to describe her," said Bledsoe with a smirk.

Weintraub tendered a smirk of his own and said to the sailor, "Are you thinking what I'm thinking, Jim?"

"Probably. My guess is that Kozlov arranged for her to get the job, the senator had an affair with her, not knowing who she was of course, and she milked him for every scrap of information she could until the good citizens of Montana voted him out of Congress. Afterwards she needed a new job, so he sent her down here to Norfolk, where she has since hooked up with Pike."

"You hit the proverbial nail on the head," nodded the FBI agent. "In fact, now that I think of it, it might be beneficial to have a little chat with the former senator. Maybe he knows something about her that can help us."

Gallagher interrupted, "What are you two implying? Are you suggesting that Mary Young was sleeping with a United States senator and stealing government information right out from under his nose?"

It was Bledsoe who answered, "Well, like the president, senators handle hundreds of classified documents each year. As

Brubaker's secretary, she could've had access to them at one time or another, with or without his knowledge. She may have been able to read them or even had time to make duplicate copies. If they were top grade military documents, it's certainly the kind of stuff the Reds go for."

"A good point," added Weintraub. "I'll have the Bureau investigate Brubaker's background to see if he'd belonged to any defense committees on Capitol Hill."

Davis asked of Bledsoe, "Is there anything I can do to help, Commander?"

"Well, you did meet with Pike and the girl, right? What was your impression of them?"

"Like I told Bill, Pike didn't strike me as the type who would murder his wife, let alone anyone. I also don't think he's the kind of man who would sell out his country to the enemy."

"Another guess, Mr. Private Detective?" chirped the cynical Weintraub.

Davis hesitated. He didn't like the man and let it show on his face.

"Call it what you like, Mr. Weintraub," he fired back.

"What about the girl?" Bledsoe asked him.

"Well, sir, she struck me as the cautious type, and yet she's always in control. She's shifty and clever—a real pro, in my opinion."

His analysis sparked an outburst of sarcastic laughter from Weintraub.

"That's very interesting," he said, "especially coming from someone who makes a living peeking into dark bedrooms."

Davis' eyes flared.

"Yes, I'm a peeping Tom, Mr. Weintraub, if that's what you want to call me. But don't underestimate me. I've helped the police many times catch wanted criminals in compromising positions. In fact, one was a local government official who was embezzling city funds."

Bledsoe said, "So, Mr. Davis, it's your professional opinion that Miss Young has the qualities to be a first-rate spy?"

"Yes, sir, no doubt about it."

"Well, that's important information indeed. However, my primary concern is how Pike fits into the picture. If we find out that he's helping her, he could get life in prison...or even the hangman's noose."

"We've already wiretapped his telephone," said Weintraub, regaining the floor. He opened the note pad on his lap. "This past weekend he made two phone calls. One was to an auto repair shop around the corner from his apartment. Something about getting his brakes adjusted. The other call was to his parents in Falls Church, Virginia. It was typical family chitchat."

"Catching him won't be easy, Mike, if in fact he *is* providing information to the girl."

Gallagher said, "In other words, the investigation could take weeks, months, or even longer."

"Maybe, maybe not. The *Roosevelt* sails in a few weeks. NATO deployment in the Mediterranean, I'm told. In the meantime anything can happen."

The meeting broke up an hour later. Weintraub and Davis exited the base and returned to their respective offices. Bledsoe and Gallagher lunched at the officers' galley, then afterwards took the latter's car to Pier 12 where the mammoth *Roosevelt* was moored.

The morning cloud cover had since scattered, and it was a lazy afternoon, warm, relatively peaceful. There was constant activity aboard the supercarrier, sailors arriving and departing, moving about in work.

From stem to stern the *U.S.S. Roosevelt* measured 1100 feet: the length of nearly four football fields. Assembled with loving skill by the artisans of the Newport News Shipbuilding Company and launched in October '64, the great warship was powered at sea by eight nuclear reactors, generating 280,000 horsepower from her four Westinghouse-geared turbines. Fully laden, her maximum cruising speed was thirty-two knots. Equally impressive was her complement of fighting aircraft, ninety in all, including the A-4 Skyhawk and F-8 Crusader.

"A floating city," said Bledsoe thoughtfully. He swiped a thin line of perspiration from his brow. "The greatest warship in the world."

"That's a fact," seconded Gallagher.

"And scary too. She operates solely on atomic energy. And when she's at sea, all those men and jet planes and aviation fuel, not to mention all those munitions and supplies. One accident and *boom!*"

"I served on the *Independence* during my tour in 'Nam," Bill told him. "I know what it's like."

"Can you imagine how many millions it cost to build her?"

"The price of freedom, sir."

Nodding, Bledsoe took a moment to adjust his glasses. He stared at the marine at length, his blue eyes brimming with purpose.

"Bill, you've been in the service, what, four years now? Tell me, do you still believe in our democracy?"

"Naturally."

"Let me put it another way. Do you consider yourself a patriot? Are you still willing to sacrifice your life for our country, to preserve its freedoms guaranteed by the Constitution?"

"I do that everyday, sir. It's my duty as an officer."

"Yes, of course. But the same holds true for Pike. In fact, in his case, it might even be more so."

Bill frowned, perplexed by his choice of words.

"What do you mean, Jim?"

"Well, Pike is Annapolis bred, the son of an admiral who, I'm told, was somewhat of a legend. No doubt great things are expected of him. I suspect that if he stays in the service and doesn't retire an admiral, he'll probably consider himself a failure. See what I'm driving at?"

"So you don't believe he's involved with Mary Young and her Commie friend either? You believe he's unaware that she's a spy and that she sleeps with him to bleed him of military information, like she did with the senator."

"Yes, I believe Pike is a patriot. It's in his blood, so to speak. You've met him, Lieutenant. Tell me, how do you feel about him?"

"I despise him!" Bill told him, not sparing the hate in his voice. "He's everything I find reprehensible in a human being."

"Why, because he's successful? Because you think he murdered his wife? Because he might be a traitor to the same ideals you swore to uphold when you joined the service?"

"Sir, can I be frank? I know you don't care one way or the other if Pike killed his wife, but I do. I knew what Marlene endured when she was married to him. Pike may be a genius and son of a war hero, but he abused her during their marriage, had even threatened to kill her. In my mind, he *did* kill her. Maybe it'll never be proven, but he did it—I know it! And if he's a traitor working for the Russians…well, it'll just give me another reason to hate him."

"Will you feel vindicated if we find out he's working for the Russians?"

"No, but I'll feel better knowing I had helped expose him as a traitor."

"And if he's not working for the Russians?"

"I'll still hate him."

As Gallagher and Bledsoe were discussing the finer points of duty and patriotism, Major Yevgeny Kozlov was lying in bed with a slight fever. He had caught the summer bug over the weekend and been bedridden ever since. Normally he would be on an express train to Pennsylvania to honor his weekly rendezvous with his undercover operative at the Philadelphia Naval Shipyard. His appointment in Norfolk with Maria Brandt scheduled for the following morning would have to be postponed as well.

He gently massaged the top of his bald head and sighed. Getting far too old for this kind of work, he mused. He had always enjoyed it when his life was more regimented. The discipline, the comradeship, issuing orders and leading his armored command to victory in simulated combat over his Warsaw Pact "enemy" were more to his liking.

The proud son of an infantry commander who had fought and died heroically in the rubble of Stalingrad in 1943, Yevgeny Kozlov had also seen service in the "Great Patriotic War" as a T-34 tank commander in Hungary. Since the end of the war, he had dreamed of leading his battalion of super tanks against the docile NATO forces manning the border that separated East from West. He had known then and still believed his tanks would have given the enemy a bloody nose had it come down to the ultimate confrontation of war.

But those days were but a whisper in the past. He had been forced into semi-retirement due to a perforated eardrum and offered work in the foreign service of the KGB, mostly because of his unique knowledge of America and its military potential. His eldest son, Mikhail, was now serving as a junior officer in the Red Army, which pleased him to no end. At least the Kozlov military legacy would continue long after he was dead and buried. That in itself was comforting.

The bedside telephone rang. Kozlov grunted as he reached for it and picked it up.

"*Da?*"

"Good morning, Comrade Major," said the female voice in his ear. "Feeling better?"

"A little."

"Shall I make plane reservations for your trip tomorrow?" asked his secretary.

"Yes, Irina, but I might have to cancel them if this damned cold doesn't improve."

"Would you like me to call the doctor?"

"Yes, ask him to come up right away. There's a baseball game on television tonight and I don't want to miss it."

He hung up and lay back on the bed, pillowing his head in his hands, smiling as he thought of the upcoming game between the Washington Senators and the Boston Red Sox. He was a devout spectator of the game, one of the few things he had learned to enjoy during his two and a half years in the West. Specifically, he would be rooting for Frank Howard to hit one of his titanic home runs. It was what he liked best about the silly game.

That same afternoon Kozlov's undercover operative in Norfolk, wearing a pink chiffon blouse, black miniskirt and knee-high black leather boots, left her boyfriend's apartment and climbed aboard a waiting taxicab. It transported her to the waterfront section of Norfolk known to the locals as Lambert Point. Unbeknownst to her, the two men who followed her in the white Plymouth Barracuda were watching her every step. She emerged from the cab, paid the driver and strolled along the sidewalk until she found an empty bench not far from the waterline. One of the FBI watchers followed after her at a discreet distance. The other remained in the car.

Maria Brandt had a splendid view of the Elizabeth River. Directly across the way was the navy refueling depot on Craney Island. It was not really an island, and from the air it looked like a tooth jutting out into the anchorage of Hampton Roads, where the famous 1862 Civil War battle between the Union's *Monitor* and the Confederate Navy's *Virginia* had been fought.

Boat traffic along the river was sporadic. She fed the loitering pigeons breadcrumbs from a brown bag she had brought along as several construction barges plowed back and forth through the murky green waterway, an occasional tug or fishing smack chasing after them. To the FBI man on foot, she seemed totally uninterested in the river parade until the gray frigate came into view. The ship had just left the Portsmouth Shipyard and was churning toward the Roads, heading for deployment in the South Atlantic.

She reached inside her purse and yanked out the camera. "She took several pictures of the frigate," the watcher would tell Michael Weintraub when he made his report later. When the ship had disappeared from view, she rose from the bench, walked over to a nearby phone booth and made a brief call.

The taxicab, which arrived fifteen minutes later, delivered her to a camera shop on East Tidewater Drive. The cab driver waited for her to return, which she did eight minutes later, and dropped her off at the apartment building at 3:45. She didn't reappear until almost an hour later, where she was picked up by her friend in the green Mercury. Mary Young and her co-worker stayed at The Gunslinger tending bar and flirting with the "cowboys" until one o'clock closing.

At 7:30 that evening, the kitchen wall phone in Timothy Davis' Chesapeake home trilled. The PI was helping his wife with the dinner dishes, both hands immersed in a sink of soapy water. His wife answered the call.

"Hello?"

Janet Davis listened to the caller, who told her in a polite voice that he needed to speak to the man of the house.

"One moment," she told him. She pressed the phone against her chest. "Dear, it's for you."

Her spouse dried his hands with the dish towel hanging from his shoulder and grabbed the telephone from her.

"Yes?"

"Mr. Davis?"

"That's right."

"Mr. Davis, my name is John Wilcox. I've got a problem and thought you might be able to help me."

"What's your problem, sir?"

"I need to hire a private detective."

"I'm always interested in new business," Davis told him. "Would you like to make an appointment?"

"Actually I was hoping to see you tonight."

"Sorry, Mr. Wilcox, but I never see clients at home."

"I was hoping we could meet at your office," persisted Wilcox. "I know it's late, but it's very important."

Although reluctantly, and despite his wife's pledge to give him a slow massage at bedtime, Davis agreed and met Wilcox outside his office at 8:21. The PI unlocked the door, flipped on the light switch and led the way in.

"Have a seat, Mr. Wilcox." Davis indicated the empty chair by his desk.

"Thank you."

Davis opened the windows and switched on the fan, sat down and produced a notepad and pencil from the top drawer.

"So what can I do for you, Mr. Wilcox?"

"I'll explain as soon as my friend arrives."

"Friend?"

"Yes, he should be here any minute."

In fact, Wilcox's friend was already there and listening at the door. Without knocking, he opened the door and stepped through the portal, startling the PI. Davis rushed to his feet, fear showing on his face, heart drumming.

"What is this?" he demanded, glaring at Wilcox. "What's going on?"

"Relax, Mr. Davis," said Sean McCormack.

The spymaster stepped up to the desk and reached inside his brown tweed blazer. He produced his CIA identification card and gave it to the PI. Davis read and handed it back.

"But I don't get it," he said, shaking his head. "What do you want?"

"Please sit down and relax, Mr. Davis, and I'll explain why we're here." McCormack dipped his hand into his breast pocket and yanked out a pack of cigarettes. "By the way, you don't mind if I smoke, do you?"

CHAPTER 19

The Chesapeake Bay Bridge-Tunnel is seventeen and a half breathtaking miles of pure driving adventure. The journey begins at the southernmost tip of the Delmarva peninsula, skips across Fisherman's Island by way of the North Channel Bridge, disappears through a pair of mile-long tunnels, and ends up on the north shore of Virginia Beach which the locals refer to as Chic's Beach. Depth of seawater along the great causeway fluctuates between 25 and 100 feet. Opened to the public in April 1964 and awarded the American Society of Civil Engineers' "Outstanding Engineering Achievement of 1965," the Chesapeake Bay Bridge-Tunnel had taken three and a half years to construct at a cost of two hundred million dollars.

For Walter Conway, driving along the "Eighth Wonder of the World" that Tuesday morning was a dream come true. A second generation hardware store owner from Salisbury, Maryland,

Conway and his wife had pinched pennies for several years in order to make the trip to the famous resort town. For the next six days they would enjoy a well-earned vacation, something they had been dying to do ever since he had experienced a massive stroke three years earlier. They were determined to relax and not worry about the business, which was in the capable hands of their eldest son, Walter, Jr., who would inherit the business following their retirement in seven years.

As they exited the southern end of the northernmost tunnel, Walter glanced at his wife and said with a toothy grin, "You can open your eyes now, dear."

Shirley Conway dropped her hands from her face, peered through the windshield of their Chrysler Imperial and sighed with relief at the sight of bright daylight surrounding her again.

"Glad that's over with," she said. "Never did like tunnels."

"Well, get ready for another one," he said, chuckling between words.

She applied lipstick to her mouth, using the mirror on the windshield visor to guide her, glanced to starboard and saw a gray freighter steaming westward toward Hampton Roads, wondering what kind of cargo she carried. On her husband's left was a vast green sea better known to the world as the Atlantic Ocean. The sky above the horizon was a hazy pale-blue picture with no clouds attached. She opened the brochure on her lap.

"The next one is called the Thimble Shoal Channel Tunnel," she said. "According to this pamphlet, there's a fishing pier and gift shop when we come out on the other side." She glanced at him, adding, "Can we stop there, dear? I want to buy some souvenirs for the grandchildren."

"We can do that on the way back."

"Oh, Walter, I'm so excited about this vacation. All these years and we're finally going to Virginia Beach. It's like a dream come true."

"They say the seafood's great down here."

"You have a one-track mind, Walter. Don't you ever think about anything besides food?"

"It's my favorite hobby," he said with a grin.

"Yes, I know." Giggling, she leaned closer and pinched the part of his stomach that hung over his belt buckle.

"That's not my fault," he said in defense. "If you weren't such a good cook…"

"Is that the real reason you married me, because of my cooking?"

"What do you think?" he said, trying to keep a straight face.

"I thought it was because my dad gave you a loan to renovate the store."

"Well, you're wrong, dear. I did it because I was madly in love with you."

Blushing, she changed the subject when she said, "You think we could go to Williamsburg tomorrow?"

"I thought you wanted to do that on Saturday."

"I've changed my mind."

"Well, if the weather's okay, I suppose we could. It's only an hour from the beach."

"Look at all those seagulls," she said, switching topics again. "There's one on each lamp post."

"Yeah, they're looking for food too—fresh fish."

"Food, food, food. It's all you think about, Walter."

At the same time Walter Conway was paying the attendant at the bridge-tunnel toll plaza, Jim Bledsoe was making a cup of fresh-brewed coffee in his office at the naval base. A half hour earlier he had been in conference with his ferret aboard the *Roosevelt,* Andrew Lewis. So far the young ensign had uncovered nothing unusual or suspicious about Commander Pike. He's efficient, likeable and well respected, he told Bledsoe. "A model officer."

Bledsoe pondered as he sipped from his cup. Today was the day they had been waiting for. Would Kozlov make his weekly rendezvous with Mary Young at the airport? Time of course would answer that question, but he was skeptical. Although rarely involved in monitoring the comings and goings of KGB field agents, he knew for a fact that their methods were never predictable. Then again…

Bill Gallagher arrived in the office at ten minutes to eight. He looked overly tired, as though he had not slept a wink. Bledsoe gave him a cup of coffee.

"Bad night, Lieutenant?"

"Yeah." Bill sprinkled powdered cream on the dark brew and stirred. "This'll help."

"Today's the big day, huh?"

"Could be, sir."

"Mike Weintraub called earlier and said everything's in place. He's even got a hidden camera set up in the coffee lounge at the airport. He's hoping to get some snapshots of Miss Young and her Russian friend."

"That's *if* they show up."

"Yeah, I was thinking about that too."

"What if they don't show up, Jim? What then?"

"We'll just keep watching them. What else can we do?"

Weintraub arrived in the office a half hour later. Unlike Gallagher, he had enjoyed plenty of sleep the night before and seemed eager as a pup. He never needed coffee as a stimulant.

"We're as ready as we'll ever be," he told Bledsoe. "My boys on

Granby will call as soon as she leaves the apartment. And I've got another team waiting at the airport."

"Are you going to make an arrest today?" Gallagher asked him.

"No, I doubt it," was the answer. "We want to see what goes on between the lady and her Commie friend and get what we can on film. We must be very careful about this. We need to be absolutely sure what's going on before we make any kind of move against them."

"Agreed," nodded Bledsoe. "Timing is everything."

The radio-phone call from Weintraub's stake out team on Granby Street happened at 9:24. "She's on the move," said the FBI watcher. Weintraub ordered him to relay the information to the airport.

Exactly fifteen minutes later Joe Renner spotted Mary Young entering the passenger terminal. Wearing a loud red blouse, white skirt, knee-high red leather boots, sunglasses, glossy red lipstick, and toting a white purse large enough to hold five envelopes, she walked at a leisurely pace as she made her way through the concourse, eventually ending up in the waiting area near Gate 2. She smoked a filter cigarette as she watched the plane from Philadelphia arrive on time.

But there was no Kozlov.

She waited until the last passenger debarked before starting back through the concourse. She stopped in the lounge for coffee, where she was photographed three times from three different angles by Weintraub's hidden cameraman. Finished, she paid the bill, visited the rest room, walked out five minutes later, vacated the terminal and hailed a taxi. The watchers on Granby confirmed that she arrived at the apartment building at 10:41. Weintraub hung up the phone and swore.

"Well, that's it," he said, addressing Bledsoe, his voice a

cauldron of frustration. "The Russian never showed up." To Gallagher he said, "Seems your private eye friend may have some explaining to do."

"But Kozlov *should* have been there," countered Bledsoe. "Let's face it, why else would she have gone to the airport?"

"Jim, for all we know, maybe she likes airports or just hanging around people. Hell, this whole thing could be a waste of time. She may be what she seems—a good-looking piece of skirt that works at an all-night club, is restless in the morning and needs something to do with her free time." He punctuated his statement with sarcastic laughter, to which Gallagher took exception.

"If you're trying to make me look like an idiot, you've succeeded, Mr. Weintraub."

"Hold on, Bill," interjected Bledsoe. "Yes, Mike's being facetious and cynical. But he has to be. It's his job to consider all possibilities. This is a serious business we're involved with. It's not a game of checkers."

"So what now, sir?"

"Well, like I said, we'll keep watching. You agree, Mike?"

"Yes. We'll continue to keep a close eye on both of them. In fact, my guess is that Kozlov had to abort today for some reason or other, which means he might have an alternate day he'll show up. Maybe later in the week."

"Or maybe he'll wait until next Tuesday," suggested Bledsoe.

"Or maybe next month," added Gallagher gloomily.

Weintraub regained the floor when he said, "There's another possibility. Perhaps Kozlov was aware of Davis tailing him last week, and that's why he aborted. You're right, Jim. He should have been on that plane."

Bledsoe said, "If indeed Kozlov is running Mary Young, he may abandon her altogether if he thinks her mission has been compromised. Which means we'll never find out what she was up to."

His comment provoked a puzzled look from Gallagher.

"I'm lost, sir."

Weintraub said, "What he means, Lieutenant, is that Miss Young is expendable. That is, if in fact she is a Soviet agent and Kozlov feels her mission has been compromised. He might send her back on the next flight to Russia, or even liquidate her so that she never reveals what she knows to anyone. Our KGB friends are famous for that. It's one of the reasons they're so successful at this game." He stood out of his chair. "I'm going to the airport," he told Bledsoe, and left the office at the march.

Gallagher waited until the door was shut before he said, "I got a nasty feeling Weintraub thinks this whole thing is a joke, a waste of time."

"Don't worry about him, Bill, he's just overly cautious. I've worked with him before. He's certainly not the most likeable guy, but he knows his job."

At noon, Sean McCormack and John Wilcox were having lunch in their ground-floor suite at the Hilton hotel. The window curtains were open in front of them, allowing them a clear picture of the Norfolk Airport. McCormack was munching on a cold roast beef sandwich, Wilcox a bacon-lettuce-tomato on toast which made a crunching sound each time he took a bite.

"Well, Davis was right," said the latter, chewing between words. He grabbed his cup of iced tea and sipped. "What now, Sean?"

"What I want to know is, why did Kozlov abort?"

"You think he's still in Philly?"

"That's if he ever got there in the first place. We'll know for sure when Osgood makes his report."

"Jeff should have called by now. Want me to check on it?"

"No, give it some more time. We're not in any hurry."

The telephone call from Osgood, their contact at the Philadelphia Airport, happened just after they had finished eating.

Kozlov never arrived, Osgood told Wilcox, who answered the call. After he hung up, McCormack told him to call Langley and ask them to confirm Osgood's report. "He never left the embassy," was the reply.

"Interesting," said McCormack, lighting a cigarette. "The plot has thickened."

"So friend Kozlov decided to call off his usual routine. What do you think, Sean?"

"God knows. Maybe he changed his itinerary for some reason or other. Then again, maybe he didn't feel like flying today."

"Maybe he'll take a bus next time to throw us off balance," suggested Wilcox.

"Well, whatever he's doing, he's the only one that knows about it. The girl was expecting him, that's for sure."

"Yeah, and so were those FBI clowns."

McCormack opened his mouth to respond, but then flinched when the telephone trilled. Wilcox picked it up.

"Oh, yeah!" he said, answering the caller. He covered the mouthpiece with his free hand. "It's Joe Renner, Sean. Said he just saw Weintraub snooping around. He went into the coffee shop and disappeared behind the counter. Joe thinks he has a hidden camera there."

"Yeah, that figures."

McCormack grabbed the telephone from him and spoke to Renner. Afterwards he took a moment to admire his manicure of the other day, appearing pensive. Wilcox thought he seemed anxious, worried about something.

"What is it, Sean? You don't look so good."

McCormack chewed on the fingernail of his left middle finger, spat out what he bit off, and said, "I'm going to call the DCI. This thing's moving faster than I thought. That fool Weintraub will screw up everything if we don't intervene."

"Want me to call Langley?"

"Yeah, thanks," nodded the spymaster. Then quickly added, "And, John, tell 'em it's top priority."

When Mary Young left for work later that day, her mind was racing. Why had Kozlov aborted? She knew she didn't need an answer to that, but it still bothered her. Today was the first time he had missed their weekly appointment, almost six months after she had moved in with her sailor boyfriend.

She sighed. Strange to think that she considered Pike her boyfriend. He was an American, the most repulsive kind of human being on the face of the earth. Then again, she was half American and reminding herself of that fact made her skin itch.

Her job playing barmaid that evening turned out to be predictably tedious. Eight overly friendly customers asked her to go home with them, but she spurned them by flashing her bogus engagement ring in their faces. They're all drunken swine, she told herself.

On the way home, Kozlov still dominated her thoughts. Would he fly in on Thursday to collect her envelope as per their backup plan, or would he wait until next Tuesday? In any event, she would need to be at the airport Thursday morning.

When she stepped into the apartment, she was surprised to find her lover wide awake. He was lying on the sofa, head propped against two couch pillows, watching a Randolph Scott western on television.

"What are you doing up so late?" she asked, pretending to sound concerned.

"Couldn't sleep," he told her.

She glanced at the television and frowned.

"That's silly," she said. "Would you like a drink, darling?"

"Only if you're having one."

She disappeared into the kitchen and returned with two martinis. She gave him one and snuggled in beside him.

"How was your night?" he asked.

"Oh, just lovely. Some jerk old enough to be my grandfather asked me to marry him." She sipped her martini and giggled.

"Why do you keep that crummy job? Why don't you get a day job like normal people?"

"Because I'm not normal," she said, thinking how true that was. "We'll talk more about it when you get back from sea, okay?"

He nodded mechanically, and as he sipped his drink, she glanced at the empty corner where he usually stored his briefcase. She slipped off the sofa, stretching her arms.

"I'm going to bed. Coming, darling?"

"Soon," he told her.

She gave him a sexy smile, went to the bedroom and switched on the overhead light. She scanned the room: no briefcase.

She went to the bathroom, removed her clothes and stood in front of the mirror, smiling with pride. Yes, her figure was quite magnificent. The curves at her hips were perfectly rounded, the tanned legs sleek and firm, like a professional dancer's. She fondled her breasts and tingled inside, thinking of the handsome sailor in the other room touching her like that. She winked at the beautiful face as she dabbed Chanel Number Five behind each earlobe, adding a splash more on her chest and thighs. She then left the bathroom and slipped into her green silk negligé, the one that always drove him wild.

"Time to get something out of this dreadful night," she whispered in German.

She left the bedroom, stood in front of the television and beckoned him with her index finger.

"Darling, I need you."

CHAPTER 20

On Wednesday morning Tidewater awoke amidst a clear sky and a gentle southwesterly breeze. It would be pleasantly warm by midday, with temperatures hovering in the low eighties. It was ideal weather for vacationers who had come to the region to take advantage of the September sunshine and the off-season hotel prices.

Two time zones away in Great Falls, Montana, it was twenty-five degrees cooler as former senator Russell Nathaniel Brubaker heaved himself out of bed and headed for the bathroom. He took care of some necessary business, dressed and enjoyed a cup of tea with his wife in the dining room. Finished, he excused himself, donned his fleece-collared suede windbreaker and white Stetson, and made a beeline for the horse barn, where his favorite stallion Dusty was saddled and waiting for him.

He took the reins from the groom, walked the black beast out of the barn and climbed into the saddle. He inhaled a breath of fresh air and grinned. Another glorious day for a ride.

He tapped his heels into the horse's flanks and left the ranch. He took his usual route along the southern bank of the Missouri River, his destination anywhere, thinking it might be fun to do some trout fishing later. Yes, retired and free, with no hassles, responsibilities or annoying constituents to please. That was the way to live.

When he arrived back at the ranch, he was surprised to see his wife, her bleached hair still in curlers, standing outside the mansion waving for his attention. Behind her were two men in dark business suits, both taller than his corpulent spouse. The red-and-white Ford Thunderbird in which the strangers had arrived was parked in the gravel driveway not far from the three-car garage. As Brubaker dismounted and passed the reins to the groom, his wife turned suddenly and scampered into the house. Brubaker approached with caution.

"Good morning, Senator," said the man on his left.

Brubaker looked them over judiciously.

"Sorry, gentlemen, but it seems you have the advantage of me."

The newcomer who had spoken, a pale-faced man of dark hair and neatly trimmed sideburns who, Brubaker estimated, was not much older than his eldest daughter, apologized and produced his FBI card for the Republican.

"My name is Allison," he said cordially. He indicated his colleague, a grinning Negro with linebacker shoulders and a thigh for a neck. "And this is Mr. Smith."

Brubaker examined the card and handed it back.

"What can I do for you, gentlemen?"

It was Smith who answered, "We'd like to have a word with you, Senator. Do you have a few minutes to spare?"

"Well, I was about to have breakfast with my wife," replied the ex-congressman. "Would you care to join us?"

"Actually, we need to speak to you in private, sir."

"Oh, in regard to what?"

"It's about a government employee who used to work for you during your last term in office."

"And who might that be?"

It was Allison who told him.

During his drive to the naval base on that lazy morning, Bill Gallagher reflected over the events of the past few days, feeling strangely uneasy. As incredible as it seemed, his quest to find Marlene's murderer had evolved into a full-scale espionage caper, with secret agents, a suspected traitor, the FBI, and the Office of Naval Intelligence as the principle players. He wondered what other surprises were waiting for him in the wings.

Yes, the new turn of events had begun as a result of his girlfriend's murder. Seemingly a thousand years ago, and yet… He swore as he thought of his nemesis, Charles Pike. A possible murderer and turncoat? Even if neither was true, the idea of the blond bastard harboring an enemy agent left a sour taste on his palate. Privately, he hoped the boy wonder would soon be caught dealing with the enemy, tried and convicted for his crime.

He veered off the highway and applied the brakes, stopping the Mustang along the shoulder. He took a deep breath and exhaled slowly.

He had changed, was a different person, no doubt about it. He glanced at the grim face staring at him from the rearview mirror: the same man physically, but not the same person. Yes, Watson had been right all along. His obsession to prove that Pike killed his wife had taken its toll on him. Hate for the man had suppressed his ability for rational thought. His visit to the fleet psychiatrist proved that and would always be a part of him, a permanent stain on his once unblemished record and reputation.

Yes, it had all started with the brutal murder of a woman whom he had adored more than anyone else, and yet someone he had barely known. Maybe Marlene *had* been the runaround type as Pike had proclaimed and not the innocent girl next door he had always believed her to be.

He wiped the moisture from his eyes with a handkerchief. It was another long minute before he put the car in gear and accelerated onto the freeway.

At the main gate of the naval base, he returned the sentry's textbook salute, leaned on the gas pedal and followed the road to Bledsoe's office. When he marched into the room, he found the ONI officer involved in a spirited telephone conversation. He fixed himself a cup of black coffee, took a seat at the front of the desk and waited.

"Was just speaking to Mike Weintraub," said Bledsoe as he hung up the phone. "He told me he'd keep monitoring Pike's apartment, but said it's impossible to have his men at the airport on a constant alert basis. There was some trouble in Newport News last night involving the state police, and his men had to be reassigned there to help out."

"So if Mary Young decides to visit the airport again, his men on Granby will be on their own?"

"Yes, I'm afraid it's all the support he can give us for now. But I seriously doubt she'll be making any new trips too soon. I've a feeling the rest of the week will be quiet."

"Sir, do you absolutely need me here anymore?"

1"I know you're getting itchy, Bill, but I'd appreciate if you'd stay on the case a little while longer, at least until next Tuesday.

Remember, you're the key player in this affair. Without you—"

"I know, I know. If I hadn't been so stubborn in trying to find the man who killed Marlene, none of this would have happened. But if you think that makes me feel like some sort of hero, you're wrong, sir. Actually I'm not sure *how* I feel about this whole sorted mess anymore."

"Bill, the last thing I want to believe is that an officer of the United States Navy is a traitor selling military information to the Russians."

"And when it's all over and done with, then what?"

"Life will go on. I'll continue my job here and you'll return to Oceana to serve your country as a flyer." Bledsoe proffered a short grin, adding, "And I've no doubt you'll continue to serve with distinction."

At three o'clock, Bledsoe received another phone call from Mike Weintraub.

The conversation lasted ten minutes, with Bledsoe taking mental notes during the interval. When he hung up, there was a strange faraway gleam in his eye.

"Interesting," he muttered, as if speaking to himself. "The FBI made a house call at Brubaker's ranch this morning."

"And?"

"Well, the former senator reluctantly acknowledged that he'd had an affair with Mary Young. According to him, the girl was hired by his campaign manager, who admitted after the election that *he* had had a fling with the girl too."

"This whole thing is getting more bizarre by the minute, Jim. Like a TV soap opera."

"To make matters worse, it seems that Brubaker had also been a member of the Senate Armed Services Committee while he was in office. Which means he was privy to classified documents regarding defense spending, the kind of stuff the Commies would be interested in."

"What a mess," moaned the head-shaking marine.

"Yeah, I wouldn't want to be in Brubaker's shoes now."

"But, Jim, it still doesn't prove that Mary Young is a spy."

"Maybe, but the theory is perfectly feasible, don't you agree?"

Gallagher shrugged his shoulders.

"It's beyond me," he said. "This whole thing is so bizarre, I don't know *what* to believe anymore."

"Relax, Bill. Before you know it, the fog will clear and the whole picture will come into focus. It'll happen—you'll see."

Sean McCormack received the telephone call from his superior in Langley at 7:23 p.m. When the twenty minute conversation had ended, the spymaster turned pensive. His partner, John Wilcox, who had been out scrounging around for a late-night snack, appeared in the hotel suite ten minutes later with a box of pizza and a six-pack of Miller High-Life.

"Hungry, Sean?" Wilcox placed the items on the table by the window and sat. McCormack lit a cigarette.

"Just got off the phone with the DCI," he said to the window.

"Yeah, what did he say?"

"He's scheduled a meeting with the FBI director first thing tomorrow morning."

"Does that mean we move in?"

"No, not until he gives me the green light."

"Sean, we might need some extra help with this."

"I already took care of it. Randy James and two of his heavies are on their way down here as we speak."

"You expect things to get rough?"

"At this point I don't know what to expect, John. But to make sure things don't get out of hand, I want you to take charge when Randy and his boys get here. Have them ready to move at a moment's notice."

Nodding, Wilcox chewed some pizza, swallowed and frowned; it was already cold. He opened a bottle of beer with his Swiss Army knife.

"Why can't life be simple and uncomplicated?" he said, but McCormack was not listening.

Earlier in the afternoon Andrew Lewis informed Bledsoe that Lieutenant-Commander Pike had left the *Roosevelt* at 17.55 hours. Was his briefcase with him? "Yes," was the ensign's reply.

Later that night as Pike slept, Maria Brandt went to work in the kitchen with her camera. When she had finished, she removed the roll of film, replaced the camera behind the box of cereal, dropped the film in a secret place in the lining of her raincoat, put the briefcase back where it belonged and tiptoed back to the bedroom. She nuzzled in beside her lover and fell asleep with a satisfied grin on her face.

CHAPTER 21

Thursday in Norfolk dawned as a carbon copy of Wednesday: spring-like warm and complemented by a fluttering southwesterly wind. Having slept little the night previous, Bill Gallagher arrived in Bledsoe's office at half-past seven and found the sailor sitting at his desk munching on a cinnamon bun, a full mug of coffee within reaching distance of his fingers.

"Hello, Bill."

"Good morning, sir."

"Doughnuts and sweet rolls on the table next to the coffee pot," Bledsoe told him. "Help yourself."

"No, thanks, just coffee for me."

Gallagher fixed himself a mug and sauntered over to the window. He saw a crew of civil service employees working to repair a section of broken sidewalk across the street, jackhammers chattering nonstop, then disappear as a truck convoy passed in front of them. High above the motor parade were four parallel streaks of white tail vapor stretched across the pale blue sky: navy fighter jets in formation showing off. He shook his head.

That's where I should be.

He watched the lead fighter, picturing himself in the cockpit. He glanced from side to side, making sure his wingmen were there with him. Then, suddenly, they veered away and vanished to port, swallowed up by the dark thunderheads which had magically appeared out of the southeast.

He radioed them to return to formation—there was no response—and he felt alone, a weird, cold sensation. No, none of it was real, he told himself. It was a dream—it had to be—and yet the lush jungle below seemed all too genuine. Where was he going? What orders had he received?

Rain peppered the cupola, blurring his sight. Then, suddenly, orange tracers lit up around him, like fireworks on the Fourth of July: canon bursts from the Russian MiG bolting toward him at nine o'clock.

Gallagher throttled to maximum in a steep climb toward the heavens and God, the enemy fighter rapidly losing ground. The dogfight was on.

The rush of adrenaline seized him, his heart racing in response, drumming against his breastbone as if trying to break out. The training, the experience, every skill he had mastered was in play now. He was ready; he would win.

You're gonna die, gook!

The MiG appeared again, was back on his tail. Bill glanced over his shoulder and saw the angry face of his Vietcong rival. He zigzagged, expecting to lose him, but the gook was determined, remained glued to his butt. More tracers, and the marine banked to starboard, taking the Skyhawk down, the MiG still chasing, still closing. A hard yank on his stick, and he reversed course, circling over the MiG as it charged under him. He was the hunter now. Victory would soon be his.

Semper fi!

The North Vietnamese zigzagged, desperately looking to escape, but Gallagher was there, closing fast. The MiG climbed, nose-dived, climbed again, but to no avail. Bill had him exactly where he wanted him—in his gun sight crosshairs. The Hawk shuttered as he squeezed the trigger, watching the canon bursts gut the MiG's fuselage, with yellow flames following, engulfing the dying jet. A thunderous explosion, and the MiG disintegrated, its nuts and bolts showering the jungle below. No parachute. Bill clenched his fist in celebration. His fifth kill. Just as it had happened two years ago…

He smiled, but then lost it in a hurry as that glorious moment from the past faded, returned to the files of his memory. Eyes still locked skyward, the navy jets had vanished. He turned and walked away from the window, frowning.

He heard Bledsoe say, "What is it, Bill? You seem anxious this morning."

"Oh, just contemplating the future."

"Still thinking of leaving the Corps?"

"Maybe."

"Why, because of this wretched spy business?"

"That's part of it." Bill hesitated, as if reluctant to elaborate, but then switched topics when he said, "Did you watch the news last night?"

"No, but I can guess what was on. Vietnam jungle fighting and antiwar protests, right?"

"Yeah. Life in this country is pure hypocrisy. We fight and die in Vietnam while no one supports the war here at home. What's happening to America, Jim? Where's a real leader when we need one?"

"I know what you mean. Ever since Jack Kennedy died, the country hasn't been the same. It's almost as if someone pulled out the plug and we're washing down the drain. If we don't put back the stopper soon, the whole country will end up in the sewer."

"When I was in 'Nam, I thought the war wouldn't last long. Let's face it, we have superior air power, not to mention the best army in the world. It's almost as if the big shots in Washington aren't concerned with winning the war at all."

"It's hard to win a war or even justify it when the citizens at home don't support it. If we *don't* win, how do we account for all the men who've died? The ramifications of this war will no doubt haunt us for generations to come. Without a doubt, it's the most unpopular war in our history."

"It bothers me now that I was a part of it."

"Well, when it finally ends, we'll still be left with the war with the Russians. The Cold War won't go away no matter how hard the natives protest. In my opinion, it's the real war."

"That's what Pike said, Jim. Marlene told me he was against the war too. Said it was a sideshow meant to keep the defense contractors in business."

"Bill, I know how you feel about Pike, but there's something else, isn't there?"

"I don't like him, Jim. Nothing will ever change that."

"But you do have a certain amount of respect for him despite what you think he may have done?"

Gallagher did not answer. Instead, he reached for his mug and sipped, aware Bledsoe had touched a nerve of truth despite how repulsive it sounded.

*   *   *

At 9:15, Bledsoe received a phone call from Michael Weintraub. His stakeout team on Granby Street, the FBI man told him, had just seen Mary Young leaving the apartment building in a taxicab. The watchers started after the cab in their gray Dodge sedan. The taxi continued north along Granby, then made a right-hand turn at Little Creek Road, his obvious destination the airport. The watchers continued their not-too-close pursuit as the taxi made the obligatory turn onto Military Highway, but then were forced to give up the chase when the unexpected happened.

The left front tire burst apart with a bang, and the Dodge veered sharply into the left-hand lane, nearly sideswiping a UPS delivery truck. The driver skillfully regained control of the wheel, swung back into the right-hand lane and brought the car to a rickety halt along the shoulder.

"What the hell!" cried his partner.

"We got a blowout!" shouted the driver.

They went outside and examined the damage. The bottom of the tire was flatter than a Blue Ridge pancake. The driver swore, but he was a professional and quickly regained his composure.

"You better call the boss," he told his partner.

Michael Weintraub received the bad news three minutes later. Like the driver, he reacted with his favorite four-lettered expletive. He relayed the story to Bledsoe.

"She was heading for the airport," he added.

"Mike, do you have any men available to help out?"

"'Fraid not, Jim. They're still on assignment in Newport News. Is there anything you can do?"

Bledsoe pondered furiously. Finally he said, "I'll go over there myself. By the way, what was she wearing?"

Weintraub told him, adding, "I'll join you there as soon as I can."

Bledsoe hung up, vaulted out of his chair and reached for his cap dangling from the coat rack. At the same moment Gallagher strolled into the office, returning from a visit to the bathroom. He frowned when he saw Bledsoe donning his cap.

"Going somewhere, Jim?"

"Yeah, and you're coming with me."

"Where to?"

"The airport," was the sailor's reply. "Come on, I'll explain on the way."

In his hotel suite at the airport, Sean McCormack hung up the telephone, ending his eight-minute conversation with his boss in Langley. He glanced around the room for Wilcox but didn't find him.

"John?"

No answer.

"John!"

Wilcox appeared from the bathroom holding a safety razor in his right hand, the left side of his face covered with shaving foam.

"Yeah, Sean?"

"Just got off the phone with Langley," McCormack told him. "The DCI gave me the go-ahead to proceed. Said he had just finished ironing things out with our FBI cousins. They're notifying their man in Norfolk now."

"Weintraub, you mean?"

"Yeah. I think it's time I had a little chat with him and set him straight. In fact, I think we should get Davis in on this too. Might save us some aggravation."

"Want me to call him?"

"Yeah, and make it snappy."

Wilcox flipped through his note pad. When he had found the page with Davis' phone number, he reached for the telephone but stopped when it started to ring. Startled, he glanced at McCormack, who promptly scowled at him.

"Well, John, what are you waiting for? Answer the damned thing!"

Wilcox picked up the phone.

"It's me," announced the voice in his ear, which he recognized as Joe Renner's. "The girl just arrived." Wilcox covered the mouthpiece with his free hand and relayed the news to his boss.

McCormack scratched his head as he contemplated his next move. Ready at last, he opened his mouth to speak, but Wilcox cut him off before he could utter a sound.

"Hold on, Sean! What's that, Joe?" Wilcox listened, teardrops of shaving foam dangling from his chin. When Renner had finished, he covered the mouthpiece with his other hand and said, "Joe said Gallagher just showed up too."

"Holy Jesus!" McCormack snatched the phone. "Joe, it's me. Don't let Gallagher out of your sight. If my guess is correct, he'll have Bledsoe with him. I'm sending John over there now. He'll have Randy and his boys with him. They know what to do."

Renner acknowledged, McCormack hung up, and Wilcox returned to the bathroom. The latter reappeared four minutes later with a clean-shaven face and promptly vacated the suite. When he returned, there was another man with him.

Randy James was a tall, broad-shouldered man. When his shirt was off he looked like a body builder. With it on he looked like a body builder. James was in his late twenties, had chin-length dark hair—he looked more like a campus agitator than a CIA enforcer—and wore a wide insincere smile of cream-colored teeth. McCormack told him exactly what he wanted done and James nodded obediently.

"No problem, sir."

James, wearing faded blue jeans and a green football jersey, started to leave with Wilcox but stopped when the telephone trilled. McCormack picked it up.

"It's me," he heard. The caller was Jeff Osgood, his watcher in Philadelphia. "Our Commie friend is heading your way."

Sean McCormack lost his temper.

"Why the hell didn't you call sooner?" he shouted into the phone. Osgood babbled something in return that sounded like an excuse but McCormack was not interested. "Never mind, dammit! What's the flight number?"

Osgood told him and McCormack slammed the phone down. He glanced at his wristwatch, lips pressed together in nervous thought. His wrinkled face was cherry red with anger.

"Kozlov's on his way, John—Pan Am flight 111. Get over to the airport and take care of this business now." He stared at James, his wide eyes bayonets. "And no rough stuff, Randy, unless John says so."

"Yes, sir."

McCormack said to Wilcox, "You know where I'll be. Meet me there when it's over." He shook his head angrily. "Dammit to hell!"

"Don't worry, Sean, I'll take care of it." He tapped James on the shoulder. "Let's go, Randy."

"One more thing, John?"

"Yeah?"

"Davis' phone number—let's have it."

Wilcox read the number on his note pad, waited until McCormack had written it down, and then he and James left the room at the march. Mumbling to himself, McCormack grabbed the phone and dialed.

Although Michael Weintraub was the head man of the Norfolk branch of the FBI, he was still subordinate to higher authority. It was at the same moment Wilcox and James were sprinting to the airport when he received the telephone call from his boss in Washington.

Twelve minutes later he hung up the phone. He stared at it for a while longer, his mind churning. He switched on the intercom and told his secretary to connect him with his watchers, who were still involved at the corner of Little Creek and Military Highway. When the connection was made, he told them to report back to the office as soon as they had replaced the flat.

At 9:59 the intercom buzzed. He flipped the switch.

"Yes?"

"Sorry to bother you, sir, but there's a gentleman here to see you."

"Who is it?"

"A Mr. McCormack."

Weintraub frowned, wondering who he was.

"Peggy, tell him I'm too busy to see him right now. Ask him to make an appointment."

The moment he had finished, the door swung open and Sean McCormack marched into the office. Weintraub's secretary, a not-too-natural red-haired, middle-aged lady, was standing behind the CIA man, her face flush with embarrassment. Weintraub vaulted from his seat.

"What is this?" he demanded, addressing the intruder.

"I…I'm sorry, sir," muttered Peggy. "I tried to tell him but he was very insistent."

McCormack said, "I know you're a busy man, Mr. Weintraub,

but I've an important matter to discuss with you that can't wait." He stepped up to the desk and showed his credentials. "I thought you could make an exception in my case."

Weintraub, his wrinkled face a white cloud, said, "It's all right, Peggy, you can leave." She did so, closing the door behind her. "What can I do for you, Mr. McCormack?"

"I believe you and I have a mutual friend," said the spymaster. "His name is Timothy Davis."

"Davis! You mean the private dick?"

"That's right. He's on his way over here as we speak."

"Really, what for?"

"Oh, but you already know, sir. Have you not received a phone call from your superior?"

Weintraub seemed bewildered, wondering how the stranger knew that, but then saw the connection and answered with a nod.

"Good," was McCormack's reaction. He lit a cigarette. "Now, sir, would you please buzz your secretary and tell her to admit Davis when he gets here?"

Weintraub did so with reluctance as McCormack made himself comfortable in the vacant chair at the front of the desk.

"Do be seated, Mr. Weintraub. And please relax. We're both on the same team." McCormack grinned hugely. "Now, let's talk shop, shall we?"

"There she is, Jim!"

Gallagher and Bledsoe had arrived at the airport just as Mary Young was emerging from the back seat of the taxi. A pure stroke of luck on their part. Her long hair tied back in a smart ponytail, she was wearing the green-and-white-striped blouse, black leather miniskirt, and knee-high boots of the same color and fabric which Weintraub had described over the phone earlier. Bledsoe stopped the car as she leaned through the open window and paid the driver. She then turned without hesitation and started toward the terminal entrance.

"You sure it's her, Bill?"

"Yeah, it's her all right, no doubt about it."

"All right, get out and follow her. I'll park the car and join you as soon as I can."

"But she knows me, Jim. I met her at that night club she works at. If she recognizes me—"

"But she's never seen you in uniform, right? Besides, I doubt she'd remember you." Bledsoe produced a pair of sunglasses from the glove compartment. "Here, wear these, just in case. Just don't get too close to her."

"Yes, sir."

Gallagher donned the glasses and slipped out of the car. He waited until Bledsoe accelerated before he turned and headed for the building.

There was a moderate-sized crowd inside the terminal. Bill walked in at a leisurely pace—another military uniform among many—and remembered the last time he had been there. It was on the night he had returned from San Diego: four days following Marlene's death.

He spotted Mary Young. She had just appeared from the women's rest room carrying a leather purse that matched the color of her miniskirt and boots. As she made her way through the lobby, heads started turning, the majority male admirers. Gallagher let her get ten yards ahead, glanced over his shoulder, didn't see Bledsoe, picked up his momentum and went after her.

Joe Renner, who was monitoring the marine's every move from the telephone stall, signaled with a nod to a panting John Wilcox, who had just arrived in the terminal with Randy James and his two muscular cohorts. Wilcox correctly interpreted Renner's gesture and whispered something to James, who nodded dutifully and left at the march, following in Gallagher's wake. His long-haired, over-sized buddies in bell-bottom jeans chased after their colleague. Wilcox watched with a satisfied grin as the enforcers were gobbled up by the crowd before making his way over to the magazine stand, where he bought a copy of *Time* from the proprietor. He then sauntered over to a vacant spot nearby, opened the magazine and waited.

Pan Am Flight 111 arrived at Gate 2 at 9:59.

Maria Brandt, smoking a filter cigarette, greeted Yevgeny Kozlov with a handshake when he stepped into the waiting area. A brief conversation ensued, and then the two started through the concourse with the other passengers from Philadelphia. Still hiding behind the sunglasses, Gallagher followed them at a discreet distance. Trailing not far behind was the grinning James.

Baldy, outfitted in a gray pinstripe suit and toting a tan briefcase, kept reaching up to his face with a handkerchief, sniffling, as if he had an unstoppable runny nose. Gallagher ended his pursuit when Young and the Russian strolled into the coffee lounge, where they were escorted to a vacant table by a smiling waitress. Gallagher took a deep breath and exhaled slowly, aware of his heart hammering against his rib cage.

He scanned the lobby, looking for Bledsoe. At last he found him standing near the magazine stand chatting with a stranger, a tall, thin man with oily-looking dark hair. The stranger was wearing a short-sleeve white shirt and candy-striped red and white tie, a rolled up magazine in his right hand. Gallagher wiped sweat from his palms over his trousers, took another deep breath and started toward them. He stopped when Bledsoe spotted him and shook his head: a signal for him to stay put. Bill reluctantly nodded in answer, found an empty chair near a group of chattering out-of-towners, sat and waited.

Maria Brandt and Yevgeny Kozlov had their usual ration of coffee. At 10:36, the girl rose from her seat and vacated the lounge, heading in the direction of the women's rest room. She disappeared inside, reappeared four minutes later and made a casual beeline for the exit. Gallagher stared at Bledsoe to gauge his reaction, but the ONI officer was still engaged in conversation with the stranger with the magazine.

Kozlov left the coffee lounge at 10:47 after having paid the bill and placing the yellow envelope Brandt had left behind inside his briefcase. He was followed to Gate 3 by Randy James, who remained in the waiting area until the Russian had boarded the D.C. shuttle.

In the terminal lobby, Gallagher had grown tired of waiting, was beside himself with anxiety. Back on his feet, he removed the sunglasses and started across the lobby. Bledsoe and the man with the magazine met him halfway. Bill confronted the sailor, ignoring the stranger's presence.

"Well, Jim, what now?"

"We're leaving," Bledsoe told him. He indicated the dark-haired man beside him. "Bill, this is Mr. Wilcox."

"Hello, Lieutenant," said McCormack's right-hand man. Then quickly added, "And this is my colleague, Joe Renner."

The bespectacled Renner, having appeared seemingly out of nowhere, was standing directly behind the marine. To the left of him was the smirking Randy James, his brawny pals flanking him, both wearing similar facial expressions. Gallagher turned pale as he struggled to swallow the lump in his throat.

"What's going on here, Jim?"

"Like I said, we're leaving," was the sailor's reply. "We're going downtown with these gentlemen."

"But…I don't get it. We're not going back to the base?"

It was Wilcox who answered, "No, Lieutenant, you're not." He smirked at the bemused marine, adding, "You're coming with us."

CHAPTER 22

The executive conference suite at the FBI building in Norfolk was located on the second floor, west wing. To the left of the immaculately polished conference table, a trio of windows offered a broad view of the city skyline. Across the murky green Elizabeth River in the background was blue-collar Portsmouth. The sleek conference table, rectangular in shape and rounded at the corners, had enough maroon leather chairs to accommodate a dozen people.

Special Agent Michael Weintraub was seated at the head of the table, his usual place when conducting a meeting. Opposite him at the far end of the table sat the chain-smoking Sean McCormack. On the spymaster's left was his partner, John Wilcox. Facing Wilcox across the table was Bill Gallagher, who was sandwiched between Jim Bledsoe and an atypically anxious Timothy Davis. Weintraub had the floor.

"Now that we've dispensed with the formalities, shall we proceed with the briefing, gentlemen?" His statement was a suggestion, not a question that needed an answer. "Mr. McCormack?"

"Thank you." McCormack cleared the cigarette frog from his throat. "First of all, I'd like to apologize to Mr. Bledsoe for the unceremonious way in which he and Lieutenant Gallagher were spirited away from the airport. However, what was done was absolutely necessary.

"Mr. Weintraub has already been briefed regarding the facts of this case. Since this has been a CIA operation from the beginning, it would be prudent of me to start the meeting by saying that the ad hoc investigation by the Navy and FBI, although commendable, terminates as of this moment. The decision was not mine, you understand, but entrusted to me by higher authority. My colleague, Mr. Wilcox, will keep a stenographic record of the meeting." He turned. "John, would you like to add anything?"

"No, Sean."

"Very well." McCormack stared down the table and inclined his head. "Mr. Weintraub?"

"On behalf of the Bureau, I'd like to reiterate my full cooperation in this matter," responded the FBI chief.

"Excellent." McCormack turned, facing Bledsoe. "And the Office of Naval Intelligence?"

"Likewise," nodded the sailor. "To say the least, I'm anxious to get to the bottom of this."

Wilcox's boss lit a cigarette, inhaled hungrily and discharged the smoke through his nostrils. Watching him, Gallagher said, "Excuse me, Mr. McCormack, but don't you think it's time we cut through all the polite chitchat and get to the heart of the matter? Commander Bledsoe and I were picked up like wanted criminals by Mr. Wilcox and his Gestapo buddies without explanation. What kind of game are you playing at?"

"If you'll allow him a moment of courtesy," cut in a piqued-sounding Weintraub, "he'll be happy to explain."

"It's all right, Mr. Weintraub," said McCormack. "In fact, I sympathize with Mr. Gallagher. If I were in his shoes, I'd be upset too. But the game, as you put it, Lieutenant, is a matter of national security, much more than just a routine investigation of a foreign agent on American soil."

Bledsoe said, "You're referring to Mary Young, of course?"

It was Wilcox who answered, "Her real name is Maria Brandt. And you're right, sir. She is a trained Soviet agent."

McCormack said, "For the record, Commander, she's not Russian, but German, a citizen of the German Democratic Republic, or East Germany as we know it. She was recruited and trained as an undercover operative by the KGB. We think she slipped across the Canadian border on a false passport sometime in early 'sixty-seven."

Wilcox said, "She used to work as a secretary for an ex-senator named Russell Brubaker, a Montana Republican who has since been voted out of office. During his term in Congress, Brubaker was a member of the Senate Armed Services Committee. In early October we received an anonymous tip that he had been shacked up with her during his tenure on the committee. We investigated, of course, and not long thereafter her fingerprints were found on a number of classified documents that Brubaker had been privy to during his time in Congress."

McCormack added, "In other words, gentlemen, it was enough evidence for us to initiate round-the-clock surveillance of her."

Davis said, "Why didn't you arrest her?"

"We certainly could have," was McCormack's reply. "However,

before I explain why we didn't, I'd like to indulge everyone's patience, if I may, and tell a brief story." He paused for a drag of cigarette, coughed harshly when he exhaled, and aimed his next words at Bledsoe.

"Commander, I was told that you're somewhat of a history buff. In particular, the history of naval intelligence in the Pacific theater during the Second World War."

Bledsoe nodded in response, wondering how the man knew that.

"Yes, I've done some research along those lines," he said. "In fact, I'm contemplating writing a book on the subject."

"Indeed!" Another puff, another gravelly cough, before the spymaster continued, "During your research, sir, tell me, did you ever come across the phrase, *Higashi no kaze ame?*"

Bledsoe leaned forward in his seat, elbows on the table, and stared at the white-haired gentleman through narrow slits, his mind churning.

"Yes, I know it," he said finally. "It's a Japanese phrase."

"For the benefit of those in this room who don't understand the Japanese language, would you please explain what it means, Commander?"

"It means 'East wind, rain'."

"Yes, that's the literal translation. But in December 'forty-one, that simple phrase, a routine weather forecast, was code for something much more profound in meaning. Do you know what that was, Commander?"

"I do. Decoded, 'East wind, rain' meant war between Japan and the United States."

"Thank you, sir." McCormack rose from his seat. He took another puff, this time without coughing, and began a back-and-forth pacing routine.

"Gentlemen," he said, "before the Pearl Harbor tragedy, our intelligence apparatus in Washington had broken the enemy's diplomatic code—called the Purple Code by our military cryptanalysts. By late November 'forty-one, relations between Washington and Tokyo had become so strained, war was inevitable. Anyway, to make a long story short, the Japanese government alerted their embassies and consulates throughout the world via the Purple Code that war would commence when they issued the 'East wind, rain' directive.

"During this time, contrary to popular belief, there was but one enemy spy working in the Hawaiian Islands. He was an ensign in the Imperial Japanese Navy, assigned to their consulate in Honolulu. His name was Takeo Yoshikawa. His job was to spy on the Pacific Fleet and keep his government up to date on all naval activity in and around Oahu. When he received the 'East wind, rain' directive, he knew that war was imminent.

"And since we had broken the enemy's code, we knew it too. Although naval intelligence was aware of Yoshikawa's covert activities and that war was forthcoming, there was still a multitude of skeptics within the ranks of our military hierarchy who refused to accept it, and for some reason or other failed to alert our base commanders in Hawaii.

"Why did our government fail to heed the advice of our intelligence experts and act accordingly to the threat of Japanese attack? Well, I suppose that's a question for historians to answer. Although we paid a heavy price at Pearl Harbor, we licked our wounds and hitched up our pants, vowing never to let that mistake happen again. The Battle of Midway, for example, and others that turned the tide in the Pacific were won in part thanks to the brilliant code-breaking work of naval intelligence, whose efforts were finally being recognized by our esteemed leaders.

"Yes, gentlemen, Pearl Harbor was the event that opened our eyes to the value of intelligence and what it can lead to when used responsibly. Since the end of the war, we've continually strived to improve our intelligence-gathering methods. Let's face it, we've no other choice. Our new enemy, Soviet Russia, is a most formidable and cunning adversary. To combat the Reds, we need to be just as formidable and cunning, if not more so. And that includes all areas of intelligence, from the most sophisticated spy satellite in outer space to the average field agent working behind the Iron Curtain. Bluntly speaking, if we are not vigilant in our duty twenty-four hours a day, the ghost of Pearl Harbor may come back to haunt us, only this time the results could prove to be much more severe. And by that, I mean, nuclear war."

McCormack stopped pacing and reclaimed his seat. He stubbed out the cigarette in the ashtray provided, and sponged the excess moisture from his brow with a handkerchief.

"Forgive me, gentlemen," he added, "I didn't intend to sound like a lecture."

Pin-drop silence followed. It was Gallagher who ended it.

"So what's the moral of your history lesson, Mr. McCormack? Are you trying to tell us that Mary Young—or whatever her name is—is a modern-day version of that Japanese spy?"

Wilcox said, "Had you not interrupted, Gallagher, he would have explained."

McCormack said, "Your analogy is right on the mark, Lieutenant. However, in the case of Maria Brandt, there's much more to the puzzle."

"And that would be Comrade Kozlov?" The question had come from Bledsoe's lips.

It was Weintraub who answered, "Yes, Jim."

"But I don't get it!" It was Davis again. "You know these

people are spies, yet you take no action against them. Hell, what must they do before you arrest them? Blow up the Pentagon...or the White House?"

McCormack laughed.

"If only it were that simple, Mr. Davis." He lit another cigarette. "Explain it, John."

"You see, it's like this, Mr. Davis. Maria Brandt is not just one spy working alone, but part of a network of Soviet agents. They're run by the man you discovered by accident, Major Yevgeny Kozlov."

"*Major* Kozlov?" spouted the perplexed Gallagher.

"That's right. Kozlov is a former Red Army officer who now works for the foreign service of the KGB. We believe he's the ring leader of the network. So far we know he's running two agents. One is Maria Brandt. The other is a man we've identified as Pavel Yakovenko. Yakovenko works undercover at the Philadelphia Naval Shipyard as a civil service employee. A pipe fitter, or something or other."

Davis said, "So that explains baldy's weekly trips from Philly to Norfolk."

Ignoring him, Wilcox went on, "We also have another man under surveillance who, we believe, is a Cuban national. He's employed at the Naval Air Station in Pensacola, Florida, works as a stockroom clerk at the base commissary."

McCormack regained the floor when he said, "Yes, gentlemen, it's all true. There are spies everywhere, it seems. Of course, we play the game too. We have agents working in Moscow, Havana, East Berlin, and places you've never even heard of. It's the part of the Cold War no one ever sees. And like all undercover work, it's extremely dangerous and unpredictable, not at all glamorous like it is in those idiotic spy movies and TV shows."

Davis said, "I still don't get it. What about the information Kozlov is getting from Mary Young and that Pavel what's-his-name? If you know what they're doing, why don't you arrest them?"

"Because the game of peacetime espionage is played differently from the days of Yoshikawa," McCormack told him. "To arrest these people at this stage would do more harm than good. Kozlov, for example, has diplomatic immunity. We just can't walk up to him on the street and arrest him like a common jaywalker. Besides, we don't want to bust up his network until we know everything that's going on and how many agents are involved. We have to move with discretion."

Wilcox said, "In fact, leaving him alone to continue his dirty business works to our advantage."

More silence. Not long thereafter Bledsoe revived the debate by making a startling revelation.

"I believe I understand what you're leading up to, gentlemen."

"Indeed!" McCormack shot a glance at Wilcox, who also seemed rattled by the sailor's remark. The former swung his eyes back to Bledsoe. "Do go on, Commander."

"Well, correct me if I'm wrong, but you're involved in the game of disinformation, aren't you? Take Mary Young, for instance. When you suspected her of stealing classified documents from the senator, you could have arrested her then but you chose not to. Instead, you let her continue to operate, only this time it was you supplying the documentation. In other words, documents with false information attached."

"Bravo, Commander! Very astute of you," said the grinning McCormack. "If you ever decide to leave the service, please look me up. I'm sure I could find suitable work in the Agency for a man of your talents."

Wilcox said, "When Brubaker was voted out of office, Miss Brandt found herself out of a job. But that didn't stop Kozlov. He transferred her to Norfolk hoping she would find another pigeon to squeeze."

"And that pigeon, as John put it, is Commander Pike."

The sudden mention of Pike's name prompted an immediate reaction from Gallagher.

"Yes, what about Pike, Mr. McCormack? How does he fit into the puzzle?"

"But isn't it obvious? He's the one providing her with the false papers. You see, Pike is more than just a naval officer doing his duty for God and country. He's also a CIA operative." McCormack smiled proudly, showing nicotine-stained teeth. "In other words, Lieutenant, he's working for *me.*"

A brief adjournment for lunch before the meeting resumed. McCormack picked up where he had left off.

"So there it is, gentlemen. Lieutenant Commander Charles Jefferson Pike is a patriot, *not* a traitor. He is a real life spy—or I should say, counterspy. For several months now he's been feeding false information to this present-day Yoshikawa we know as Maria Brandt. To a credulous world, Pike is just another sailor doing his duty. Those in this room and a few select others know that he is a spy and hero to his country. A man whose job must remain obscure for the sake of national security. It's extraordinary men like Pike who will help us win the so-called Cold War." His eyes met Gallagher's. "And that's why you and Mr. Bledsoe were picked up at the airport this morning. Pike's cover had to be protected at all costs."

Davis said, "But what happens if the Russians find out that what they're getting from Mary Young is useless information?"

"A good point," chimed in Wilcox. "We suspect that Kozlov will reassign her, or perhaps abort her mission altogether and send her back home."

McCormack said, "The Reds are not stupid, gentlemen. They're as good at this game as we are, at times even better. They know of Pike's reputation and importance aboard ship. They also know that the Navy would never allow him to leave base with classified material on his person, especially that which would compromise national security. What Pike allows her to see is declassified papers. However, to keep her sweet and coming back for more, he sometimes allows her to see top-grade material. Unbeknownst to her, it's material that he himself has doctored and in no way can jeopardize our nation's security.

"However, there are many other ways for an agent of Maria Brandt's caliber to acquire bits and pieces of military information, and that's why she's planted where she is. For example, from gabbing sailors who frequent that night club she works at. Information such as ship deployment, sea orders, et cetera."

More quiet. McCormack lit a cigarette.

"Gentlemen," he said, "I think we've reached the end of the briefing. Are there any questions?"

"I have one," spouted Gallagher.

"Lieutenant?"

"Mr. Davis, Commander Bledsoe and Mr. Weintraub got involved in all this because I was convinced Pike killed his wife. In my wildest imagination, I had no idea it would come to this. But now that you've admitted the CIA has been involved from the beginning, tell me, Mr. McCormack, what do you know about the murder? Did he do it? If not, do you know who did?"

"This is irrelevant to the business at hand," said Wilcox, an annoyed tone attached to his words. "I'd suggest—" McCormack cut him off.

"Wait a minute, John." To Gallagher he said, "I know very little about the murder of Mrs. Pike. From what I do know, however, it seems to have been an unfortunate coincidence."

"Oh, what kind of coincidence?" fired back the marine. "The planned or the unplanned kind?"

"What are you hinting at?" urged a bemused-sounding Weintraub, but Gallagher ignored him as if he was not there.

"Well, Mr. McCormack?"

"I don't understand."

"Oh, I thought the CIA knew everything. At least, that's the impression I've got the past few hours listening to all this crap! Come on, Mr. McCormack, why don't you come clean and put my conscience at ease? Did Pike kill his wife? Or...did you do it?"

"You're mad!" snarled Wilcox.

Bledsoe elbowed Gallagher's arm, snaring his attention.

"Bill, do you know what you're doing?"

"It's all right, Mr. Bledsoe," McCormack told him. To Gallagher he said, "Go on, Lieutenant, I'm fascinated."

"Very well, I'll be blunt. I've got a theory about what's *really* going on here."

"Theory?"

"That's right. I believe Marlene accidentally found out about her husband's secret new job, and that you and your henchmen eliminated her so that his cover wouldn't be blown. Yes, somehow she got too close to your precious secret agent and you killed her, didn't you? Of course, you didn't perform the sordid act yourself, but you arranged it, all in the name of national security."

McCormack jabbed the cigarette between his lips and puffed, no emotion showing.

"And Pike?" he urged. "What about him?"

"Maybe he knew, maybe he didn't. But it doesn't matter now who killed her. What matters is whether you or someone in the CIA arranged for her death." His brow dotted with beads of sweat, Bill's hands shook, like his voice as he continued, "So why don't you tell me the truth, Mr. McCormack? Put my mind at ease so I can sleep tonight. Convince me that my theory is wrong and that you had nothing to do with the murder."

"You're out of your mind!" shouted Wilcox. "What gives you the right to accuse Sean McCormack—"

"Because it all finally makes sense to me!" retorted the marine. "This whole rotten stinking affair finally makes sense. Pike the patriot, Pike the hero. And his wife—dead! But why, for the sake of national security?" He looked away from the red-faced Wilcox, eyes big and alive, chest heaving.

"So tell me, Mr. McCormack of the CIA. Climb down from Mount Rushmore and tell everyone the truth. Did you murder Marlene Pike, or were you ordered to do so by higher authority?"

Wilcox vaulted from his chair, was fit to be tied.

"This is preposterous!" he thundered. "They'll throw you out of the service for this outburst, Gallagher. I swear to you, you'll rot in Leavenworth for the rest of your life if we have anything to say about it."

"Yes, by all means, Wilcox, write it down and tell the whole stinking world!" Bill salvoed back. "But you won't, will you? No, you…you'll just liquidate me when I'm not looking, like you probably did with Marlene Pike and God knows how many others that got in your way. In fact, why don't you save some time and do it now? You can chalk it up as another coincidence!" Bill turned to McCormack, his eyes flamethrowers.

"Come on, McCormack, I'm waiting! Why don't you tell us the truth? Did the CIA do away with my girlfriend because she knew too much about your precious hero and his German whore?"

"Mrs. Pike was murdered, Lieutenant, by someone unknown to you, the Norfolk police, and myself," replied the spymaster. "Whether or not you believe me...well, that's up to you. I can't change the way you think. Believe me, I sympathize with your loss. I know what you're feeling inside."

"No, Mr. McCormack, you've no idea what I'm feeling inside," Bill corrected him "However, I'll come clean and tell you. People like you make me sick to my stomach! You hide behind this...this bogus façade claiming that everything you do is for the good of our national interest while innocent people like Marlene Pike get trampled in the process. It's people like you and Wilcox who give our country a bad reputation."

"It's obvious you had deep feelings for the girl, and still do," said McCormack. "Mr. Davis, in fact, made that quite plain to me the other day. As for your theory, although I hate to admit it, you're absolutely right. Mrs. Pike did indeed stumble upon the fact that her husband was involved in clandestine work designed to feed false information to the enemy. However, I can tell you here, now, and for the record, the Agency was not involved in your girlfriend's death."

"At least, not that you're aware of," commented a smirking Tim Davis.

For the first time McCormack appeared agitated. He ground his teeth together.

"Yes, you're absolutely right, Mr. Davis. Then again, I'm not God. I don't know everything." To Gallagher he said, "Are you satisfied, Lieutenant? Will you be able to sleep tonight?"

Gallagher made no effort to respond, was seemingly at a loss for words. To everyone there, he seemed drained of energy. McCormack flaunted a smirk, satisfied he'd gotten in the last word.

"Very well, any other questions, gentlemen?"

"Yes, I have one." It was Bledsoe's voice. "Why did you bother to mention the story of Yoshikawa and the Purple Code? What's the connection to all this?"

"No connection, Commander. 'East wind, rain' is the cover name I've designated for this project. In this case, 'East wind' meaning Kozlov's gang of spies, and 'rain' the danger they pose to the West."

"I see."

McCormack turned, facing Wilcox.

"John, is there anything you'd like to add?"

"No, Sean."

"Very well, the meeting is closed."

At the naval base later, Bledsoe and Gallagher were reviewing the events of the day.

"Made a fool of myself, didn't I, Jim?"

"To be honest, Bill, your theory made perfect sense to me. If you remember, McCormack never said the CIA wasn't responsible for Marlene's death. He only admitted what *he* knew."

"Yeah, thanks to Tim Davis." Gallagher looked up from the floor. "He's a pretty sharp guy."

"Still, this whole thing seems like a bad dream."

"Yeah, I know what you mean. How could Mary Young and the others be a danger to national security? For instance, what kind of damage could that grocery clerk in Florida do?"

"It's hard to imagine, isn't it? But step back and think about it for a moment. There's a commissary at all naval bases around the world. As a grocery clerk, he could determine how much food and supplies were stored in inventory, and then estimate from that just how many personnel were stationed there. He could also learn the names of wholesalers and how they go about supplying the Navy with goods and the like. In peacetime as in war, it's valuable information."

"I never thought of it that way."

"Yes, it all seems so trivial, doesn't it? But that's what we thought about Yoshikawa before Pearl Harbor. We didn't take him seriously and look what happened."

"What about Marlene, Jim? How could she have jeopardized her husband's cover?"

"Don't know. But maybe the CIA didn't want to take any chances with her. They seem to be an organization unto themselves. There are some, in fact, who claim they work at times like organized crime. Some people I know in the intelligence community believe they may have been secretly involved in the JFK assassination and others, including Bobby Kennedy and Martin Luther King. If it's true, killing Marlene to protect her husband's cover is not beyond what they're capable of. It's the proverbial end-justifies-the-means principle."

"It makes me nauseous, Jim. If they do stuff like that, how do we know they won't do the same to us?"

"Now you're getting paranoid, Bill. But I know what you're saying. It *is* a little scary."

"So what now, sir? Is it all over?"

"Yes, Bill." Bledsoe put a comforting hand on his shoulder. "It's all over."

At 5:30 that afternoon, Lieutenant William Francis Gallagher stood alone on the waterfront dock where the *U.S.S. Roosevelt* was moored. For almost a half hour he had been waiting at Pier 12 for the sailor to appear. Although mentally worn out from the day's activities, he forced himself to continue to wait.

It was five minutes later when the broad-shouldered officer walked down the gangplank of the great ship. Gallagher stiffened as the man approached, the rugged features on his face becoming clearer with each step.

Charles Pike was dressed in khaki uniform and peaked cap, a black leather briefcase dangling from his right hand. He stopped when he recognized the marine, but then picked up his momentum and joined him. It was Gallagher who took the initiative and spoke first.

"Good afternoon, Commander."

"So we meet again," said Pike unnecessarily. "Tell me, is this a social visit or did you come here to make more accusations?"

"No, I've come to offer an apology." Bill's words had come out of his mouth dry, were barely audible. He cleared his throat. "It seems I was wrong about you."

"Indeed!"

Pike stared at the marine at length, as if trying to look through him, but then the light went on and he nodded in comprehension.

"I see. Anything else?"

"Yes, sir, there is." Gallagher brought his heels together with a soft click, lifted his chin and raised his right hand in salute. Later he would tell Steve Watson it was the hardest thing he had ever done in his life.

Pike seemed hesitant to respond, but then switched the briefcase to his left hand and calmly returned the salute.

"Good day to you, Lieutenant," he said, and marched away from the pier.

CHAPTER 23

"Y ou're absolutely sure about this, Lieutenant?"

"Yes, sir, I am."

Watson let the typed letter of resignation slip from his fingertips. He sat there for a moment longer, studying his friend, but then rose out of his chair, stepped over to the window and peered out at the busy airfield.

"I'm losing a good instructor," he said to the window.

"I'm not indispensable, Steve."

Watson turned away from the window, a disaster of a smile attached, and said to the flyer, "I'm still losing a good man." He returned behind the desk. "So what are you going to do when you get out?"

"Not sure," was Gallagher's answer. "Maybe I'll go back to Florida and try my luck at grad school." He shrugged. "Then again…"

"You'll miss it, though."

"What, the marines or flying?"

"Both."

"You're probably right, sir. But maybe it's time I explored other opportunities out there. Haven't you ever had the urge to leave the service?"

"Believe it or not, the thought has never crossed my mind. Shows you how comfortable a man can get when he reaches a certain rank in the military. Maybe I'm just too lazy to leave the navy."

Smiles were exchanged before Watson switched topics.

"Bill, how about having dinner at my house tonight? My wife's making lasagna."

"Thanks, Steve, but Chet Greaves beat you to it. We're going into Norfolk to meet a friend for dinner." His smile widened. "I'll take a rain check, though."

Gallagher and Greaves met Roger Morrison at the Steak Pit restaurant a few minutes before six o'clock. The ex-sailor turned air traffic controller had already reserved a table and greeted them with a huge smile.

"Just like old times, eh, guys?" Morrison waved his hand, beckoning a waitress nearby. "And everything's on me tonight, got it?"

Greaves said, "Gee, Roger, life in the outside world must be treating you good. Why so generous?"

"Because I've been a cheapskate most of my life and I'm trying to make up for it."

Laughter from the trio as the waitress appeared. Morrison ordered a pitcher of Budweiser, which she delivered moments later. He gave her a dollar tip.

Slim, petite and brunette, she was an attractive young woman who had, Gallagher noticed, the most compelling smile and chocolate brown eyes. It was the first time a female had caught his attention since the day he had learned of Marlene's death. Their eyes met, he smiled, she blushed in return, and he watched as she reluctantly left the table. When he turned back, he found his friends studying him, smirks attached.

"What is it?" he urged.

It was Morrison who answered, "I think she likes you, Bill."

"Yeah, maybe there's hope for you after all," added Greaves, barely keeping a straight face.

Gallagher said to Morrison, "I'm leaving the Corps, Roger. Talked to Steve today and made it official."

Morrison's jaw went south. He glanced at Greaves, skepticism describing the mood in his eyes.

"This guy on the level, Chet?"

"'Fraid so, buddy."

"But why, Bill?"

"It's a long story, Roger. And don't ask me to explain it, 'cause I won't."

Morrison reached for his glass, sipped, swallowed and said, "I never thought I'd live to see the day. I thought you'd be a jarhead forever."

"Yeah, so did I," nodded Gallagher. "But I'm leaving now and there's no turning back."

"How are you going to make a living?"

"He's going to run for president in 'seventy-two," butted in Greaves, chuckling between words. "Right, Bill?"

"Sure, why not? The country's a mess and needs a new leader." His fake sarcasm provoked another outburst of laughter from his friends. When it subsided, he went on in a serious tone, "First, though, I'm going to get an apartment in town and start looking for a job. You know, check out my chances with the airlines." He clapped Morrison on the shoulder, eyes hopeful. "Think you can help me?"

"Hell, you bet! I've got some pretty good contacts at the airport. I can ask the pilots and get some names for you. It's the least I can do for an old buddy."

Greaves said, "Thought you were thinking of moving back to Florida, Bill."

"I've changed my mind."

"So soon?"

Morrison said, "By the way, Bill, whatever happened to that private detective you hired? Is that all over with?"

"Yeah."

"So what happened?"

"I can't tell you, Roger. Maybe later, maybe never."

"So you don't want to talk about it, is that it?"

"That's right." Gallagher took a deep breath and changed the subject. "Let's order some food, guys. I'm starved."

At 9:34 that night, the police station in Ocean View received a telephone call from a hysterical woman who identified herself as Sally Ann Collins. She had just finished her evening shift at the Crab Cake Diner and returned to her apartment, where she found her roommate and co-worker, Carol Lombardi, lying dead on the living room sofa.

At 9:51, a fairly good-looking, fair-haired man was cruising west along Route 564 in his 1963 Impala at fifty miles an hour. He was enjoying the pleasant evening air with the window down while smoking a Camel cigarette. His destination was the Norfolk Naval Base, where his ship, due to sail at the end of the month, was stationed. His duty watch was scheduled to start at midnight.

The red Pontiac GTO that swerved out of the eastbound lane and struck his beloved Chevy broadside was driven by a teenager whose name the police would identify later as Chucky Hartenstein. Chucky had no idea that the sailor he had just crushed to death was a murderer, nor did he care. When the wrecker pulled the two mangled cars apart, Chucky had lost consciousness. Not long thereafter he would lose his left leg in the emergency room at Norfolk General. Four days later when he came out of coma, most of his memory was gone too, particularly the part when he had guzzled down that last can of whiskey-spiked beer before taking the wheel of his car on the night of the accident.

At 11:13, Jake Wharton appeared at Sally Ann Collins' apartment on the insistence of Fuzzy Hostetler, who had arrived at the murder scene an hour after the killing had been reported. When he saw the naked body of the dark-haired Lombardi girl lying on the sofa, he shook his head sadly.

"Are you thinking what I'm thinking, Matt?"

"Yep, she was strangled, no doubt about it. Just like Marlene Pike and the Hingston girl."

"Which means we got a lot of work to do."

"Yep." Hostetler nodded grimly. "Let's get started."

When Shirley Conway walked out of the gift shop on the southern-most man-made island of the Chesapeake Bay Bridge-Tunnel, she found her husband standing alone at the end of the fishing pier. He was admiring the goliath ship making its way toward Thimble Shoal Channel at a speed he had amateurishly estimated at ten knots. The sight of the great ship nearly took her breath away. She stepped up behind him and put an arm around his waist.

"My God, that's a big boat, dear."

"That's the *Roosevelt*," he said. "The largest ship in the world."

"What kind is it, Walter?"

"An aircraft carrier."

To her it looked like a gigantic sea monster, but she didn't tell him that. She knew he would only laugh at her.

"Look, dear, there's a man on board waving at us." She indicated the tiny figure in khaki to which she was referring, a sailor standing by himself on the flight deck not far from the ship's superstructure. "See?"

"Yeah, I see him, honey." Walter Conway watched in awe for a while longer, but then turned back and smiled at his suntanned wife.

"It's almost lunch time," he said. "Let's get something to eat?"

"Food, food, food—it's all you think about, Walter."

As the Maryland couple walked away from the pier, the tall, broad-shouldered, blond sailor aboard the *U.S.S. Roosevelt* stopped waving and sighed. He glanced toward the bow of the ship. Ahead was the mighty Atlantic and three months of training maneuvers in the Mediterranean Sea.

He reached inside his breast pocket and yanked out a pack of Camels. He shook one out and stuck it between his lips, but then remembered the smoking lamp was out and tossed it into the sea. Smiling, he took a healthy breath of salt-spiced ocean air and promptly returned to his duty station in the nuclear ship's engineering control room.

Author's Note

God bless and long live the United States Navy and Marine Corps.

Books by T. K. Marion

Kill the Devil
East Wind, Rain